MAMA, I'M IN LOVE (. . . WITH A GANGSTA)

From *Essence* magazine best-selling author of
If I Ruled the World and *Dollar Bill*

MAMA, I'M IN LOVE (. . . WITH A GANGSTA)

Two novellas 'bout real ghetto love
by
JOY

URBAN BOOKS LLC
www.urbanbooks.net

Urban Books
10 Brennan Place
Deer Park, NY 11726

ISBN 1-893196- 67-4

First Printing November 2006
Printed in Mexico.

10 9 8 7 6 5 4 3 2 1

*This is a work of fiction. Any references or similarities to actual
events, real people, living or dead, or to real locales are intended to
give the novel a sense of reality. Any similarity to other names, char-
acters, places, and incidents is entirely coincidental.*

Submit Wholesale Orders to:
Kensington Publishing Corp.
C/O Penguin Group (USA) Inc.
Attention: Order Processing
405 Murray Hill Parkway
East Rutherford, NJ 07073-2316
Phone: 1-800-526-0275
Fax: 1-800-227-9604

BEHIND EVERY BAD BOY... is a

bad-ass bitch

A novella by
JOY

My Mother's Womb

'I'd much rather had suffocated in my mother's womb than to endure life in this fucked-up world.

But for some reason, I was deemed deserving of a slow, excruciating death out here, a place where I can't breathe anyway.

Every time I do take a breath I inhale suffering and pain, which inevitably will result in a fatal wound. Killing me slowly. Killing me softly. Killing me.

So I'll hold my breath until I die.

But this drawn-out demise could have been avoided if I had just suffocated in my mother's womb.'

This story is dedicated to those who got past the pain and can breathe again, and especially for those, like myself, who sometimes find themselves still gasping for air.

JOY

Prologue
Fuck the World

I'm sure most people figured me as that ghetto-ass girl who wouldn't amount to shit in life. I didn't finish high school. Couldn't read when my ass *was* going to school. My mother chose crack over me at a time in my life when a girl really needs her mother. My fuckin' granny, one I had no relationship with as a little girl, had to teach me how to plug my pussy up when it was that time of the month. I laugh at the shit now, but it really ain't funny at all. Hurts like a muthafuck. But I guess I laugh to keep from crying.

I spent most of my life holdin' back tears. Not even at my own daddy's funeral, the man I thought was my daddy anyway, did I cry. He died while he was in the prison system doing time for the death of my baby brother, the one I never got to see grow up. The one who never got to grow up. I was only eleven years old when he was born, and in no time at all he was tryin' to cling to my titty more so than our own mother's.

The day my baby brother was brought home from the hospital all I could do was sit there and stare at him with pity. "Baby bro, you have no idea of the fucked-up mess you've been born into," is what I wished I could have said to him, but he wouldn't have understood. Unless our mother could put baby brother in a pipe and smoke his ass, he would get no love from her. I ended up being the one who would tend to him in the middle of the night when he'd wake up crying— not that his mother was ever home to tend to him no how and Daddy worked from twelve midnight to twelve the next afternoon, so he wasn't home either.

I was the one left there to change my baby brother's diapers, if he even had any. I was the one left at home to feed him his bottle, if there was anything to put in it. There were times when there wasn't any milk to give, and he wouldn't take water. He wouldn't take his Binky either, so he'd just cry and cry. I thought his crying was going to drive me insane, so one time I remember putting his fist in his mouth, making him suck on it so I could get a moment of silence. I'd watch him suck away at his tiny little fist, trying to get just a drop of something out of it. Only, there was nothing. He'd look at me and start crying again, like it was my fault. I could see it in his eyes. I could hear it in my baby brother's cry; he blamed me.

I knew what it was like to be hungry, but the difference between me and my baby brother was, I was old enough to understand the pain, and cope. I understood the choice our mother had made. She chose to take all of the money Daddy had given her to take care of the home and feed her high instead of her children.

My father was a hard-working man, blinded by love. He had to be blind, or else how could he not see his home deteriorating? His wife deteriorating? His family? But, most of all, how could he not see the change in my mother's appearance? Shit, back in the day, Moms had been one of those fine-ass redbones. She was one of them "high-yella" gals that all the girls hated out of jealousy. She never did anything but look cute every day, and for that, other chicks hated her. She had long, black hair and a nice thick, not fat, physique, and she always wore nice threads. She went from all that and a bag of Gripos, to a skinny, nappy-headed geeker. Her appearance didn't keep my father from loving her, though, from wanting her, from touching her. In love with a crackhead, imagine that.

He wanted so much to believe that his wife was still the beautiful queen he had married. He loved her so much. More than his own children even. He had to have loved her more than me and my brother, or why else didn't he pack us up and take us away from the madness, leaving the cause behind? Instead, he turned a blind eye to the situation and hoped that it would take care of itself or dissolve. But things only got worse. Things would only get worse for me anyway. My baby brother got lucky—he died.

I felt as though God didn't love me enough to take me. No, He forced me to endure some ol' fucked-up shit by allowing me to live, to breathe, inhaling such insanity. I hated God for that for so many years. It would take me going through even so much more devastation to realize that no matter how I felt about God, or what beef I thought He had with me, He had always had my back. Not no homegirl, homeboy, Blood or Crip got a muthafucka's back like God do.

God carried me through everything, right down to the unimaginable, grimy shit (pardon, my language; He's still working with me in that area). But the outcome of those situations I found myself in would mold me into the person I am today—a strong, bad-ass bitch that can't be fucked with or fucked over.

Lookin' back, I wish I had done some things differently, but I regret nothing. Everything that played out in my life led me to the life I live now. It's a life I can honestly say that I love. Hell, what broad wouldn't love to be in my shoes right about now? Every day I can look around and enjoy all the

nice things I have—a car that's paid for, a home that's paid
for, a few choice pieces of jewelry, a nice wardrobe, a very
successful business and a very handsome and successful
businessman to call my own.

I recognize now that I have always been blessed. Even the
death of my grandmother was a blessing. I hadn't been in
her life that long when she passed away, but because I was
her only living next of kin, I inherited everything she and
my grandfather, who had passed away several years before
her, had worked for all their lives. My days of financial struggle would be no more. And, once I did obtain somewhat of a
mini-fortune, to make sure that from that point on I would
always have, I gave nothing.

I don't owe nobody in this world shit anyway, not even my
own mama for having me. I mean, yeah, she and I are cool
now. I forgave her for a lot of the shit she put me through, so
I definitely looked out for her. As for the rest of the world . . .
fuck the world. Like Biggie said, "Don't ask me for shit." If
muthafuckas want something out of life, they gotta work
hard for it and go through some bullshit just like I had to. To
whom much is given, much is required. Otherwise, they
ain't even gon' appreciate the shit they do get.

My pops used to tell me that all the time. He'd say,
"Harlem, you ain't always gon' be able to get everything you
want handed to you on a silver platter. You gotta sometimes
go through things and work harder than you ever imagined
you would have to in order to get just a small slice of the pie.
Sometimes you have to watch somebody else eat the whole
damn pie in your face and leave you nothing but crumbs.
But that ain't God punishing you; that's just His way of allowing you to appreciate thangs once you get them so that
He can bless you with even more."

My daddy always had some ol' logical shit to kick. I just
wish he'd used his logic to get us out of the situation we were

heading towards. But deep down inside, I knew where he was coming from. I, too, knew what it felt like to love my mother so much that nothing else mattered. I didn't even care that she felt that exact same way about crack and not about me. But it was when I realized that she loved the streets more than me that I took my love back from her. I never minded as much when she would leave me home alone to run the streets; it was bringing the streets home that really fucked me up.

There were times when I'd walk in the door from school and find my mother fucking and sucking for the pipe, and on the pipe, right there on the living room floor. With her daughter standing there in the doorway lookin' dead at her, she would never even budge or even try to hide what she was doing. There was no shame in her eyes or in her heart. I'd try to hide from what was going on in the living room by escaping to my bedroom, but oftentimes she would use my bed to pay for her habit with her pussy.

Our apartment was the official "Taj Mahal" for smokin' crack and fuckin' for crack. My resting spot became the one and only bathroom in our apartment. I'd hide out in the bathroom, putting my pillow in the tub, lock the door behind me, turn off the lights, and go to sleep with my eyes open. If anybody had to piss, they pissed outside or in the kitchen sink, because once I locked that door behind me, wasn't nobody gettin' in that muthafucka.

Eventually, I was taken from my mother and put into the system. Foster home after foster home, I found myself trying to keep grown-ass pedophiles away from my young, ripe pussy. As sadistic as what I'm about to say might sound, I used to wonder if other little girls were going through what I was going through. Actually, I hoped they were. I didn't want to be alone. I wanted God to hate another little girl just as much as He hated me. I wanted Him to hate her so much that she would go through the same things I was going through. I suppose that gives new meaning to the saying, misery loves company.

As a child I managed to escape the sick sexual clutches and thoughts of perverted old men. Ironically, it would be later in life, in my adulthood, that I would no longer be able to escape the male beast. I, along with my best friend, would experience the most brutal, life-changing event to ever happen in our lives. At first, I thought maybe I deserved it, but eventually I came to realize that I didn't deserve any of it. And it didn't take hours of talking with some counselor or shrink to figure that out. All it took was hours of precise planning and a will to seek revenge. If I had to pay the piper—hell, as far as I was concerned, we were all dancing to the same tune—goddamn it, somebody else was going to pay the piper too.

In the blink of an eye, my well-thought out, premeditated actions would change many lives. In a matter of minutes, I would forget about it all and my life would go on.

Today, as I sit back and analyze shit, I don't know what the fuck I was thinking by hoping that my past would never come back to fuck with me, that God wouldn't find a way to make me accountable for my past sins. I suppose that at some point in life we all must be held accountable for our acts, no matter how much we believe that they were justified.

Too late to cry over spilled milk now. I remember there was a time in my life when I'd rather cut my arm off with a dull, rusty blade than to cry. Then after holding so much shit inside, it all finally caught up with me, all the pain. Then I could do nothing but sit back and cry. But now a bitch is all cried out; that's why I got two teardrops tattooed on my face.

A lot of people think the two tattooed teardrops represent death, losing someone, or taking someone's life. Some people think it's cute, while others say it's straight-up gangsta.

But the tats are real tears, as far as I'm concerned; the only tears that will ever run down my face.

I've overcome situations that most people would use as an excuse to live that ghetto life. Some people liked to justify their lifestyle based on the hand they were dealt. I don't let circumstances determine the life I'm gon' live. I never put down those cats that craved the hood life, but I was on some other type shit. That's why I surprised my own self when I fell in love with a gangsta.

All my life it seemed as though I had tried to steer clear of the street life and niggaz with street ways. But then one day, in walks Jazzy into my life. I should have known his ass was a hustler, from jump. He had "bad boy" written all over him. He wasn't the biggest man on campus, but he was headed for the "dean's list," so to speak. He made some noise in the streets, and mu'fuckas knew to respect.

But the same way, after so much drama and bullshit, I left my old ways behind me, eventually Jazzy left his old ways behind him too. Now we depend on each other to hold one another down.

Jazzy might have changed his ways, but them for-real street bitches can sniff out the scent of a true-to-the-game bad boy like a fuckin' K-9. They test me, but they all fail. Hell, not a bitch out there is a challenge to me. Yeah, I'm twenty-nine years old pushin' thirty, but even them young broads with perky nipples and a gap between they legs can't put it down like me. So I ain't pressed. I never worry about Jazzy strayin'. I don't need to be on Jazzy's arm constantly for bitches to know what time it is, that he got a real bitch holdin' shit down. Hell, it's just an unspoken fact that behind every bad boy, holdin' him up is a chick like me, Harlem Lee Jones, a bad-ass bitch.

Chapter 1
The Devil Himself

Two dudes pulled up behind my Mustang. My best friend, Morgan, and I had just finished doing a little shopping. We had bags galore from almost every department store in the mall. We walked across that parking lot like *Pretty Woman* or some ghetto princesses or some shit. We were loading up my trunk with all of our bags, when they rolled up on us, these two clean-cut muthafuckas. They claimed that they wanted my parking spot. I should have known that some foul shit was up then—Why the fuck would they be waiting around on the furthest parking spot from the mall entryway?

I always parked my Mustang far away from other cars. Since I didn't have any kids, my ride was my baby, and I didn't want some triflin' muthafucka driving a hooptie parking their raggedy, uninsured shit next to mine. Them the type of jealous cats who would purposely ding my door, simply because they hatin' on my whip.

"Do you love her?" the dude who had been sitting in the passenger seat asked me, referring to Morgan.

I could see him. He wasn't a bad-looking guy at all. He was a little edgy, with a nice, clean shave. His skin complexion

was light. He had a nice, soft, curly grade of hair and beautiful gray eyes. He was what Morgan and I would refer to as a
cutie pie. He was wearing a nice lightweight V-neck sweater
that revealed the hair on his chest, and his sparkling dia-
mond earrings were blinding.

The next thing I know, his equally attractive friend was behind me. I could smell him. He was wearing the cologne
Very Sexy for men. He was so close to me, every time he exhaled, a draft traveled down my neck. His breath was making
the hairs on my neck stand. Just thinking about the smell of
his breath made me gag. It reeked of stale Miller Genuine
Draft.

"Do you love her?" the guy repeated, with much more bass
and anger in his voice. It was an eerie tone.

I blinked.

He had a knife to Morgan's throat. Specks of her blood
spotted the blade.

As I looked around, I saw nothing but trees. It was dark, so
fucking dark, except for the headlights from their car. I
couldn't remember how we got from the parking lot to this
dark place.

My face hit the ground. It hurt like hell, but I didn't
flinch. I wanted to cry, but crying was for sissies. Besides, crying wasn't going to get me out of that living hell, so why shed
a tear for them muthafuckas? Pain . . . I'd felt worse. Besides,
my father had always told me that crying wasn't going to get
me nowhere, so I sucked that shit up. I was stunned as hell,
though.

I was face down, and he was right there on top of me. I
could feel him, his hands violently pulling my panties off of
me. I couldn't believe this shit was happening to me. Not
me. Not Harlem Lee Jones. I was the baddest bitch ever
born to the streets of the Midwest or, at least, so I thought.
Someone once told me that everybody gets broke down. I

guess you could say I was on deck; my number was being called.

I was clawing my nails into the ground. My nails filled with dirt. A woman with dirty fingernails was so fucking disgusting to me. Dirty fingernails and nails with chipping nail polish was just some ol' nasty ghetto shit.

This bastard was only moments from being inside of me, taking what was mine against my will, and all I could think about was the dirt underneath my fingernails. Call me neurotic, but I couldn't wait to wash my hands and scrub underneath my nails. I couldn't wait to get home and scrub the dirt away. Not once did I even consider the fact that I might not even make it home.

I saw the trees again. He had turned me over onto my back. I looked over to my right where Morgan was laying, and the same thing was being done to her.

"Morgan!" I yelled frantically. "Morgan, Morgan!"

"Harlem, baby." Jazzy made his way upstairs from the living room and into my office, which was actually the third bedroom in my home that I had turned into an office.

Before my mind had wandered off to that horrible night almost three years ago, I had been going over inventory logs for our bookstore and music shops, "Harlem's Blues."

Jazzy had been downstairs playing "Grand Theft Auto" on the game station. "Harlem World, you okay?" he asked, out of breath from running up the steps.

I blinked my eyes back into reality. The trees were gone. The driver and the passenger were gone. So was Morgan. Morgan was gone. My best friend was gone. My eyes watered. I wanted to cry. Instead, I closed my eyes and placed my fingers on my tat.

"You cool?" Jazzy entered the room. "You were calling out Morgan's name."

"Yeah, yeah." I blinked my eyes, shaking that shit off, trying desperately to get back to the reality of things. I straightened myself up and began scanning down the inventory log, as if everything was gravy. Like I hadn't just been calling for my best friend who had been dead for well over two years now.

Jazzy rubbed his strong hand, the color of a smooth manila envelope, down my long, dark-brown ponytail. His touch, just what I needed at the moment, felt so good, so soothing. Jazzy's touch was electric; it always settled my nerves and tamed me. *What a priceless antidote for the crazy bitch I could sometimes be.*

"Look here . . ." Jazzy took me by my chin and pulled my face to him.

I knew right then and there that he was very concerned about me. Since moving to Columbus, Ohio from Atlanta, Georgia, he had managed to rid his speech of that strong Southern drawl he had brought here with him, but every now and then, when he was either worried or pissed off, that down-South accent made a cameo.

"Look dead at me, woman," he ordered, staring into my eyes.

I looked deeply into his dark browns. I loved looking at myself in his eyes. I loved how he saw me. I smiled.

He smiled back; I passed the test.

If I hadn't, he would have shaken his head and said, "Come clean." That nigga wouldn't have let me be, until he found out exactly what was on my mind. Like some people learned how to trip a lie-detector test, sometimes I could do the same with Jazzy.

"Satisfied, Superman?" I said in an I-told-you-so manner.

Jazzy claimed he could see right through me, that he could read me like a book. So whenever he was worried about me and thought that I might not want to burden him with my troubles, he made me look into his eyes.

Only Superman was notorious for being able to see through shit, so I sarcastically began calling him Superman. But what was strange is that sometimes I really felt as though he could see through me. He could see things that I didn't even know were there.

"You had me worried there for a minute," Jazzy said, relieved. "What did you do? Doze off or something? Were you having a nightmare?"

I looked away from Jazzy and fiddled with the inventory log. "Yeah," I stuttered. "I must have dozed off while doing inventory for the bookstores."

"Why don't you take a break? Come downstairs with me and play "Grand Theft," or let me whoop that ass in a game of acie-deucie."

"You ain't beat me in a game of acie-deucie since we bought the backgammon board," I bragged. "I'm starting to think you one of them undercover kinky niggaz—you like for me to keep spankin' dat ass, huh?"

Jazzy laughed, running his tongue across his top row of teeth. They weren't pearly white, but they weren't yellow either or crooked. It was so sexy how he did that; every little thing he did was so sexy to me.

"Put your money where your mouth is." Jazzy raised his arms in the air.

This fool was challenging me. I stood up from my desk, walked over to him, and got all up in his space. "That's too easy—put your clothes where your mouth is." I licked my lips.

The smell of his breath was turning me on. He must have been downstairs drinking a Hulk because I could smell the Hpnotiq and Hennessy on his breath. That, and the smell of weed on him, always made me want to do him up; the shit was like an aphrodisiac.

"Shawty, you ain't said nothing. I'm 'bout to go get the

board out. You find you a stopping point with that there log and hurry your ass on." Jazzy turned to exit the room. "Oh, yeah, and earrings don't count."

"Huh?"

"You heard me—when it comes time for you to start stripping, earrings don't count, damn it."

I smiled and watched him as he walked away. I swear, every time he walked, the shit was in slow motion. He had this sexy-ass stride about him. Couldn't no other nigga fuck with his swagger. Jazzy was definitely that mu'fucka, and the best part about it, he was my mu'fucka.

The smile on my face faded away slowly as I thought about how I had just lied to him. I hated lying to him, even if it was just a little white lie. I was always afraid that he would be able to read the truth between the lies. There were times when I know he could, but just gave me a pass. Sometimes I wondered if that muthafucka really was Superman.

Fortunately, he hadn't the foggiest idea that I really hadn't dozed off at all. I had been having another one of my nightmares while wide-awake. I had been sitting there with my eyes wide open, when, all of a sudden, it started happening again. This was the third time this month. I could see Morgan and me with them. *Those sick sons of bitches.* It was so real. It was like it was actually happening all over again; I could feel the pain once again.

It seemed like forever since all that shit went down. I had never, not once, had a nightmare or anything about that night. It wasn't something I ever wanted to think about again, so I buried it deep, so deep that a hypnotist couldn't have forced me to recall the event. If asked if that shit had ever actually happened to me, I could have denied it and still pass a lie detector test—that's how deep I'd buried it. Now, all of a sudden, I was being haunted, not only in my sleep, but while I was wide-awake. It was starting to freak me out; I couldn't figure out why now. Why, after all of this time, were these thoughts starting to fuck with my head?

I had this awful feeling in the pit of my stomach. You know that feeling you get when something just ain't right? Well, this was that feeling. I'd know it anywhere. I'd had it one too many times before in my life. But what in the hell could possibly be brewing? It had only been for the last couple of years that my life had finally been blissful. Before that, it was like a dark cloud had been following me around from the day I was born.

I used to wish that I had just suffocated in my mother's womb. Back then I'd much rather have suffocated than to be in this fucked-up world. I felt that, for some reason, I was deserving of a slow death out here, a place where I couldn't breathe anyway. Every time I took a breath I inhaled pain, which I thought inevitably would result in a fatal wound. So I went through life figuring that I could simply hold my breath until I died.

But God had something else in store for me. Only, I didn't know it then. So just like every other muthafucka I encountered, God was the enemy. He had to be, or why else would He have just sat by and allowed all the fucked-up shit that happened in my life to go down? I used to ask myself, "What kind of God watches a little girl's mother nurture a crack pipe more than her own child? What kind of God watches a little girl witness her baby brother be driven away dead in the back of an ambulance? What kind of God watches a little girl lose her daddy, then her grandmother, and then her best friend?"

Even after everything, I tried, 'spite all the bullshit I went through, to make something of my life. That's when I started my own bookstore, The Suga Shop. Business was booming. Then, at the hands of a vengeful hater, my entire store was destroyed, vandalized to the point where nothing could be salvaged, nothing but the bell that hung over the entry door.

It was unreal. At that time I felt that if there were a God, no way would He just sit by and allow life to treat me so badly.

At the end of the day, though, once the dust settled, God would be the only one there for me. The lessons cut like a knife, but God stitched the wound back up. Now, God doesn't hide my blessings from me and force me to figure them out. I feel as though He places them right into my hands, because now I see every little thing as a blessing.

Through my fucked-up childhood, where my mother's drug habit caused the death of both my little brother and my father, to my young adulthood, where me and my best friend were victim to a crime so brutally violent that my best friend would lose her life, through all of this, my eyes have been opened to allow me to see how every event in my life had meaning. My life has been brought full circle, especially with my mother, Reese.

I never imagined that Reese and I would have the relationship we have today. It seems like just yesterday when she would show up at my store, begging for handouts, that I'd put her ass out like she was a stranger. I would be dishonest if I said that sometimes I still didn't resent her. Back then, though, my heart was full of hate to the point that, if she had died, I wouldn't have even gone to her funeral. But God restored her. She counted her blessings and fought for the one thing that could keep her from going back to that shameful life of a crack fiend. That one thing turned out to be me.

As far as Jazzy, words can't explain what having him in my life meant. From the moment he walked into my bookstore and I laid eyes on him, I knew I had to have him. Oddly enough, he ended up kickin' it with Morgan at first, but they never had anything serious though.

I ended up kicking it with his boy, York. It was a strange relationship. I had deep feelings for York. I can honestly say that he was the first man who ever truly brought out the woman in me. I had always been hard and edgy, but I eventually grew to have love for York. Now that was crazy, considering love didn't come easy from my heart. Even so, with all the emotions I had for York, I still craved Jazzy. It was just this unspoken energy Jazzy and I had between us.

Some ol' crazy bullshit went down with York and me that had to do with his sister, Yvette. We never patched things up to the point where we became a couple again, but I didn't hold that shit against him as a person. So "just friends" was what would eventually define our relationship; good friends, but just friends nonetheless. So I ended up losing the one person who had managed to soften up my rough edges a bit and make me feel that I could possibly love and be loved.

But then York ended up going to jail with a sentence of ten to twenty-five years. On top of that, I ended up losing Morgan as well. I thought I was going to lose my fucking mind. It was almost too much for me to bear.

Once all the dust settled, though, Jazzy and I, the two people who should have been together in the first place, ended up together after all. The love he offered was right on time. It was a love I was starving for; he became my ultimate "all-you-can-eat buffet."

The Suga Shop was rebuilt, but without Morgan, the person who had helped me run it from day one. I didn't want to go back to doing it without her, so I put the business up for sale. It sold almost immediately to a man named Jason Fields, Jazzy's government name.

Jazzy let me back on as part owner, and we ended up becoming partners in running the store. It became the go-to literary spot in the city. We offered author book signings, hosted book club meetings, had open-mic poetry, and even a gallery showing every now and then. Since Jazzy's favorite pastime was drawing, we featured some of his work at the showings and made his prints available for purchase on a regular.

We eventually opened up a second store, which Reese ran.

So even though I lost two people almost simultaneously, I ended up gaining two people. I was no longer hungry for the certain types of love I needed to fulfill my life. Now, I was able to breathe again.

Recently, though, I was starting to feel as though harmful fumes were invading and contaminating my air. It was a scary feeling. I didn't ever want to go back to that deep, dark place I had dwelled in for so long. Back then I had remained in such a state because of my determination to fight God, blocking his blessings like the world heavyweight championship belt was on the line. I feared that the visions I'd been having lately were an attempt to take me back there.

I had a strange feeling that this war I was about to engage in wouldn't be the same type of battle I had fought before. Before, I thought I had been fighting God, only to learn that He was, in fact, my ally. I had, in actuality, been battling myself, but I could feel deep down inside that once again I would have to armor up for a fight. Only, this time it was very clear who the enemy was—none other than Satan, the devil himself.

Chapter 2
Locked Down

"Damn, I need to put some money on that nigga's books," Jazzy said, as we sat waiting in the prison visiting room for York to come out.

"I already put money on his books this month," I told him.

"How much?"

"Enough; he's at max."

Jazzy paused for a minute, almost as if he was concerned about the fact that I had hooked his boy's books up. "Oh, all right. Cool then."

He said it was cool, but I knew better. "What?" I asked. I didn't know what his problem was. It wasn't anything out of the ordinary that I'd put money on York's books; he had asked me to several times, so pretty soon it just became second nature to look out for York's books.

"Nothing. I said it's cool."

"That's what your lips are saying."

"Look, you think into shit more than I do. Don't go there with me, Harlem. Next time just tell me you put money on his books, so I don't waste time worrying about it."

What he was worrying about was what else I was doing for, or with York that I wasn't telling him.

I loved it when Jazzy got jealous. I thought it was cute—stupid, but cute. *Jealous of York?* Like I was gon' break into the prison to fuck that nigga. Please. York was my past, not my present, nor my future. Nothing and no one could ever come between Jazzy and me—never. Especially not York.

For over two years, Jazzy and I had been visiting York, in a prison in Chillicothe, Ohio. It felt strange sometimes.

This was the same prison where my father was introduced to the Grim Reaper. After serving only six months of a ten-year sentence, he was shanked, his jugular vein cut.

Charged with neglect, child endangerment, and manslaughter, he was incarcerated for the death of my baby brother, for allowing him to drown in the bathtub. The judge felt that the ten-year sentence was as lenient as he could be on him.

Little did the judge know—it wasn't my father who was the cause of my baby brother's death—it was Reese. She had left him in the bathtub to go answer the door. When she saw her "get high" buddy Sharmane standing at the door, ready to smoke, she forgot all about my baby brother. Once she finally remembered, it was too late—his little lungs had already filled with water, and he died.

Daddy didn't want to see his Queen go to jail, though, so he took the blame instead.

When it was all said and done, it didn't matter how much more time the judge gave my father. In only six months, prison life had taken his. Seems inmates didn't take too kindly to other inmates who had harmed a child. What's fucked up is that he wasn't even the one who killed my baby brother.

* * *

So it's crazy that I was sitting in the prison, waiting for a man who's doing time for holding another man's shit—shit that just happened to be my man's.

"What up, dawg?" Jazzy said to York as York made his way over to the table. They hugged one another. I stood up to hug York as well.

Maybe it was all in my head, but for some reason whenever he hugged me, it felt as though he never wanted to let me go. In fact, he never freely let me go. I always had to initiate the separation. Even then, I could feel his resistance, him trying to keep a hold on me. So initially the beginning of our visits were always a bit awkward for me.

"Same ol' shit, different mafuckin' day." York was all smiles.

He had to be the happiest nigga in the joint. Not once had we visited him and he didn't have a smile on his face from ear to ear. He had always been upbeat and positive.

Me, I think it was all an act. I think that he just didn't want Jazzy to ever feel guilty about his being locked up. After all, he was on his way to make a drop for Jazzy, when the cops pulled him over. He was holdin' two kilos and had ten grand in the center compartment of his vehicle. The feds tried to get him to turn state's evidence, but York wasn't about to snitch. Not only because, in the game, it's death before dishonor, but because he felt that he owed Jazzy for puttin' him on when he didn't have a pot to piss in or a window to throw it out of.

In return for York's loyalty, Jazzy hired him one of the best criminal defense attorneys in the city. Referred to as a street lawyer, all the hustlers used him. He had an obscene flat rate of twenty thousand dollars for his initial legwork. Jazzy ended up shelling out five thousand more on top of that.

When all was said and done, the attorney filed an appeal on York's initial sentence. He got several of York's charges dropped and managed a six-year plea, one year served. Jazzy had always kept York's books tight, to let him know that he appreciated the sacrifice that was being made. Even though freedom had no price, York was obliged.

With a little over half of his sentence left to serve, I suppose York did have something to smile about. Although he had only served less than half his bid, he saw the cup as almost half-full. What I don't think he ever thought about was what the fuck he was going to do with himself once he did get out.

Before, York was nothing more than Jazzy's right-hand man. Not to say that he was his flunky or anything, but he didn't make no noise in the game. He had no connects. Jazzy was the nucleus between him and the dope. If York was to try to jump back into the game, he'd have a hard time getting put on. He'd have no choice but to start out being somebody's flunky.

Jazzy was completely out of the game now. Although the bookstores bring in major revenue for Jazzy, it ain't that easy-come, easy-go type of money that both Jazzy and York had gotten addicted to. Jazzy had to come down off of his high slowly. He had stacked plenty of loot over his years of hustling. Having to tap into money he hadn't touched in years was a little strange for him at first, but once the stores started doing better than ever, he was able to replenish, plus add to. He was still stacking loot; it was less money in smaller increments and took longer to make, but it was legit.

York, on the other hand, had to quit cold turkey. Against his will. I don't think that's something that anybody can get used to. I suppose being locked up made it a little easier, but once let out and back on the streets, who the fuck wanna go back to being hungry?

This was a fear I'd always had in the back of my mind. You see, back in the day, if Jazzy was still in the game, he would have been able to put York on at one of his car washes once he got out of jail. Jazzy, before giving up the life, had used his chain of local car washes as a business front to keep his dirty money clean. In no time at all, York would have been back to ballin' out of control.

But shit had changed. Hopefully York would be fully detoxed from making fast money; otherwise, slowly but surely, he'd start fiendin'.

It wouldn't have surprised me. It was typical for cats to come out of the joint and go back to doing the same old dumb shit again. I just hoped that York wouldn't try to get Jazzy back in that game in any way. Matter of fact, I made Jazzy promise that no matter what, he wouldn't even stick his big toe in to test the waters.

Jazzy had been good at what he did. He moved his shit quick, was never short, and none of his crew was ever short. He ran a tight shift. Even them New York niggaz couldn't fuck with his hustle. His connects would have rather seen him dead than to see him leave the game, but they took their chances. They figured that, like all the others who tried to leave the life, Jazzy would be back, and they promised him that they'd always leave the door wide open for him, that he didn't even have to knock, he could use his key.

That open door was the foundation of my one and only insecurity with Jazzy. It wasn't bitches, it was the game. So I made a vow to myself to cater to Jazzy's every need. I was bound and determined to keep him honest with love, never allowing him to doubt how much he meant to me and how much I needed him. I vowed to keep him honest by making sure that I worked equally hard, if not harder, so our business would continually rake in money. Money could never become an issue for us. I'd rather hit the block in a G-string for money than for Jazzy to get back into the game, because I knew if he did, this time there would be no walking away. There would only be two other ways out.

Last but not least, I'd keep him honest with pussy, throwin' ass at him like it was lined in gold, givin' it to him whenever and whatever. I just hoped that the bond between him and York couldn't stand up against any of what I had to offer. So I made it a point to be a ride-or-die bitch with my man.

"What's been up with you, Harlem?" York's eyes burned through me.

"Same ol', same ol', baby." I leaned back in my chair, gangsta-like.

I had always had this tomboy edginess about me, but it seemed as though, around York, I displayed it even more. It was my way of not sending him mixed messages.

Ironically, the same man that had brought out the woman in me, I now had to tuck it away when in his presence. Because what York and I had was no more.

I was in love with his boy. I didn't want York to look at me and see the girl he used to bend over the tabletop counter and hit from the back on his tippy-toes. I wanted him to see me as just one of his homies who had his back. I was his down-ass bitch too, but just in a different way.

"How you holdin' up?" I asked, genuinely wanting to know.

"You know me," York said with a smile. "You knew York first."

I put my head down and smiled. I couldn't help it. That was York's inside line with me. When he and I were kickin' it he had purchased me a personalized gold nameplate necklace with my name. The *H* in the nameplate had sparkling diamonds embedded in it. Later on, as my special gift to him, I took the necklace to my jeweler and had them add the words "Knew York" to the plate so that it read "Harlem Knew York." The night I presented it to York, I swear that nigga was almost in tears. I can't front; it was special. York and I were special, but now we were just friends. Special friends. Special good friends, but just friends. And although I knew York first, Jazzy was the melody to my soul.

"I did, didn't I?" I said, giggling, not knowing how that stupid schoolgirl giggle slipped out.

"A'ight, a'ight, cut it out," Jazzy joked. He proceeded to change the subject and the mood. "So you holdin' up?"

"Yeah, man. You ain't heard me complain since the day they put the bracelets on me and brought me to this mutha-fucka. I'm just doing my time, yo."

"I feel dat." Jazzy shook his head then looked down.

I noticed that Jazzy had a hard time looking York in the eyes. *Guilt could grip a nigga's nuts like a pair of pliers.* I often wondered if it was because Jazzy got with me once York went to jail.

Jazzy cleared his throat. "You want something from the machines, man?"

"That's cool," York said, turning to look at the vending machines. "Some chips and a soda or something is straight."

"You want something, baby?" Jazzy said to me, standing up.

"Something sweet," I replied.

"Oh, I got that all day long." Jazzy winked as he walked away.

I couldn't take my eyes off of him. I could feel York watching me watch Jazzy. I could tell that he wanted to know what I saw in him. He wanted to know what Jazzy had that could possibly make me pull a stank-ass move like fuckin' with him. He wanted to know, I could just feel it, but he never asked.

"So how you and *my boy* doing?" York said, exaggerating the words *my boy*.

Even though at first York wasn't cool with Jazzy and my being together, he eventually got over it. It probably had something to do with the way he found out. Some half-Asian half-black girl named Zondra, who had a thing for York and Jazzy both (hey . . . who am I to talk?) saw Jazzy and I at church together one Sunday. She and I had words before, one time when York and I were out together, so she knew ex-actly who I was. Needless to say, her ass sent York a letter, pri-ority, dropping the bomb on him. Once he brought it up to

Jazzy on the phone, Jazzy went to visit him so that he could tell York everything about us.

After hearing it from his boy, York was cool with it. He didn't have a choice. Jazzy and I were going to be together regardless. York told me that he didn't have any hard feelings against me, that as long as I was happy he was good, but lately, through his subtle actions, I was starting to beg to differ.

"Why you say it all like that?" I asked, snapping my neck back.

"Like what?" York said, shrugging his shoulders.

"Nothing." I wasn't in the mood to play games.

"So you gon' answer my question?" York leaned in, forcing me to look him in his eyes.

York wasn't as nearly as cute in the face as Jazzy, but he was easy on the eyes for sure, especially now that his physique was all tight and shit from lifting weights. He was a smooth, creamy-brown, chocolate brotha. Picture the color of a buckeye and that was York's complexion. He had light-brown eyes and he used to have a nice little mustache growing in, but now he had a full goatee. He still wore his hair in his signature zigzag braids, edged out with his *good* baby hair.

"We good," I said, almost nervously, turning away from him.

"And the stores?" York asked as if he purposely wanted to keep me talking. It was like he was eventually trying to get at something else.

"Great." With my legs crossed, I kicked my foot back and forth and swept the visiting room with my eyes.

"You can't look at me, Harlem?" York asked in a serious tone.

"What?" I squinted my face up. "What are you talking about?"

"You tell me. It just seems that all of a sudden I'm getting this different vibe from you is all I'm saying."

"I could say the same fucking thing about you," I said,

snappin'. I know he wasn't trying to call me out on no shit when it was his ass that was having a change of heart after all of this time.

"Whoa," York said in surrender, "it's all good derre."

"How you gon' try to say my vibe is changin'? You the one who all of a sudden is acting like you got some bitterness happening."

" 'Bitterness'?" York laughed. "You think I'm bitter?" His tone changed into a more serious one. He looked me in my eyes. "Why should I be bitter? What reasons do I have to be bitter? Can you name just one, Harlem?" York burned a hole through me with his eyes.

Lucky for me, Jazzy approaching the table prevented me from having to reply to York's inquiry.

"Y'all look all intense, damn," Jazzy said, setting down a bag of Lays and a Coke in front of York. He then slid a pack of cookies to me as he opened the soda he had bought for himself.

"I was just telling York how great business is going," I replied.

"Oh yeah." Jazzy's eyes lit up, as they did every time he talked about the bookstores. He had been a hustler all his life. Selling books was still a hustle, but it was honest. He was truly proud of himself, as was I. "We boomin', man, selling books like hot cakes. Can't nobody never tell me that black folks don't and can't read." Jazzy looked over at me to make sure that he hadn't offended me with his last comment.

For the years Morgan and I had run the store together, no one knew that she was my eyes. I was running a bookstore and could barely read, due to my being dyslexic and shit. It wouldn't be until after Morgan's death, when I was asked to read the eulogy at her funeral, that everyone would learn that I didn't know how to read. Eventually I did get help with my disability, got my GED, and went to community college. It wasn't a sore spot with me or anything I was embarrassed about any more. The fact that I could now read on a better level was one of the greatest accomplishments in my life.

"Word? Business is boomin' like that?" York nodded. "Let you tell it, the book business sounds better than the car wash business." He winked.

A feeling of uneasiness fell upon the mood. Jazzy ignored York's last statement, and I interjected to talk about something else. For the remainder of the visit we talked about everyday shit and past presidential elections, how people's votes really don't count or else they would have counted the muthafuckas. We talked about the lawmaker's views on niggaz coppin' drug charges getting longer sentences than niggaz who actually kill muthafuckas. After the visit was over, Jazzy and I headed back home.

Jazzy and I didn't say much on the ride home. Normally we were all talk when we weren't working together, but lately it seemed as though everything had been changing. It was only a matter of time before I'd find out if shit was changing for the better or worse.

"Get the hell away from here, goddamn it!" I yelled to the raggedy-ass crackhead that was hanging outside of my store, begging for change and shit from all of my customers.

My store on Main Street was in a neighborhood that always had 'ho's, mules, and crackheads hanging out. I normally let them be, as long as they didn't fuck up my money. But this particular crackhead, Do-Rag they called him, was a nuisance. I hated to see his ass coming. He wasn't as easy to get rid of as the rest of the loiterers. He was crazy and had a "fly mouth." Not only would he beg the pretty women for change, but he would flirt with them and pretend as if he was trying to feel on their booties just to taunt them. It got to the point where, if some of them saw him out there, they would go in the other direction rather than come and patronize my store and have to deal with his crazy ass. That's when I'd have to step in.

"Keep bringing your bummy ass around here, scaring my customers off, and see what happens," I spat.

"Man, fuck you, you evil-ass bitch." He grabbed his nuts through his dusty army-green pants. "I ain't in yo' store. I'm on the sidewalk. Sidewalk is for public use, and guess what?— I'm the public, and I'm using it." He began laughing until his laugh turned into a nasty cough.

I put my hand on my hip and walked up to dude. "Look, nigga," I said, pointing my finger dead in his face, "you come around here one more time yankin' at your nuts and harassing my customers, and I'ma have them nuts of yours in a jar."

His eyes bucked open. That fool thought that crazy talk of his would scare me, but somebody should have told him that a sista like myself don't scare so easy.

I gritted my teeth and took my hand that I was pointing at him with and balled it tight as if I was crushing his nuts inside my fist. I could see the discomfort in his eyes as he just stood there cringing, almost as if he was imagining the pain that such an act would cause him.

Staring dead into my eyes, he snorted up a wad of mucus and spat on the sidewalk. "Humph," he said, walking away while twisting his lips up at me, "how easily we forget. Wasn't too long yo' own mama was out here begging and trickin' right in front of yo' store. Think you'd have a little more compassion."

I just stood there shaking my head. What a sista had to go through to maintain her place of business in the hood. I turned around to go back into the store, and standing there, holding the door open for me, was a face that almost made my knees buckle.

"Miss Jones," he said, a snide look on his face, "long time no see. I bet you thought I had forgotten about you."

Suddenly I felt faint. My body moistened as if I had just coached my team to the Super Bowl and they had showered me with a tub of water in celebration. My heart began to race ninety-five miles per hour as shit started coming back to me. Shit from the last time I'd encountered this pig that was now standing in front of me.

"Detective Somore," I said, almost under my breath, forcing myself to speak.

Detective Somore was the same white bastard of a detective who was assigned to Morgan's and my case. He tried to act all concerned and shit, like he really wanted to find the men who had harmed me and Morgan and bring them to justice. But I didn't trust the po-po then, nor did I now. As desperate as him and his partner seemed to act like they wanted to find the men who assaulted Morgan and me, I knew that even if they did get the fuckers in their hands, they wouldn't do what needed to be done to them. Those fuckers needed to die; they deserved to die, and I could only trust one person to see that that got done—fuck handcuffs and rehabilitation. A 9 mm was justice enough in my book.

"Hey, you remembered my name even." He chuckled like he was Jolly Old St. Nick, but I could sense the Grinch lurking behind his laugh.

I just stood there looking at him, this white, suburban, suited-up, $75,000-a-year cop who had eventually made detective. He wasn't to be made to feel uneasy by a little colored girl's glare, though.

"I heard you had sold this place." Detective Somore looked up at my store. "I guess somebody's giving me the wrong information."

"No, you're getting the right information; I did sell it."

"You bought it back?"

"Something like that. But you're a smart detective." I looked him up and down. "I'm sure you already know the details."

He nodded and grinned, informing me that I was correct in my assumption.

"Come inside, why don't you?" he said, opening my store door even wider.

I brushed by him, entering my store.

He was close behind me. "Really nice spot you got here," he said, looking around. "Not a bad little crowd for early morning either."

I had about six customers in my store. Two were regulars, this black couple that attended Capital University further up Main Street. They stopped in almost every morning before class, shared a cup of coffee, and did some last-minute studying. The other four were some stylists from the shop next door.

"I didn't know you people got up this early." Somore chuckled.

I stopped in my tracks. I swear on everything I wanted to go for my gun that I kept under my register for security purposes and just blast his cracker ass. That's just how heated his comment made me. But I knew how this flatfoot rolled and I wasn't falling into his trap. He liked getting a rise out of his mark, thinking he could piss them off so much that whatever he was trying to hear would just fly off of their tongue out of anger.

"Yeah, we gotta get up early so that we can go to work and pay our taxes. We have to have something to give to Uncle Sam to help raise all that white trash that's on welfare around here."

He laughed under his breath at my comeback. He knew I was on to him.

"As you can see, Detective, I have some customers to tend to, so if you can just get to the reason why you are here, I'd appreciate it." I paused. "And I'm sure it's not for a cup of latté."

"Oh yeah," he said, playing dumb, "I almost forgot."

I rolled my eyes and sucked my teeth. I was in full "Jada Pinkett mode" . . . before she added the Smith.

"I, uh, just wanted to touch bases with you," he said, pulling out a pen and notepad. "It's been a while. You know your case has never been solved? We never did find the two animals that raped both of you, and killed your best friend."

I remained silent, looking off as if I was truly more concerned about my customers than what he was talking about.

"Actually, I found it strange that you didn't keep in touch with us, Harlem—Is it okay if I call you Harlem?"

"Miss Jones is fine."

"Well, Miss Jones," he enunciated, "again, I found it kind of strange that you never hounded us, or even called us once about the status of your case. The Kleininghams, your best friend's parents, call us all of the time. I know you don't like to talk about what happened to you and your friend; at least that's what you tell Mrs. Kleiningham when she tries to talk to you about it."

I snapped. "Look, detective, if I had any new information to tell you, then I would. I'm just trying to get on with my life. I'm trying to forget that it ever happened. How am I supposed to forget, if I spend the rest of my life rehashing it with the police? I just want to move on with my life."

"Is that why you changed your phone number, so that we couldn't call you any more? Is that why you never answered your door when we came by to discuss your case . . . because you wanted to move on?" Detective Somore looked around my store. "Looks like you've moved on pretty well. Most victims involved in a crime as tragic as yours tend not to move on as well as you, unless the criminals have been brought to justice."

He stared at me, as if expecting a response, which he didn't get, of course.

"I mean, one minute you and your friend are in the parking lot of the mall, and the next minute you find yourself carrying your best friend down the road. If those Good Samaritans driving along the road hadn't stopped and brought you to the hospital, you might have been buried next to your friend right now."

As Detective Somore spoke, thoughts about that horrific day filled my head. All of a sudden my private area began to throb in pain as I thought about the feeling of both men running in and out of me like I was nothing but a hole in the ground. I felt Morgan's pain for her. I felt the pain of being sodomized, of someone's entire fist ramming up inside of me. I wanted to vomit. I took a deep breath and looked away.

"Didn't mean to stir up bad memories, Harlem—I mean, Miss Jones. It's just that I have a job to do. My job is solving crimes, and it just so happens that your file, marked *unsolved crime*, turned up on my desk again."

" I don't have anything to say to you now about the case that I didn't say then. I try to forget about it. Like I said, I just want to move on. I know your job is solving crimes, but mine isn't, and I just don't know how to help."

He put away his pen and notepad and started walking slowly towards the door. "Speaking of solving crimes," he said, stopping in his tracks, "I'm working another unsolved homicide case as well. I don't know, you might have heard about it—two corpses over in a wooded area out near Alum Creek—does that ring a bell to you? Actually it was about a mile from where those Good Samaritans said they found you walking with your best friend. They were two African-American males, one around 5-11, the other around 6-2. Figured that out from their bone structure. Their bodies had deteriorated from weather and animal life, you know. Their bodies had been there a while before they were dis-covered. We got some clues . . . and two possible witnesses that we believe they were last seen with at a party, a couple of females. They say they don't know anything, but if you ask me, they know more than they're saying. But it's like something's got them too scared to talk."

"Well, good luck solving crimes." I turned away and headed for behind the latte counter. I was no longer about to entertain Detective Somore.

"Thanks." He nodded his head.

I didn't look up at him, but I could hear the bell ring on the door, letting me know that he was exiting.

"Or someone," he called back into the store as he was halfway out.

"Excuse me?" I was now extremely agitated.

"Those two witnesses," he said, refreshing my memory. "I said that something's got them too scared to talk, but I'm thinking it's probably more like someone. Anyhow, good day, Miss Jones." He walked out of the door.

I just stood there frozen. The most paranoid feeling came over me as if I had just done a line of coke.

For the rest of the day I couldn't think straight. I knew my drawer was going to come up fucked-up because I was forgetting to give customers their change, the correct change. Or I was just giving them change back, when they didn't even have any coming.

My mind was all over the place. I couldn't focus. Detective Somore was picking on me. I could tell that his entire purpose with coming to the store was to start feeding me rope with the hope that eventually I'd hang myself.

Chapter 3
And on the Seventh Day

I loved Sundays. It was the only day I got to sleep in and be up under Jazzy all day long. We usually didn't even get dressed on Sundays anymore. We just lounged around watching movies, playing acie-deucie, and eating. Of course, we made love, had good conversation. Then we fucked. This Sunday, though, I was going to have to break up our little ritual.

Over a month ago I promised Reese I would go to the Mother and Daughter dinner at church. If it ain't Mother and Daughter Day, then it's Friendship Day. If it ain't Friendship Day, then it's Women's Day. If it ain't Women's Day, then it's Men's Day. If it ain't Men's Day, then it's Friends and Family Day. And all of those days are exactly why I stopped going to church so much. God didn't care about that shit. That's man's doing. Every day was God's day and that's it. Period!

What happened to just praising the Lord? That's how my my dad's mother, grandmother Jones' church was. Before she passed away, she never missed a Sunday or a Bible study. Them folks put on a show praising the Lord, but they didn't make up days just to get dressed up, show off, and have an excuse to keep passing that collection plate around. Once I felt that God's ways were being removed from the church, I removed myself. He had been looking over me just fine before I started attending church; I didn't see any reason why he would stop now.

But I ain't gon' knock Reese's faith or her ways of expressing it. There was a time when she would have gone to church simply just to wait for the collection plate to make its way to her so she could grab a handful of its contents and go get a hit. I'm not exaggerating either. Crack will not only have a fiend stealing from they own mama, but it will have them stealing from the Lord too.

As a child, watching Reese grow to love crack more than her family was something that was hard for me to set aside. That's what made it so difficult for me to learn to love her again. For so long I had hated the ground she walked on. Things hadn't always been that way between us though. As a small child, before my baby brother was born, as Reese and Ray's only child, they gave me all the love and material things I needed to make me happy. The love Reese and I shared then, we were finally able to share again.

As I looked around my walk-in closet, I was undecided as to what to throw on to wear to church. I wasn't in the mood to get all dressy-dressy, wearing stockings and shit. "I don't know what to wear," I said to myself in a frustrated tone.

"Can I make a suggestion?" Jazzy entered the closet, walking close up behind me.

I could feel his stiff dick poking against my ass. "I'm always open," I said in a sensual tone, tilting my head to the side— He planted a wet kiss on my neck—"to suggestions."

"I think you look your best when you don't wear a goddamn thang," he said smoothly. Jazzy turned me around and stuck his tongue deep in my throat.

I sucked on it like I was trying to get to a creamy middle or something.

He slowly began to remove the boxer shorts I was wearing.

"Um, uh, we can't," I said with a sigh, pushing him away. "Reese is picking me up and I'm already running late trying to figure out what to wear."

"So let her wait," Jazzy said, continuing his strategy.

My shorts dropped to my ankles, and Jazzy pulled my "wife-beater" over my head. I stood there in the closet butt-ass naked.

"You the shit." Jazzy checked me out, licking his lips and shaking his head.

"I'm what you make me," I said with a smile. And I meant that shit too. Jazzy made me feel sexy. He made me feel wanted. He made me feel loved. He never had a problem telling me that. More importantly, he never had a problem showing me. He was the shit; I was merely a reflection of him.

I slid my body down his, kissing every inch of him along the way. I squatted down on my tiptoes, pulling his pajama pants down with me. Maintaining my butterfly position on the floor, I proceeded to stroke his dick with my hand. I looked up at Jazzy, and he was looking down at me smiling. He knew what time it was.

I inhaled every inch of his thick, juicy vessel. It was the submarine, and my mouth was the ocean. "Ummm," I moaned. I cupped Jazzy's nuts with my hand and moved my head back and forth on his dick.

"Oooh, Harlem, baby, shit!" Jazzy put his hands on his hips and began to thrust them back and forth.

When I first started giving him head, he used to like to grab my head and thrust himself into my mouth. That was some ole' degrading porn star-type shit that I wasn't hav-ing—some nigga grabbing me by my hair and bobbing me on his dick like I'm some fuckin' puppet. Hell no! Sometimes he would still catch himself doing it, not knowing what to do with his hands. That's when he just started putting them on his hips and letting me do my thang, which is exactly what I was doing. My head game had never really been on point because I never really did that kind of shit on the regular. I always questioned what was in it for me. But seeing the way that it pleased the man I loved damn near brought me to climax.

With my free hand I grabbed his dick and slightly squeezed it. It was as hard as an alcoholic trying to pass a sobriety test. I then swirled my tongue across the tip of it, which absolutely drove Jazzy crazy.

"That's right," Jazzy moaned, "spell your name on that dick with your tongue. Spell your name. It's yours."

"It's mine?" I pulled it harder into my mouth. "Is it mine?"

"Hell yeah! Do dat shit, girl."

I pulled Jazzy out of my mouth but continued fondling his nuts and jacking off his dick as I stood up. Looking him in his eyes, I placed the tip of him against my clit and proceeded to grind against him.

"You like that?" Jazzy asked.

"You know I do." I gave him a peck on his lips.

"Now put it in."

Jazzy lifted my left leg, and I slid his dick deep inside of me. The next thing I knew, he had lifted my right leg too and had me in the air, fucking the shit out of me. Stumbling out of the closet to the bed, Jazzy cupped my ass cheeks in the palm of his hands and lifted me up and down as I threw my head back in ecstasy.

After throwing me down on the bed, Jazzy stood over me as if he was a starving man who hadn't eaten in days and I was his main course. "Girl, I'm 'bout to tear that shit up." Jazzy smiled and came down on top of me.

"I ain't scared of you," I said with a mischievous grin on my face.

Just as he placed himself inside of me, the doorbell rang.

"Aw, shit!"

"Reese!" I exclaimed.

The doorbell rang again.

"Fuck that! Let it ring." Jazzy began humping me. He slowly slid himself inside of me and then slowly pulled it out until only the very tip of the tip was touching me. He then quickly thrusted himself back in and slowly pulled himself back out, pushing the right button each time.

"Oh, Jazzy," I moaned as I started to work with him, pulling my hips away slowly as he pulled out, and thrusting myself hard against him as he re-entered. We were grooving.

And then the doorbell rang again.

"I can't just leave her out there." I placed my hands on his shoulders and tried to push him off of me, tightening my pussy around his dick, trying to get one last feeling of pleasure in.

"Umm, umm," Jazzy said as he thrust inside of me. "I'm getting mine." He began pumping in and out of me. "And if you knew what was good for you, you'd shut the fuck up, lay here, and get yours too." Jazzy planted his teeth into the side of my neck as he sucked.

I spread my legs as wide as they could go, allowing him to quickly get the both of us off. We pumped and grinded each other wildly like two animals.

"Oh, shit. That's right. Keep that shit wide open for Daddy. Hold dem ankles."

The doorbell rang again.

I tried to block it out as I grabbed my ankles and arched my back. "Fuck me, Jazzy, fuck me." I pumped my ass high up off the bed so that Jazzy could visit deep inside of me.

"Oh Jazzy." I bit down on his shoulder as he released himself inside of me, trembling as I came right along with him.

Our bodies jerked until they were weak.

"Oh shit, Harlem World," Jazzy said as he rolled off me, and onto his back. He lay there looking up at the ceiling, his chest rising up and down from breathing so heavily.

Just then the doorbell rang again.

I jumped up. "Shit, Jazzy!" I ran into the closet and snatched up my navy blue suit. "Throw on your clothes and go let Reese in while I clean up and get dressed real quick."

"I can't believe you 'bout to go to church just after committing such a sinful act," Jazzy joked as he got up to slip his clothes on.

"Fuck you, Jazzy." I laughed as I headed to the bathroom. "Like all them other backsliding Christians say, 'God knows my heart.'"

I closed the door behind me and jumped into the shower. I didn't even use my sponge. I just used my hands to do a quick wash up. As I stood there allowing the water to run down my body to rinse the soap, I thought to myself, *God knows my heart all right. He knows everything.* I looked up. *God, I hope you can keep a secret.*

Chapter 4
I Know What You Did
That Summer

It was late and it would be dark soon, but I needed to visit Morgan's grave. I was running the Main Street store alone, so I had to stay until close. But I needed to get to that grave and I needed to do it tonight. It was daylight savings time, but it was still getting dark. I wasn't worried about visiting a graveyard at night. All I was worried about was finding the damn plot in the dark.

I hadn't been to Morgan's grave in a grip. There was a time when I could have gotten to her plot blindfolded. When she first died I used to visit quite frequently. I would spend the entire day reading to her. Reading was Morgan's favorite pastime, that and passing time with dudes.

Looking and built like Naomi Campbell, Morgan could have had any man she wanted. Problem was, she always wanted some gangsta, thug-type nigga; she claimed she only liked them to play with. That's how I knew she didn't really have any feelings for Jazzy, even though he was one of the nicer ones she had ever been with. That, and the fact that she never talked about Jazzy much. Only to complain that he wasn't buying her gifts and stuff like York was buying me. If she really liked a guy, I knew about it.

I knew eventually I would have gotten Morgan together in the men department and she would have gone on to get married and live happily ever after with her 2.5 children. But all that was taken away from her that dreaded night. Now I was left with nothing but a memory and an oversized engraved rock I could come talk to whenever I got a chance.

Once Jazzy took over The Suga Shop and turned it into Harlem's Blues, things started changing so quickly. Our workload tripled because Jazzy had so many plans that he wanted put into motion. Sometimes I thought his plan should have included a bedroom in the back of the store for as many times we damn near spent the night there.

I ain't no punk; I can admit that I buried myself in work to forget that I had buried my best friend. I wanted to run from that part of my life. But the nightmares reminded me that I can run but I can't hide.

The sun was incognito by the time I reached Greenlawn Cemetery. I drove right to Morgan's grave without even second-guessing myself. It was a warm evening, but all of a sudden, as I exited my car, a cool breeze kissed the left side of my face. I imagined that it was Morgan, glad to see me.

I slowly walked over to Morgan's headstone, touched it, and then sat down. "Hey," I said, as if she was sitting right across from me. "I know it's been a minute, but shit has been crazy. I've been so busy running the stores and shit." I put my head down, not knowing what to say next.

I could see Morgan sitting there with her arms crossed like, "Bitch, please—I am not trying to hear those lame-ass excuses."

"Okay, so I haven't been that busy," I confessed. "But I figured that you must miss me as much as I miss you because you keep visiting me in my dreams." I chuckled, paused and then got right to the point. "Morgan, what do you want from me?" I asked in a desperate tone, holding out my hands. "What else could you possibly want from me? I thought you would be able to rest in peace. Your blood was on their hands, and now their blood is on mine. So you rest now and leave me alone. No more messing with my head and stuff, okay? No more. I'm not trying to be hard on you, but you don't understand—this shit is driving me crazy! It's so real. It feels so real that I can't take it. It feels so real that some days I feel like I'm going to walk into the store and find you there working . . . not that you ever got to work before me."

I took a deep breath and buried my face into the palms of my hands. I felt nuts. I felt trapped because I couldn't talk to anyone else but Morgan about what was going on in my head, the nightmares. I wanted to talk to Jazzy, but I couldn't. He was my best friend now, and I shared everything with him. Everything, but this. I mean, What was I supposed to do—Walk up to him and say, "I see dead people"?

Before Jazzy there was Morgan. She was the one who knew everything about me that there was to know. So here I sat talking to her and waiting there, almost if she was going to respond.

"What more do you want?" I yelled at Morgan's grave. "What more?"

I wanted a sign, any sign. I even ended up going to church with Reese that following Sunday after visiting Morgan's grave in hopes that my sign would be there. In something the pastor preached about, in something the choir sang about, in something the dance ministry danced about. I must admit, it did seem like the pastor had a word for me as he preached on being baptized, the remission of sins, and living life on a new slate, so to speak. The dance ministry danced to a song titled "Yes," by Shekinah Glory that insisted that there was so much more required of me. It was now up to me to figure out just how much more I had to give, and exactly what more consisted of.

* * *

For the next few months I continued having nightmares. I thought it was just a phase, and that it would all be over soon, but with Detective Somore paying me yet another visit, I knew that my nightmares were just beginning.

"Miss Jones," Detective Somore stood on the doorstep of my front porch. "How'd I know that this time you'd answer your door?"

"Detective," was all he got from me.

"I just have a couple questions I need to ask you."

"Well, can you make it quick, because I have to head to work?"

"Is that so? Hmm . . . I just left the store, looking for you actually, and the nice lady informed me that you had left for the day because you weren't feeling well."

Fuck! I had left the store earlier because my stomach was giving me problems. I actually hadn't been feeling well for a couple of days. I had been feeling sick to my stomach and light-headed. I hadn't gotten much sleep either and was just worn out.

"Yes, but I'm feeling better now, so I decided to go back in."

"I see." He rocked back and forth from heel to toe. "I'll make it quick then." Somore took out his notepad and pen. "What kind of car did you say those two men who picked you and your friend up at the mall were driving?"

"I didn't say. I didn't remember. Remember?"

"Oh yeah, that's right." He paused. "You know there was a car found where we found those two homicide victims I was telling you about. A uhh . . . what kind of car was that again?" He flipped through his notepad. "A red Nissan Altima."

I swallowed slowly as Detective Somore immediately looked up at me for my reaction. He didn't say anything, he just stared at me, and I stared right back.

"You said a couple, as in two—What's your other question?"

"Oh, yeah, I'm sorry." He pretended to snap out of his daze.

It all seemed so rehearsed, like he had been watching and emulating that weird-ass detective on *Law and Order*, the one who blew his brains out in the movie *Full Metal Jacket*. He kind of resembled him too, only he was a little heavier and had lots of gray in his hair.

"You know what . . . that other question has slipped my mind. I guess I'll just have to come back and see you when I can remember what it was. You know better than anybody how easy it is to forget things."

"Yeah, you just do that. Now if you don't mind, all of a sudden I don't feel too well again, so I'm going to go lay back down."

"Oh, I'm sorry to hear that, Miss Jones. Anyway, thanks for your time." He made his way down the steps.

"Which case are you trying to solve anyway, Detective?" I couldn't help asking. I was tired of the game he was trying to play with me.

"Excuse me, Miss Jones?"

"Which case are you trying to solve anyway?" I said louder, and with more attitude. "You show up at my store, you show up at my home talking about you're trying to solve my case, but yet you're always focused on that other case. Maybe that's why you can't solve my case."

"Finally, a little emotion. I was starting to worry there for a minute, Miss Jones."

" 'Worry'?" I sucked my teeth. "You'll never have to worry about me, Detective. I've always taken care of myself just fine."

"For some reason I don't doubt that. Anyway, good day, Miss Jones." He continued toward his car. "And to answer your question—I have the strangest feeling that if I can solve one of the cases, I'd be killing two birds with one stone." On that note, Detective Somore got into his car and drove away.

"Baby, you all right?" Jazzy walked into the bathroom.

I was leaning over the toilet and puking.

"I really think you need to go to the doctor. You've missed four days of work in the last two weeks. Let you tell it, you ain't missed a day of work since you first opened the bookstore."

"Yeah, yeah," I said nonchalantly. "I'll make a doctor's appointment."

"This is serious. You said you were going to go to the doctor last week, and you didn't go. You ain't getting no better—you look like shit."

"Thanks a fuckin' lot." Before I could say anything else, my face was buried in the toilet bowel again.

"Harlem . . ." Jazzy paused to gather his thoughts. He got this real serious look on his face and then took a deep breath. "Do you think you might be pregnant? I hope not, because the last thing I want is a kid, man."

"Well, damn! Let's hope I'm not pregnant then. Thanks for your comforting words."

"You know I don't bite my tongue; you don't bite yours either. That's why we have such a good relationship."

"Up until five seconds ago."

"I just want to let you know where I stand from jump."

"Well I feel a lot better now knowing that if I am pregnant, you're going to be right there holding my hand while I get the baby sucked out of me."

"*Fetus.*"

"What?"

"It wouldn't be a baby yet; it would be a fetus."

"Look, I personally don't give a fuck about pro life, pro choice, a fetus, a baby or shit. I'm not about to debate with you right now. But, if it makes you feel any better, I don't want a goddamn baby either. The last thing I'd ever want to do is to bring a baby into this fucked-up world! Hell, I'll never forget what it's like to be a kid in this world. I'd never wish that shit on my worst enemy. Do you hear me? Never!" Just then I hunched over and grabbed my stomach, as the sharpest pain ripped through me.

"Harlem World, you all right?" Jazzy kneeled down next to me.

I started to sweat profusely, and the room started to spin. The next thing I know, Jazzy had me in the car on the way to the hospital.

By the time we made it to Mount Carmel Hospital's emergency room, Jazzy, typically a cool-ass muthafucka, was in panic mode.

"She just fell out! She just fell out!" he shouted to the input nurse.

"And when was the date of her last menstrual cycle?" The nurse typed into her computer.

"What?" Jazzy snapped. "What the hell does that have to do with the fact that—"

"Shhh, shah, shah." I cut Jazzy off, placing my index finger over his lips. With my other hand I was holding my stomach, my eyes were closed, and I was shaking my head at the incredible pain in my stomach. "It was three weeks ago. Around April 7th."

"Thank you," she said, ignoring Jazzy's attitude. She was probably used to that type of thing, overzealous people scared for their loved ones.

After the nurse finished gathering the basic information from me and putting it into the computer, she had us go back in the waiting area until the doctor could see me.

"What the fuck is taking them so long?" Jazzy said as he sat next to me with his arm around me.

I just gave him a moan.

"Harlem, do you think . . . do you think that maybe you might be, uh, you know . . . with child?"

I immediately sat up out of his arms. I didn't know if he was more concerned about my health or if he was going to have to deal with a crazy-ass baby mama. "What the fuck is this 'with child' shit?"

Now Jazzy and I could go at it. We loved the hell out of each other, and nothing could come between our love. But we were too much alike not to have disagreements and a frequent exchange of words, as I liked to call them.

"Nigga, just say pregnant. Don't come at me with that white people's 'with child' shit." I rested back down. Then I immediately sat back up. "And what if I am? Is this fuckin' déjà vu, or did we not just have this conversation? Did I bump my head when I fell?"

"Calm your hyper ass down." Jazzy pulled me back into my arms. "And watch your mouth. You up in a hospital doing all that goddamn, muthafuckin' cussin. You think all these sick muthafuckas wanna hear that shit?"

I just buried my face in my hands and sighed.

"Harlem Jones," a voice called.

"Right here." Jazzy helped me to stand up, forgetting all about our argument.

The nurse who'd called my name said, "Can you follow me to the back?"

We followed her to an examination room, where she took my blood pressure, checked my pulse, and asked me the same damn questions the intake nurse asked me. She then had me go to the bathroom and provide her with a urine sample.

"The doctor will be right in," she said, exiting the room and closing the door behind her.

About ten minutes later the nurse returned to the room, following behind the doctor.

"Miss Jones." The doctor extended his hand. "I'm Doctor Ward. How are you?"

I never understood why doctors always asked that question. *What the fuck do you mean how am I? I'm in the ER. How do you think I am?* I clutched my stomach as a sharp pain entered it.

"Oh, not too well I see," Doctor Ward said.

No fuckin' shit.

"Well, after looking at your chart and from the test that we've run, I don't think this is a hard one to diagnose," he said. "I do want to do one more thing, though, but I believe I already know what the cause of your discomfort is."

Once the doctor confirmed why I had been feeling the way I had been feeling, he gave me a prescription along with some instructions to follow. He then advised me to make sure that I followed up with my own doctor because it was very important in the early stages.

Jazzy and I waited in silence as we sat in the CVS pharmacy drive-thru. There was so much tension in the air that neither one of us wanted to be the first to use our tongue to cut through it.

"A bleeding ulcer," Jazzy said, finally breaking the silence. "All that arguing over nothing."

"I wasn't the one arguing," I said. "You were the one trying to drive me to the abortion clinic just on GP, like you're this God and the only thing a pitiful soul like myself was put on earth to do was to carry your seed. Nigga, you fine and all but . . ." I sucked my teeth.

"Look, if you don't want to accept my apology, then fuck it."

"What apology?—You didn't apologize."

"Well, you know what I meant."

I just looked at that nigga and shook my head. His ass was so lucky that he was fine. By now I'd be asking myself, "What's love got to do with it?" and be done with his cocky ass. But every time I looked at him, just like back in the day when he was what I wanted but couldn't have, there was just this electric current that rushed through me and made me forget how much he could get on my nerves sometimes. Like Middle Child's song says, "It was his mystery that got the best of me."

Jazzy was far from an open book. If you didn't ask, he didn't tell. That's how the man who had raised him as his own taught him to be. In addition to teaching him how to be a natural born hustler—unlike most hustlers who started hustling because they had to eat—Jazzy's pops taught him to never let anyone know everything about you. They could learn your weakness and possibly use it against you some day. Finding out what lies deep beneath the surface of a person can change the way you look at them from that point on, make you see them as something other than what you thought they were. I was living proof of that and therefore felt forced to remain secretive.

"Look, Jazzy, I don't wanna fight." I sighed. "I don't want to put no more stress on myself and make this thing in my gut any worse."

"An ulcer? I don't get it. You cool. Everything's cool. Ain't nothing been stressing you or bothering you like that where your shit should be all fucked up."

Little did my man know, I had all kinds of shit stressing me out and worrying the fuck out of me to the point where I had made myself sick. I had to figure out a way to put an end to this shit. I couldn't live with the thought of one day Detective Somore showing up to my front door with handcuffs custom-fitted for my wrists. Something had to give. All my life I had figured out a way to get out of shit and not become a victim to any circumstance. Once again, I was being tested.

"Well, I know one thing," Jazzy continued, "I almost got a

damn ulcer worrying about you being pregnant and shit, but I got a cure for that."

Before I could even ask Jazzy just what his cure was, the pharmacist opened the drive-thru window to hand him my prescription. "Do you have any questions about any of your prescriptions?" she asked.

"No," I answered from the passenger side.

"Then is there anything else I can get for you?" she asked as Jazzy freed her hands of the medicines.

"Yes," Jazzy answered. "Some condoms."

" 'Condoms'?" the pharmacist said. "What type? How many?"

Jazzy looked over at me, and then back at the pharmacist. "All of them. Every kind you got. Every size. I'll make that shit work!"

I just shook my head and laughed as the pharmacist then proceeded to bag up every type of condom they had.

"You are so stupid," I said to Jazzy.

"Oh, but I'm so sincere." He then looked at me and got very serious. "Look, Harlem, you know I love you to death. There's nothing more in the world I want than to one day live far off in a house on a hill with some kids, dogs, and cats and shit. You know. But it's gotta be right. My hustle is legit now, but it's still a hustle. We constantly put in work, real blue-collar work. That shit still takes some getting used to after being in the game as long as I was. And I ain't gonna even lie to you, Harlem—I get that taste for the life some-time."

The hairs damn near stood up on my neck.

"I do. What can I say? The streets raised me, and there's no place like home. But I'm trying to make my home with you. But before we do that, I gotta make sure that shit is shaken completely from my veins."

"It's been a while now since you've turned over a new leaf, so to speak. I didn't know it was like that."

"Yes, you did," Jazzy was quick to say. "Do you forget that

I'm Superman? I see right through you. I see it in how hard you try to please me. And you do please me. The Harlem I once knew only cared about pleasing herself, making sure her shit was in order. I know it's hard for you to give so much of yourself to me. And whether you can admit it or not, on top of that, trying to give yourself to a child too—you ain't ready for that. So with the two of us still trying to grow and remove our feet from the cement of being set in our ways, the last thing we need right now is to bring another life into the picture."

I paused for a minute. I then looked him in the eyes and touched his face. "I hear you, Jason." I felt as though he was going to melt in my hands right then and there as he loosened his body and rested his face in my hand.

"Don't call me that," Jazzy joked, regaining his composure, not about to become putty in some woman's hands. "Only my mama can call me that."

"Then when I'm up to feeling better," I teased, licking my lips, "why don't I give you a reason to call me mommy?"

Jazzy grabbed his hardening dick. "How long the doctor say it would take for them meds to kick in?"

"Boy, you stupid."

The pharmacist handed Jazzy three CVS bags full of condoms. He paid for them and then threw the bags into my lap.

"Now, we'll never have to have this conversation again," Jazzy said as he drove off.

For the next few months, once I got better, Jazzy and I had sex like rabbits, protected sex, of course. He was dead serious about us not having a baby until the time was right.

Things were really looking up for us. The stores were booming. We had some of the best-selling authors in the country, such as D.L. Moore, P.R. Hawkins, and Dakota Knight, visiting our stores to do book signings. We had the world-renowned poet, Ed Mabry, hosting open-mic poetry, and music performances that were standing-room-only by artists such as Middle Child and Foley.

In addition to helping run the bookstores, Reese was doing some work for Mary Haven, counseling women with drug addictions. There was also talk of her going back to school for her bachelor's degree because she felt that was her calling in life and she wanted to some day do it full-time.

The Columbus Museum of Art had a showing, which included one of Jazzy's drawings that he had donated to the museum. After the showing, we couldn't keep not one of his pieces of work in either of the stores.

Things had even been looking up for York. He had some good news of his own. When Jazzy and I got word of his news, the old saying of something being too good to be true came to mind. Soon enough we'd find out just how true, in fact, that saying actually was.

Chapter 5
Once a Hustler Always
a Hustler

Once we left the prison from picking up York, we headed straight to McDonald's, where Jazzy ordered damn near everything on the menu. I don't know if it was because we had just blazed on one of the fattest blunts ever, loaded with that good shit, and he had the munchies like a mug, or if it was to show York that though his lifestyle might have changed, but his ways and the things he had been able to do before in life hadn't, that he could still afford everything on the menu.

Jazzy and I had planned to take York to a first-class sit down restaurant, but York wanted to look the part when we rolled out like that. We promised him that we were going to do the damn thing Big Willie style to officially celebrate his release from jail.

The constant smile York wore on his face must have paid off swell because he was released from prison two and a half years earlier than he had copped in his plea. Evidently, that nigga was a model inmate. I didn't know there was really such a thing. I guess ol' York turned out to be the best of the worst.

All York was worried about was getting home, taking a nice long hot shower in his own private bathroom, and getting some sleep on a nice soft bed. So after leaving McDonald's, we headed straight to York's house.

It was the middle of August, and the temperature was in the upper 70s. On warm days, Jazzy normally drove with the windows up and the air on. He hated the noisy sound the wind made while speeding down the highway. However, today, he drove with all of the windows down.

I pulled my sun visor down to look in the mirror so that I could replenish the lip-gloss I had smudged off when demolishing my Quarterpounder with cheese. I could see York in the mirror. He had his head out the window, allowing the wind to suffocate him. Every few seconds he'd pull his head in to catch his breath. He was just a-grinning.

It was funny, watching him appreciate that little shit the rest of us take for granted every day, like the sound and the feel of the wind blowing.

York looked up and caught me eyeing him through the sun visor mirror. He gave me a crooked half-smile.

I flipped the mirror up without giving him one back in return. I looked over at Jazzy and he was looking at me. *Here we go,* I thought. Since I'd known Jazzy, no one had ever been a threat to him. Was that about to change?

When we pulled up into York's driveway, he started grabbing his belongings, as if someone was going to steal them from him. He was on a high that didn't have anything to do with that blunt we had just puffed on. I could see it in his eyes. That nigga was ready to get back to the hood of things.

"All right then, Jazzy, Harlem," York said as he began tugging at the door handle, arms loaded.

Hearing all the commotion, I turned around to watch him. "Why don't you go knock first, let Yvette open the door for you, and then come back and get your stuff?" I would have offered to help him carry some of his things, but the

last time I saw his sister, it was right there in that same driveway and we was brawling like two pit bulls over the last piece
of raw meat.

Yvette hated me and I hated that bitch. As a matter of fact,
had we referred to each other by any name other than 'that
bitch,' York would have known exactly who I was in the first
place, when I first told him my name.

York and Yvette had come up hard in life. Their mother
killed herself to escape their father's abuse. Stuck with a
man for the rest of their life who didn't give a shit about
them, they sometimes had to eat dog food in order to cure
their hunger pains. All they had was each other. York, as the
older brother, vowed that for as long as he lived, his little sister would never go hungry again. He made it his mission in
life to always look out for his sister. That's why he got into
the drug game in the first place, to be able to provide for
them.

"Yeah, that makes sense," York said to me, putting everything in his arms down on the back seat. "Beauty and
brains—what a combination." He winked.

Jazzy looked at York through the rearview mirror. "Man,
you trying to hit on my girl right under my nose?" Jazzy pretended to joke. "I know you fresh out the joint and shit—a
brotha can hook you up with some pussy right over there
outside the store on Main Street."

"Nigga, please." York laughed and Jazzy joined him.

"Ya sister here?" Jazzy asked. "Yvette know today is the day
you coming home, right?"

"Yeah, fo' sho. I wrote her ass and let her know. Been trying to call her, but she had some issues with the phone and
some other bills, you know? But all that's gon' change once I
get my shit together."

Jazzy turned around to look at York. "Why you ain't let me
know it was like that on the home front? You know I would
have looked out."

I turned my ass around so quick and gave Jazzy the look of death. He knew goddamn well that I wouldn't have gone for him giving that bitch a dime. I might have been able to stay cool with York, but still I hated his sister.

When York and I had gotten together, I had no idea that one of my worst enemies would turn out to be his sister.

Yvette was some girl Morgan had hung with back in the day, long before I ever thought of York. Morgan had met Yvette through some dude she was fucking. Yvette was one of his boy's girlfriends. If Morgan thought she was cool enough to kick it with, then I tolerated her being around, but when that bitch crossed me, oh I had to get wit' her.

The three of us had gone on a trip in a rental that Yvette put in her name. On our way back home, we were in a car accident. Some dude ran a stop sign. I was the only one who got fucked up so—hell yeah—a bitch like me filed a claim against the fool who hit us insurance company.

Yvette thought that her insurance company was going to have to get involved or that the shit was going to fall back on her some how, so she tried to sabotage my claim. She called the insurance company and told them I was filing a false claim and shit.

Fortunately, I still ended up settling the claim for a nice lump of change, but that bitch still had to pay for crossing me. By the time I got finished with that bitch, Uncle Sam had confiscated everything she owned.

As much as Yvette hustled and ran schemes, even if I had been faking my injuries, she was the last sheisty bitch to be turning in a muthafucka. She had rigged pay stubs and tax returns to get a house. She even had Morgan verify her employment by pretending to work at Chase Manhattan Bank in the human resources department to help get her a car financed. She told us about some brother she supposedly had who lived out of town that shot her money to take care of her. Morgan and I thought that was just another one of her lies. We thought that bitch was trickin', 'ho'in', or whatever you wanted to call it. But I would one day find out that she really did have a brother, York.

That's pretty much how York and my relationship came to a sudden halt. When he took me to his house to meet his sister the shit hit the fan. I didn't even get a chance to get out of the car when that bitch had opened the door and pulled me out by my shirt. She caught me off guard, or else she would have never gotten that one off.

All I remembered her screaming was, "What the fuck are you doing at my house, bitch? And what the fuck are you doing with my brother?"

I looked up and there that bitch was, standing in a boxing stance.

We ended up brawling, until York separated us. He didn't know what the fuck was going on until Yvette told him.

"That's the bitch I was telling you about who got me put out of my house back in the day. This is that bitch that caused me all that trouble that landed us flat broke again," Yvette informed York.

I'll never forget the look on York's face. That boy stood there like a deer caught in headlights. It was crazy because earlier that day he had just told me that he loved me for the very first time and I was just about to tell him that I loved him too—until that bitch snatched me out of the car. Now he had received the shocking news that he had been sleeping with the enemy.

That was the day when York and I parted ways as boyfriend and girlfriend. There was no way I could ask him to choose sides, me or his blood. Therefore, I walked away, literally. I walked away in three-inch stilettos and that nigga actually let me walk. He didn't even try to stop me. Hell, Kevin Costner stopped a huge jet to get Whitney Houston's ass in *The Bodyguard*. And with me being the grudgable bitch that I was, I knew I was done with his ass. But 'spite all the bullshit, in my heart, I knew that blood was thicker than water. That's why I was able to stay cool with York to this day. That and the fact that he was my man's best friend.

Nonetheless, York and I both had managed to let bygones be bygones as far as us not being a couple anymore. We had to, in order to still maintain a friendship.

I was genuinely happy for him as I watched him go to the door and knock. He turned around and looked at us, smiling. He looked like a little kid who had just stole five dollars from his crazy, old auntie's purse and got away with it.

When the door opened there was some dude standing there. He looked as though he had just gotten out of the joint himself. This nigga was huge—buff as a muthafuck— wearing nothing but a pair of jeans. His bare upper body showed off his muscular pecks. He was wearing a wave cap on his head with a New York Knicks ballcap over it. His arms were all tattooed up.

"Where's Yvette?" York had a look on his face as if to say, "Who da fuck dis cat answering my door?"

"Don't no Yvette live here, man," the dude said with a smirk on his face. "Some shawty done gave you the wrong address, my man."

"Yvette's my sister, man. This is my muthafuckin' house," York said in a stern voice.

"Then you need to get with Caldwell Real Estate, son, 'cause they sold me and my girl this shit two months ago."

I couldn't believe what I was hearing. Telling by the frozen look on York's face, he couldn't believe what he was hearing either. I mean, I knew Yvette was a dirty bitch, but I never thought in a million years that she would do her blood like that.

Jazzy could see that York was in a fucked-up state. He got out of the car to go have his boy's back. His intuition was on point because no sooner than he made it halfway to the porch, York was on his way up in the house to check out shit for himself.

"I need to see if my shit up in here." York attempted to push dude out of the way and enter the house.

"What the fuck you doing, son?" The dude grabbed hold of York's arms.

"Man, get the fuck up off me." York pushed the dude in the chest.

"Whoa, whoa." Jazzy got in between the two.

"You better holler at your boy," the dude said to Jazzy, breathing hard. "He don't want none of what I got up in here. You don't want none, son, trust."

"Fuck you, you big Melly Mel-looking mu'fucka." York still tried to walk up on dude, but Jazzy managed to keep them apart.

"Look, man," Jazzy said, "my man here just did a bid, you know what I'm saying? He just got out thinking he was coming home, only to find out that he ain't got a home. Imagine how fucked up you would be."

The dude looked over at York who was pacing, talking to himself.

I couldn't make out everything he was saying, but I did hear the word *bitch* a few times.

The dude looked at Jazzy and nodded. "It's cool." He raised his hands in truce.

"It's cool?" Jazzy confirmed, extending his arm to shake on it.

The dude nodded and shook Jazzy's hand. "It's cool."

"All right then, homie." Jazzy pulled out his wallet, peeled off a few bills, and extended them to him. "Sorry for the inconvenience, my man."

The dude looked down and took the money from Jazzy. " 'Inconvenience.' " He counted the bills. "There's no 'inconvenience' here; I can't think of anything better I could have done with my time."

After walking off the porch, Jazzy approached York. "You gonna be all right?"

I could tell that it was taking everything in York not to cry. "I'm fucked up, Jay." York buried his head in his hands. "This is some fucked-up shit, yo."

"Yeah, man, I know," Jazzy said in a somber tone as he rested his hand on York's shoulder. "Come on, let's get out of here."

Jazzy and York headed back towards the car.

"Yo, son," the dude yelled to York.

York stopped in his tracks, tightened his lips, and turned around.

"Sorry about your situation," the dude said. "Take it easy." He pounded his fist on his chest and then closed the door.

York swallowed, looked up at Jazzy and then at me with moist eyes. He sighed and got back into the car.

Jazzy hopped into the car and positioned himself behind the wheel. He looked at York, he looked at me, and then I at York. None of us said one word as Jazzy pulled out of the driveway and drove off. Shit didn't need to be said—York was our boy; he was coming home with us.

"Damn, man, I can't believe you're home," I could hear Jazzy say as I stood at the top of the steps listening. I had been on my way down the steps to grab a drink but, for some reason, I halted when I heard them speaking.

"That makes two of us," I heard York say. He must have taken a puff of the magic dragon because he got choked up, and it didn't sound as though it was for sentimental reasons.

"That was your house too. How she just gon' up and sell your shit like that, move out and leave you hanging?"

"Things must have really gotten bad and shit," York said.

I didn't give a fuck what him and that bitch had been through as kids: if I was York, I'd spend every waking moment looking for her ass. And once I found her, I'd beat her like they daddy did their mama. Not trying to be funny, but that bitch needed a good ass-whooping.

"As tight as you and Yvette were, as much as you looked out for her ass," Jazzy said, "things could have never gotten that bad to the point where she just up and leaves you hangin' like that. You better than me, dawg—if that was my sister, I'd be spending every waking moment looking for her ass, and once I found her . . . man."

Yep. Jazzy and I are too damn much alike, I thought.

"Hell, Columbus ain't that damn big. You'd find her ass."

"Unless she went back to Atlanta," York stated.

For a moment, there was silence. I heard him sigh and then I heard his voice crack as he continued, "Man, what the fuck am I gonna do? I got nothing, man. Once again, I got nothing—I can't believe this fuckin' shit! I can't believe this."

I could tell York was crying. Something inside of me just melted for his pain. Before I knew it, I had taken a step down the stairs as if York was calling me and I was subconsciously going to his rescue.

"It's gon' be all right, man. It's gon' be all right," I heard Jazzy say.

I took one step down and bent my head down in an attempt to see them. Their backs were to me, and I could see everything but their heads. They were both sitting on the floor in front of the television, where they had obviously been playing the game station.

By now, York was bawling. His shoulders were going up and down.

I could tell that he was embarrassed to be sitting there crying in front of his boy.

My Jazzy just sat there, probably looking dumbfounded.

He didn't know what to do at first, but then he did what any best friend would do. He went over to York, pulled him against him, and put one arm around him.

York threw the game controller down. I jumped back and returned to the top of the steps upon hearing it hit the base of the television.

"Damn, man. Sorry 'bout that and shit." York sniffed. There was a brief pause before he spoke again. "I'm sitting here, crying and shit. Damn!"

"It's all good, man," Jazzy said.

I heard a couple thumps as if Jazzy was patting York on the back. I heard some movement, then I realized that one of them must have gotten up and gone and sat on the couch because I heard the sound the leather makes when someone sits on it.

"I really hate to ask you this, man," York started. "I mean, you and your girl have already done so much for me."

"Nigga, please—you know you can ask me anything. It ain't nothin'. I got you."

"Word?" York said.

"Straight up." Jazzy waited for York to spit it out.

"I need your contacts, man," York said in a most sincere and serious tone.

"What?"

"Your contacts," York repeated. "Your connects, man, you know. I can't stay here with you and Harlem forever, man. I need to get on my feet and quick. You and I both know that there is only one way for a nigga like me to get on his feet quick—I gotta make some moves."

"Man, do you know what you're asking me?"

"I know, man, but—"

"I'd rather give you the money to get on your feet than to do that shit, man."

"I ain't no bitch, no kept woman," York spat. "What I look like, having my boy set me up in a place and shit? I've always put in work for mine, you know that, Jazzy. I put in work for you. I worked hard for you for years, man."

My body began to quiver as I leaned against the hallway wall. I knew that York's words was the silver bullet through the vampire's heart. I didn't want to hear any more. I knew Jazzy well enough to know that loyalty meant everything to him. I could have run down those steps and had my say, but at the end of the day, they would have fallen upon deaf ears. I knew that about my man because I knew that about myself. There wasn't anything I wouldn't have done for Morgan. Anything.

I tiptoed out of the hallway and went to the bathroom and closed the door behind me. I walked over to the sink and turned on the cold water. I splashed my face a couple of times then looked up in the mirror, and just like before, there they stood, staring at me. Not my own eyes, but their eyes. I jumped, closed my eyes, and quickly turned away from the mirror.

How could I possibly be worried about Jazzy's past, when mine was now becoming part of my present?

Chapter 6
Road Dawg

Before now, it had been easy keeping this bone buried so deep that not even Jazzy could scent it out. It was over and done with. It wasn't as if it was something I thought about every day. Besides, I thought more about how Morgan met her death than how I had avenged it. Telling Jazzy would have been fruitless, in addition to making him an accessory after the fact.

York had his own shit to deal with. On top of that, if I shared this with him and Jazzy ever found out, he would clown. If Jazzy thought for one minute that I could go to another nigga before coming to him that would be the end of us.

Turning to Reese was simply not an option. She'd have me up in the church praying and anointing me with oil. Her only solution would be turning myself in and having faith in God. That's not even what I was trying to hear.

I didn't think anyone could truly understand the desperation of my act, unless they had been in my shoes. Morgan would have been there for me, though. She would have understood. She wouldn't have asked any questions. She would have just been down for whatever. *Damn, I miss my road dawg.*

For as long as I could remember it had always been just Morgan and me. I was never into allowing people to get within arm's length. Even growing up I never ran with a bunch of females, a crew, or clique. It was sometimes a challenge to even say "Hi" to some bitches. So besides Morgan, I didn't think I'd ever met anyone that I would even have wanted to be friends with.

Looking back, I wish shit could have been different. I wish I had been different to some degree, not building up that brick wall around me. Now I couldn't think of anything I could use more than a friend. But thanks to that fuckin' wall that had been chipped open now to the size where only Jazzy and Reese could fit through, I had no one in my life who could ever understand what I was going through and be there to help me through it. *No one*, I thought, *no one but God.*

Almost as if I could hear Reese whispering them in my ear, words she had spoken to me some time ago came to my mind. "God doesn't just show up at your doorstep one day with the answer to everything. Sometimes God uses man."

Right then it dawned on me as I thought back to the one person who God might possibly choose to use to help me right now. There had been, in fact, along my journey through life, one person, besides Morgan, who could perhaps understand me and not judge me. Yes, if anybody could understand my situation, it would be her.

Since we were kids, I had only seen her a few times. She had come into the store on Main Street, where she got her hair done at the shop next door sometimes. Before she had started coming into the store, the last I saw her was that night in the bedroom we shared when her mother, Miss Laura, took me in as a foster child.

The night I ran out of that room, I was running for my life. I had awakened to Miss Laura's boyfriend standing over my bed. There was no looking back for me, as I got the hell out of that house and never went back. I never even talked to anyone about what that pervert was about to do to me. I just thanked my lucky stars that I was able to prevent it. She wasn't though. But I had to look out for number one—that's just how shit was back then. I dipped, she chose not to. That shit was on her; at least that's what I constantly tried to convince myself.

The last I remember, she said she was working for some downtown law firm by the courthouse as a paralegal. I couldn't think of the name of the firm right off the bat, but it was on the tip of my tongue. I knew that I would recognize it if I saw it, so I pulled out the yellow pages and looked under *attorney.*

I scrolled down every listing, one by one.

"Cravers and Zinel—that's it!" I said, excited. Thank goodness the name of the firm wasn't Zinel and Cravers, or else I'd been forever trying to find it.

I wrote down the address, suite, and phone number. My initial instinct was to call, but I felt as though I needed to have a face-to-face. So I decided that I'd just pay her a visit the next day during my lunch hour.

"What are you all dressed up for today?" Reese suspiciously gave me the once-over.

I was wearing my dark-wine skirt suit that was trimmed in satin. I had on some wine open-toe pumps and ultra sheer wine stockings. My hair was slicked back in a long ponytail, and I had on my dainty pearl necklace, earrings, and bracelet set.

"I have somewhere to go during my lunch today, so I'll be a little longer than usual," I said to Reese. "You can take your lunch first because I need to go late anyway.

"Hmm . . ." Reese mumbled. "Must be pretty important because you don't even clean up that nice for church."

I knew she was about to get started. She had to bring the Lord into everything.

"I dress just fine when I go to church." I rolled my eyes. "The Lord said, 'Come as you are.' "

"Now I ain't never heard the Lord say that and I talk to him every day." Reese rolled her eyes right back at me. "Besides, ain't nobody said you got to go out and buy a new dress and hat for church every Sunday, but you should always be willing to give the Lord your best. And obviously, you ain't been giving the Lord your best, 'cause that's the best I ever seen you dressed up, unless that place you got to go during lunch today is noon-hour Bible study."

I sighed, ignoring Reese. "Ain't that new girl from your church you was asking about letting come to the store and do an internship supposed to start today?"

"Don't try to change the subject with me, Missy." Reese hit me on the butt as she walked by me. "Anyway, you look nice in that get-up, is all I'm saying."

"Then I wish that had been all you said," I said under my breath.

"Watch it now, or that hit is going to get harder."

Reese headed to the back room of the store, and I proceeded on about my daily functions.

When Reese left for lunch, I watched the clock, anticipating her return so that I could go handle my business.

Reese got back to the store at about 2:00 p.m.

I pulled up at a parking meter in front of the law firm at 2:18 p.m. I hadn't even thought about what I was going to say once I got there. I was sure, though, that the conversation would go smoothly.

When I walked in the suite, there was a plush reception area. The color scheme was a deep burgundy and gold. Sitting at a huge oval-like booth was the receptionist. Her head was down staring at her computer screen as she typed away at the keyboard. She was a skinny, blonde-haired girl in about her mid-twenties, a nice, strategically placed center-piece for those rich, white male clients the firm was trying to solicit business from. On the burgundy painted walls behind her was gold lettering that read *Cravers & Zinel.*

What the hell were you thinking coming here, Harlem Jones? I stood there blank, feeling out of place. *A street-smart chick like yourself bringing a white-collar outsider into your world—since when in the world do you trust people so easily?*

I turned to walk away, but then I heard a voice say, "Good afternoon."

I stopped and turned.

"Good afternoon," the receptionist said in the most ditzy, aggravating voice on earth. She was definitely there to be seen and not heard.

I could have easily told her that I was in the wrong suite and go just as quickly as I had come, but I had never been a punk, or one to bail out and quit something I had started. It was a pride and ego thing with me. Besides that, something in me said to trust that God had a hand in planting me in that office and not to focus on whether or not I could trust in man at all, but to trust in Him and that whatever the outcome, it would be His will. On that final thought, I brushed my shoulder off and walked towards the receptionist's desk.

"Good afternoon, Raven," I said, reading her nameplate. "I'm Harlem Jones."

"With whom do you have an appointment, Miss Jones?" she said, scanning the pages of her calendar/appointment book.

"Oh, I don't have an appointment." I smiled. "I was in the area and a childhood friend of mine works here. I thought I'd stop in just to say hello if she wasn't tied up or anything."

"Oh, okay." She pushed the book aside. "Who is your friend? I'll let them know you're in the lobby and check if they have a minute to see you."

"Her name is Penny," I said. "Penny McCoy."

When Penny walked out into the lobby, she immediately opened her arms to embrace me. I was anything but the hugging type, but it was like Penny's arms were magnets, drawing me in. I know the hug only lasted a few seconds, but it felt the entire full length of the several weeks we had spent together as kids. Like lightning, it felt as if we were struck by every memory and thought of our brief past together, the good and the bad. At least I was. It was a weird feeling. I couldn't tell if the memories were making us feel close or making us feel distant. Nonetheless, I was there now, and my travel would not be in vain.

"She's cute," I said to Penny, pointing to a 4" x 6" sized framed picture of a little girl that was sitting on the credenza behind her desk. She had never mentioned having a daughter and I was sure that's the first thing she would have mentioned the few times she and I had talked. "One of your friend's kids or a relative or something?"

Penny turned to look at the photo. "No," she replied in a nonchalant, dry tone. "That's my daughter, Baby."

"That's her name, *Baby*?"

Penny nodded.

"She's a doll." I looked at the picture. "How old is she?"

The more I looked at it, the more she did resemble Penny, who was not a bad-looking girl at all. Her hair had been roller set and parted down the middle, with bouncing curls down to her shoulders. Like the little girl in the picture, she had dark-brown eyes and thick, long lashes. Her skin was the color of black coffee with a drop or two of powdered creamer stirred in.

"Yes, she's a cutie all right," Penny said flatly, as if the last thing she wanted to talk about was the little girl in the picture.

For a mother, Penny didn't sound too convincing. I didn't have any kids, so I guess I really didn't know how a mother was supposed to act. Usually it seemed as though most mothers, when given the opportunity, loved to brag about their children. Usually you couldn't shut them up, but Penny just coasted right by the open door.

The fact that the only picture of her daughter was one just above a wallet-size seemed odd too. *Hell, some people keep bigger pictures of their pets in their offices.* Not to mention, the picture wasn't even on her desk. It was *behind* her desk. What was it in her child's eyes that she didn't want to be able to look up from her desk and see?

"So, Harlem Jones, what brings you 'round my way." Penny smiled.

I hadn't been in her office five minutes and already I was stuck. I couldn't just come out and say what I needed from her. I had to vibe with her a little longer, to get a feel of where her head was at. I couldn't take her situation for granted and just assume that she would be willing to help me.

"Well, uh, well, you see—"

"You know, I've never told you this, Harlem, but of all the foster kids my mom allowed into our home over the years, you were the first one that I ever really liked." Penny smiled, but then her smile quickly faded. "So when you left—" She paused and swallowed.

I noticed her eyes watering. Deep down in me, where I could sometimes manage to dig out a little bit of what people call "compassion," I began to get a little emotional, thinking back on the night I left too. I placed my hand over Penny's and just allowed it to rest there, letting her know that I knew how she felt.

In my mind, I finished her sentence. *Alone. So when you left I felt alone,* is what Penny wanted to say to me.

"Anyway," Penny said, regaining her stiff composure, "you were about to tell me why you're here."

"Oh, yeah, yeah, that's right." I quickly searched my head

for the nearest lie. "There's this guy, this crackhead who hangs outside of my store, harassing my customers. On some days, if customers see him out, there they won't even bother coming to the store just so they won't have to deal with him. He's costing me money."

"Okay," she said, nodding and listening very intensely.

I swallowed. "Well, I want to file a suit against him or something," I lied.

"I see." Penny stood up and walked over to the window in her office. "You have a couple of options—you can file a restraining order on him to stay away from both you and your store; you could say he was a public nuisance." She paused and thought for a moment. "You said he's costing you money, right?"

"Umm, hmm." I nodded. "If the customers don't come in, I don't make any money."

She thought for a moment and then added, "You could file a civil suit. That would be a little extreme and I'm sure he doesn't have any money, but you'd definitely get your point across."

"Could you file it?"

"I'm just a paralegal. I could draft it, but one of the firm's counsels would have to represent you in court."

"Oh, okay then. Well, let me think about it, and I'll get back to you."

"No problem." She extended her hand to me. "Just let me know what you want to do, and I'll be glad to help."

"Thanks, Penny," I said as I stood up.

"Anytime. I'm so glad you stopped in, Harlem. It's always good to see you."

I looked in Penny's eyes, and they were so sincere. All of a sudden, I felt sorry for her. Did I really want to make her a part of my mess? After all, I was sure she'd gone through enough mess of her own, considering her mother was in jail for murdering the man who molested her as a child. The same man I ran away from that night. Did I really want to burden her with my own tale of vengeance? Nevertheless, who else could possibly understand better than she could?

"Yeah, I'm glad I stopped in too." I turned the knob and opened the door to let myself out of her office. "You wanna do lunch some time?" I said, to have a reason to get back in touch with her.

"I'd like that." She smiled.

"Good. Then I'll call you next time I'm out this way."

"You do that," Penny said as I headed out the door.

Before I could completely exit, she said, "Oh yeah, and, Harlem, before you leave . . ."

"Yes?"

"Pardon my French, but the Harlem I knew was a bad-ass bitch, even as a little ghetto girl back in the foster care days." She chuckled. "She wouldn't have involved some high-price law firm to handle some homeless bum." Penny's voice became more hard and stern, kind of like mine when I knew somebody's playing games with me.

"So, let's start over. You wanna close that door, come sit back down, and tell me why you're really here?—And don't fuck with me this time."

Chapter 7
Puttin' All the Cards on the Table

I walked back to my car after spilling my guts to Penny. I felt as though a huge weight was being lifted off my shoulders as I shared with her the blow-by-blow details of how I had taken the lives of the two men who had taken the life of my best friend.

I blew the words out in circles of smoke like a chain smoker. I didn't hesitate once, as I explained to Penny how I made those rat bastards lay there on the ground the same way they had forced Morgan and me to do. When one tried to get fly and come at me, I didn't hesitate to pull the trigger, aiming dead for his nut sac. I didn't exactly hit the bull's-eye, but I grazed that muthafucka, which was enough to get his attention. But that didn't stop his ass. Like two crackheads in a marathon for the last rock on earth, that nigga still charged at me, forcing me to shoot him again, this time in the knee.

By that time, the other one figured, since I was distracted, he would attempt to make a run for it, so I had to put one in his belly. Right after that is when I finally put his friend out of his miserable existence by placing a bullet right between his eyes. At that point, the poor, dying bastard knew it was only a matter of minutes before he'd be on a first-name basis with the Grim Reaper as well. He was in pain anyway and probably woulda bled to death from the bullet wound to his stomach. I did the fucka a favor and planted one in his head.

Reliving that night wasn't hard at all, not nearly as hard as reliving the night they tortured me and Morgan. So the same way I went back to my normal everyday life after I did that shit, I went back to my normal everyday life after re-telling it to Penny.

Back at the store I had to dodge Reese's questions all day about where I had been. That's why I liked working with Jazzy more than Reese. Reese used our time in the store to-gether as mother-daughter bonding time. Jazzy knew that all our personal shit stayed at home. When we were in the store, it was strictly business, all about making money.

Lately, whenever Reese and Jazzy worked a store together, I would sometimes get nervous. Because I knew how much Reese was into church and liked doing all that bonding shit, I often feared that one day she would decide to tell Jazzy about the secret that she and I did share, that the man who raised Jazzy as his own son was in fact my biological father. I mean, it really wasn't a big deal. Had Jazzy and I turned out to be blood brothers and sisters, now that would have been a different story. But just the fact that my biological father was like a blood father to Jazzy still made it weird. Weird enough where I was afraid that if I told him, it would make him look at me different, like a sister and not a lover, especially since at the time when I first found out, which was four years ago, we hadn't yet crossed that physical line.

But Reese promised, even though she hated keeping se-crets, that she wouldn't tell Jazzy. And a mother's word was a mother's word.

When I finally closed up the store, it was almost eleven o'clock at night. By the time I made it home, Jazzy had already long closed the store up north.

"Is that you, Harlem?" Jazzy called from the basement.

"Yeah, babe, it's me."

"I'm down here working on a picture."

That meant that York wasn't home. The basement was where York stayed when he was here, which was rarely. My guess was that he was back to his old line of work. Jazzy must have hooked him up. I figured as much though. York was going to do what York was going to do, although I hated the idea of him being back in the game. There were just so many more possibilities for someone like himself. Jazzy had even offered him a job at one of the stores, but he declined. In so many words, he told Jazzy that he wasn't about to be his sidekick in yet another line of work. All I knew was that even though Jazzy might have hooked him back up in the game, there were no signs of him being back in the game himself. Jazzy was still running the stores like he was supposed to and still handling his business with me, condoms and all, like he was supposed to. As long as he kept doing that, then I knew he was straight.

"I stopped at Rooster's on the way home," Jazzy yelled. "I knew y'all would probably be closing late because of it being poetry night, so I just stopped and grabbed some chicken. It's in the mic."

"Thank you," I said with an exhausted smile.

In all honesty, I didn't know if I was exhausted from my long day or from keeping so much shit from Jazzy. Carrying all those secrets and skeletons around was starting to wear on me. Talking to Penny did help though. She listened to me go on and on for over an hour without saying a word, looking at me like I was crazy, or judging me. When I left, I never even asked her how or if she could help me. I didn't care at that point. As crazy as it sounds, a part of me was hoping that she'd run and tell Detective Somore, taking away any of my options, leaving me no choice but to face the music. That way, all the shit would be done and over with. Whatever was to be would be.

"Eat down here," Jazzy called, "so I can talk to you while I paint."

" 'Paint'? You always draw. Since when do you paint?"

"Yeah, it's something new I'm trying. I want you to check it out; plus I want you to come talk to me."

My heart pace began to pick up. "About what?" My nervous mode kicked in.

"Damn! I don't know. Tell me how your day went. Can't I just want to talk to my girl?"

"I'm sorry, Jazzy. I'm just tired. I don't feel like talking. Matter of fact, I'm not even hungry. I'm gonna take me a shower and call it a night."

"You feeling okay? That ulcer ain't acting up again, is it?"

"No, babe, I'm good. Just tired."

As I headed to the bedroom, I thought about how I wanted nothing more than to talk to Jazzy. There was so much that I had to talk about. So much I wanted to say. But I couldn't. Like a dog that had just pissed on his master's favorite pair of slippers, I put my head between my legs and walked away.

I got in the shower and turned it as hot as my body could stand. As I showered, I thought about how I had just spent the afternoon talking to someone who wasn't half as important to me as Jazzy was, but yet I couldn't talk to him. At the same time, Penny and I still shared something, something that Jazzy and I didn't. Something that would allow her to put herself in my shoes and ask herself whether or not she would have done the exact same thing that I did.

As I poured the shower gel onto my rag I thought about the fact that Jazzy had been a hustler for some time before he gave up the life. I knew sometimes, with enemies and jealous cats out there in the streets, a gangster's gotta do what a gangster's gotta do. I wondered if he'd ever had to—I forced the thought away. I don't know, Jazzy never really talked about his life a whole lot. There was really nothing to talk about. Unlike York, who turned to the game to survive, Jazzy pretty much inherited the lifestyle from the man he called Daddy.

Jazzy was raised by a hustler, so it was in his blood. I guess what I'm trying to say is that there was really no struggle in his life. He attended the finest schools and even graduated from college with a bachelor's degree in art and design. He chose the game, simply following his pop's footsteps. He had choices and options, unlike some of us in life. But did it make sense for me to hold back from him just because I felt he wasn't able to fully recognize where I was coming from?

"It doesn't make any sense at all," I said to myself. I hurried out the shower to go downstairs and tell Jazzy everything. I didn't even lotion up. I had to get down there and tell him before I lost the courage.

"I thought you were going to bed," Jazzy said as I made my way down the basement. "Hey, check this out. What do you think?"

"It's real nice." I then walked over and sat down on the futon behind where him and his art easel were stationed. "I need to talk to you."

"What's up?" Jazzy brushed a few strokes of burnt orange onto the canvas. Looked like he was about to fill in a sunset.

"There's something I have to tell you, Jazzy. I've been wanting to tell you for so long."

He stopped painting and turned around on the stool he was sitting on to face me. "What's up?" He tried to act all nonchalant, but I could tell that nigga was on the edge of his seat.

I closed my eyes and just let the words fall out of my

mouth. "Peanut, the man who raised you as his son . . ." I paused.

At that moment, I decided to change my mind and not tell Jazzy. But I was on the high dive, and I had already jumped. I had no choice but to hit the water. I was at a fuckin' point of no return.

I took a deep breath then let it out. "He was actually my biological father." I closed my eyes and waited as if I was bracing for a blow to the mug. I heard chuckling, so I opened my eyes.

"What the hell are you talking about?" Jazzy turned his attention back to his painting.

"I'm not joking, Jazzy. Reese told me the truth about who my real father was. Ray wasn't my biological father. The day Reese met you when you came up to the hospital to visit me after what happened to me and Morgan, she knew exactly who you were then. She didn't tell me right away because she figured York was the one I had been seeing. But that day in the store when you told me how Peanut died and how he raised you like you were his blood son, that he really wasn't your biological father, I—"

"What?" Jazzy jumped up, his pallet flying onto the floor. "That was back when you and I first got together and you're telling me now?"

"I didn't think it mattered since we weren't . . ."

"Brothers and sisters?" Jazzy walked over into my face. "Is that what you're trying to say?" He paced a couple of times. "Ewww, that's some sick shit."

"But it doesn't matter now."

"Then why the fuck are you telling me now?" After a couple more paces, Jazzy walked over to his canvas and punched it. The entire easel fell. The painting was flat on the ground. "So we keeping secrets now? What other shit haven't you told me, Harlem?"

"I never wanted to keep secrets from you."

"Don't you get it, girl?" Jazzy came over to me and kneeled down. "It's not about the secret; it's about you keeping the secret from me. You and me, that's the first real shit I've believed in a long time. Knowing how hard you are, how you build this wall up around you and don't let anybody through, the fact that I was able to come through it makes me feel . . . I can't explain how it makes me feel, Harlem." He took a deep breath and then calmed down. He took my hand in his. "Good. It made me feel damn good. Almost special and shit."

"You are special to me, you know that. I love you, Jason." I leaned my head on his.

After a few moments of silence he said, "Look, babe, I can get over that shit, but I need you to do two things for me."

"What?"

"One—promise me you won't keep any other secrets from me."

"And?"

"And two—don't call me Jason. Only my mama can call me that."

I smiled.

He ran his thumb across my lips. "There ain't shit you can tell me that's gonna make me feel any differently about you. I mean you the girl that made a nigga go soft, keeping a nigga out the game and shit." Jazzy chuckled. "Look, I know I was a little pissed off and shit—"

" 'A little'?" I nodded towards the mess he made.

"But thanks for telling me. For a minute I thought your ass was gon' try to tell me you was pregnant for real this time. Our baby would have two heads and shit." Jazzy laughed.

"You stupid." I punched him in the arm playfully.

"For real, though, you can trust me, girl. You know I'm number one in your life. If you can't tell me, then you can't tell nobody." Jazzy stood up and walked over to where he was painting and started picking stuff up. "You got anything else you need to tell me before I clean this shit up only to mess it up again?" he joked.

I swear on my mom's that I had every intention of sharing everything about my past with Jazzy when I walked down that basement, but now there was no way I could tell him everything I had intended. "No, Jazzy." At this point, I didn't think our relationship could handle any more of the truth.

Chapter 8
Reap What You Sow

I raced down the stairs to answer the doorbell after it rang a couple of times. When I reached the bottom of the stairs, I noticed York in the kitchen sitting down at the table eating a bologna sandwich.

"You ain't hear the door, yo?" I said, out of breath. "You know I'm upstairs trying to get the inventory done."

He just shrugged his shoulders and continued chewing.

Meanwhile, the doorbell kept ringing.

"I'm coming, I'm coming." I looked out the peephole to see who it was. Surprised, I then opened the door. "What are you doing here?" I said, anxious to know.

"Been thinking," she said.

"And . . ."

Penny took a deep breath. "I'm in. Just tell me what you need me to do."

Overwhelmed with emotion, I almost wanted to cry. It was as if Penny was an angel who had just showed up on my doorstep, the same way God had sent me Morgan. Instead, I just closed my eyes and ran my fingers across my tats.

"Thank you, Penny," I said, almost in a whisper. "Thank you so much."

Penny nodded a "You're welcome."

"Well, come in." I moved aside to allow her through the doorway. "You want something to eat, something to drink, or anything?"

"No, I'm okay," she said, stepping inside.

Just then, York came out of the kitchen heading towards the basement where Jazzy was.

"Pardon me, ladies," York said, walking between us.

"Hey," Penny said to York. She squinted her eyes to peer at him. "Don't I know you?"

York put his head down and shrugged his shoulders. "Not me." He headed down the basement steps.

"I'm sure I've seen you around," Penny said, attempting to recollect.

"Couldn't have been me. I really ain't been around. Ain't that right, Harlem?" York winked at me and then made his way down the basement stairs.

"Never mind him," I said with a snicker. "He's right, though; he hasn't been around."

"Oh, he been locked up, huh?"

"You got it." I led Penny to my upstairs office. I couldn't wait to talk about my options on how I could handle my situation once and for all.

"So what did you find out?" I closed my office door and gestured for Penny to have a seat at the round end table that had the coffee pot and condiments on it. I wasn't a big coffee drinker; that was there pretty much for décor.

"Do the names Tiana Everette and Wendi Mosely mean anything to you?" Penny could tell by the expression on my face that those names were definitely ghosts from the past. "Are they the ones?"

"Yes." I sighed and closed my eyes.

When I closed my eyes, I could see those two girls standing there before me scared shitless, one with piss running down her leg. I didn't know who was who at the time; all I knew was that I was about to save their lives. They had been with the two rapists at some party the night I killed the bastards. I let them go. I didn't want to hurt two innocent people, but I would have, had they tried some shit. When I aimed the barrel of the gun at the two girls' heads, my intentions were never to hurt them, only to scare them enough so that they wouldn't think twice about going to the police about what they had seen. I even took their IDs from them and insinuated that if they talked, they'd die. Hell, it worked for Queen Latifah in *Set It Off*. And it had worked for me . . . up until now I suppose.

"Did they actually see you shoot the—"

"No, no." I stood up to begin pacing. "Fuck!"

Those ungrateful, stupid little bitches. "I saved their lives. I saved their fucking lives. They leave a party with two dudes they don't even know because they promised them they had some killer weed? They followed those perverts, those rapists, those murderers who killed my best friend, to some abandoned road for a joint, where nobody would even hear them scream. Where no one would hear them cry for help. Only young, stupid bitches do that kind of thing—leave a party with niggaz they don't know from Jeffrey Dahmer. Hell, maybe they deserved to die for being so stupid. Maybe I should have just let them die. Maybe I should have kil—"

"Before you assassinate these two women with your tongue, the police have definitely been hounding them, a Detective Somore."

"Yes, I'm all too familiar with Detective Somore."

"He had a partner who had been helping him work the case, Logan; he died in the line of duty last year, though. He was on a family domestic call. Some woman was allowing her crack-selling boyfriend to beat up on her and her kid. The kid, a little girl, finally called the police one night after the boyfriend had beaten her mother's ass. When Officer Logan showed up, the mother took the boyfriend's side. Officer Logan made the call that he was going to put the child in protective services until the home could be investigated. When he was removing the child from her home, the mother shot him in the back three times—can you believe that? She shoots the man who's trying to save her ass instead of the one who had just kicked her ass?"

All I could do was shake my head at the irony. I knew Detective Somore's deceased partner. Logan was the same officer who showed up at Reese's and my apartment in Greenbriar the time I called the police on her for abandoning and neglecting me. I was fed up, sick and tired. I had already been in foster homes before being placed back with Reese. It got to the point where I'd rather had been in a foster home than living with her, so dialing 911 was easy. But when Officer Logan showed up, Reese made it seem like I was a lying rebel of a daughter. Needless to say, he left me there with her, and she beat me nearly unconscious once he left.

It would be years later before I'd encounter Logan again. He showed up at my hospital bedside with Detective Somore, acting just as eager to find the creeps who hurt Morgan and me. I had already had one too many experiences with the cops to know that those muthafuckas didn't handle business like it needed to be handled. That's when I knew right then and there that if I wanted to see justice done to those rotten bastards who hurt me and my best friend, that I'd have to serve justice myself. So I had to wear three hats—that of the judge, jury, and executioner.

Perhaps I should have waited until another time to kill those fuckas, a time when they were alone. No witnesses. But I had been fiendin' to get at them. I had followed them all day, even sat outside of some house party they were at. That's when they came out with those two girls they had picked up at the party.

I followed them down the same road they took Morgan and me when they decided that they would rape, sodomize, torture us and leave us for dead. However, them fuckas didn't know that this bitch had nine lives. When they came out of the party with those two girls, I had seriously thought about letting them go and waiting until another time when I could get just the two of them alone, but I couldn't bank on another time. After seeing them again for the first time since that night, there was no way I could let them breathe for another day.

Penny interrupted my thoughts. "But anyway, like I was saying, Detective Somore has gotten to those girls; he's been questioning them. But if it makes you feel any better, they aren't talking . . . yet."

"Harlem!" Penny said, surprised to see me standing on her doorstep. "What are you doing here?"

"Just came to talk," I said, shrugging my shoulders.

Penny looked over her shoulder and then back at me. "Don't you think it's a good idea if we talk at your house or somewhere?"

"Oh, no. I didn't come to talk about that," I assured her, assuming someone else was in the house. "Just regular old talk."

"Oh, okay. Come on in then." She allowed me in but still seemed a little bit 'noid. "I was just in the kitchen getting ready to start dinner." She led me into the kitchen, where there was a girl who looked like she was about thirteen looking in the refrigerator.

"Harlem, this is Baby. Baby, this is Harlem." Penny walked over to the sink and began running water on the whole raw chicken she had in the sink.

" 'Baby'?" I said. I was shocked because the photo Penny

had on her desk was of a much smaller version of the girl that was standing before me. I was expecting Baby to be about five or six.

Baby looked up at me, smiled a very pleasant smile, and then nodded.

"She can't hear your goddamn head rattle." Penny threw the chicken in the roaster that sat on the counter.

"Hey!" Baby said. She turned her attention back to the fridge, as if Penny hadn't just gotten real ghetto on her. She must have been immune to it because it didn't seem to bother her at all. She pulled a can of soda out of the fridge and cracked it open.

" 'Hey'? What the fuck is 'Hey'? You ain't in the ghetto no more. Talk like you got some sense." Penny started shaking seasoning on the chicken.

Now a bitch like me who knew that there was a time and a place to get "straight hood" on a muthafucka was taken aback by what seemed like an immediate change in Penny's personality. Granted, Penny, like myself, was a no-nonsense type of sista, something I had just found out about her that day in her office, but to act like this towards her daughter just threw me off a little bit.

"Ma, all I said was—"

The next thing I knew, Penny hauled off and slapped the shit out of Baby. The hit was so hard that she damn near spun the poor child's head around like the little girl on *The Exorcist*. Baby's soda can dropped to the floor and splashed.

"Look what you did," Penny said. She was in her own complete zone, acting as if I wasn't even in the room anymore. "Now clean that shit up." Penny took the pan and threw it in the oven.

"But you're the one—"

"Are you about to talk back?" Penny walked up on her. "Huh?"

I just stood their trippin', wondering what the fuck had set

Penny off. The next thing I know, Penny slugged Baby in the face, causing her nose to bleed.

Now I wasn't one to ever get into anybody else's business, but I could not let that shit go down in front of me. When Penny hit Baby that second time it was like a natural instinct. I jumped up out of the chair and smacked Penny across her goddamn face, let her see how the shit felt.

There was an immediate look of shock on Penny's face as she placed her hand over her jaw. Before I could even apologize, I felt a sting across the side of my face that stunned me for a minute.

Need I say, at that point in time, the shit was on. I grabbed Penny by her hair to slam her onto the kitchen floor. As she was going down, she grabbed me by my hair and took me down with her. So there we were, two grown-ass women on the kitchen floor rumbling hard.

"Stop it!" Baby screamed. "Please, stop it! You the one always talking about we ain't in the hood no more, but look at you—grown women fighting like some ghetto girls."

Penny and I tussled around a little more. We heard Baby's plea, but neither one of us wanted to be the first to throw in the white towel.

"I'm getting out of here. I'm calling Celeste to come get me." Baby stormed out of the kitchen.

Just then, Penny released the grip she had on my hair, and I released the grip I had on hers. Breathing heavily as if we had just finished a workout video, we both found our way up off the floor as we heard the front door slamming behind Baby. Penny dusted herself off and shook her hair as if she was primping it. I was brushing off the knees of my pants.

Out of nowhere Penny asked, "Want something to drink?" She said the shit just as plainly as day.

Hell, my ass just followed suit to the way she was acting. "Yeah, that would be nice." I sat back down at the kitchen table. I looked around, feeling awkward as all hell, not knowing if that bitch was gon' decide to try to sneak me or something.

"Nice place you got here."

"Thank you." Penny took a dish towel and wiped up the soda that had spilled on the floor. She then pulled out a pitcher of juice from the refrigerator and poured two glasses.

"I'm sorry I slapped you like that. I know it wasn't my place. Something in me just snapped. You should understand that, because you and I are alike in so many ways."

"You're right, it wasn't your place," Penny said with an attitude. She held the two glasses in her hand. "And you and me, girly, we ain't nothin' alike." She sucked her teeth and threw her head back.

I know this bitch ain't trying to say that she's better than me just because she working in some fancy law firm and shit.

"Remember when our mothers weren't there to protect us?" I said.

Penny was about to take a sip of her juice but held her glass at her lips upon hearing my words.

"Remember how that felt, Penny?" I was still somewhat out of breath. I then looked at my arm and noticed scratch marks on it. "I think about all of the times I wasn't protected as a little girl. I remember when I called the cops on my own damn mama after she had been MIA for days in and nights out, leaving me home with no food and shit in the worst projects in the fuckin' city. I never knew when someone was gonna bust through that door and get my little ass. You know what those fuckin' cops did? Shit! They didn't do shit. They left me there like I was the one who had done something bad by calling the police. Reese beat the fuck out of me for calling the man on her. Nobody protected me. Look, I don't know what goes on in your house between you and your girl when I'm not here, but while I am here, there's no way in the world I'm gonna sit here and watch you do her like some nigga in the street. Kids are innocent, until we contaminate them. The cycle must stop. There has to come a point in time when somebody protects the children."

Penny looked at me for a second and then took a sip of her juice. "Ahhh." She wiped her mouth with the back of her hand. "Oh, so now you want to protect somebody? Now you want to protect an innocent child?" She started strutting like a rooster. "Is that what you're trying to tell me, Harlem?"

"No, that's what I *am* telling you."

Suddenly Penny walked over and slammed my glass of juice down on the table in front of me, some splashing out of the glass and onto the table. "Then why didn't you protect me, Harlem? Why the fuck didn't you protect me?"

That ball came out of left field and hit me dead upside my head. But I knew it was coming. I swear I did. I didn't see it coming right then and there, but I knew it would eventually and I had set myself up for that one. I had had those same thoughts myself, feeling as though I had abandoned Penny that night I left her. I just wondered if Penny thought it.

Every time she came into my store, she acted as if everything was everything. Now I knew it wasn't. Suddenly I couldn't help wondering if I had made a mistake coming to Penny. Perhaps all along, in the back of her mind, she had always wanted to get me right where she needed me in order to give me a piece of her mind.

Damn, had this bitch caught me slippin'? Did she, in fact, have me right where she wanted me? If so, I was fucked!

"Why didn't you protect me, huh, since you in the business of protecting? You left mc that night, Harlem. You left me alone with the boogieman. You knew that what he tried to do to you that night he was already doing to me, but you got away. You didn't even try to take me with you. So much could have been prevented, had you told them why you ran away, but you didn't. You were just glad to have saved your own ass, you selfish bitch!"

I swallowed hard because I knew it was going to take everything in me to let her slide with calling me the *B*-word. But in this instance, I had to let her get that one off.

"You didn't even tell anybody. You don't know how many days went by that I thought this is the day Harlem is going to send help. Every morning felt like Christmas as I thought today is the day. That day never came. You never told a soul. You just left me there for that fat bastard to keep sticking his dick in me every night until I was pregnant!"

The room filled with silence as Penny realized the words that had come out of her mouth. She could probably count on one hand how many people knew who had actually fathered her only child. I could tell that it was a definite slip of the tongue.

She calmly pulled a chair out from under the table, sat down, and sat her glass down in front of her. Staring down at her glass, her bottom lip began to tremble. Then she blurted out, "I hate her, Harlem. I hate her so much." Penny broke down into tears. "I know Baby is my daughter, but I hate the sight of her. When I look at her, I see him. I see him coming into my room at night." She could barely speak, crying so hard. " I see him on top of me. I even smell him when I look at her. I see my mother being handcuffed and taken to jail. I see all of this each and every time I look into Baby's eyes. I hate her. I didn't want her. From the moment I knew she was growing inside of me, I hated her."

I sat there for a moment taking in exactly what Penny was trying to tell me. Now I knew why she hadn't mentioned the fact that she'd had a daughter. I could now understand why.

"I don't want you to take this the wrong way," I said with a confused look on my face, "but why did you have her then? Why didn't you get an abortion or something?"

"I wanted to, but I couldn't." Penny wiped her nose. "They made me, Harlem. They made me have her. They knew my mother's boyfriend had been raping me, but my mother never told them that I was pregnant by him. She wanted to save me the humiliation. So to this day, she and I are the only ones who know who Baby's father is. But just me knowing ate me up inside. I begged the state to let me get an abortion, but they wouldn't be responsible for it. I was so ashamed. My mother had been hauled off to jail. Unlike you, I didn't have some rich grandma to take me in. I was pregnant, and a ward of the state. What could I do?" She paused as if I could possibly have an answer for her.

"I was so angry at my mother for not being there to tell me what to do. I was so angry that she had killed him. She knew if she killed him they would take her away from me, and that I'd have no one. I even asked her, 'Mom, why? Why?'" Penny bowed her head down and cried even harder. "All she said to me was that I was her little girl and she asked me what would I have done?" Penny looked up at me.

"She's your mother." I didn't want Penny to think that I didn't understand where she was coming from, but of course, me of all people could sympathize with her mother. "Well, what would you have done?"

"Huh?" Penny sniffed.

"If you were in your mother's shoes, what would you have done?"

Penny paused for a moment and then stared off. "Back then the answer wasn't so easy. But now, after hearing your story too and everything . . . I . . ." Penny then mumbled the rest of her response under her breath.

"What did you say?"

Penny sat straight up in her chair. "Killed him. I would have killed him." She then looked me dead in the eyes. "I guess that makes me and you alike, after all, huh, Harlem?"

"I guess it does."

"So is that why you came to me? Is that why you chose me to help you?"

"How's your little girl doing, man . . . the baby? How old is she now? Y'all don't have no pictures of her hanging up?"

I could tell by his tone that he didn't want answers to his questions. He wanted confirmation, something he never got from me because he never had the chance to get it.

Once I found out I was pregnant I quit the cheerleading squad, so I never really ran into him, which meant I didn't have to explain my pregnancy to him. I didn't feel like I owed him any explanation any way. As far I was concerned, he had his chance to make me his girl, but now it was too late because Duke had already made me his woman.

So many women wanted to be where I was. Every so often Duke would invite his boyz over to play cards, watch a game, a pay-per-view fight or something. Some of them would bring their old ladies or even a girlfriend or two. With green eyes of envy, them old broads would all sit around and watch the way Duke looked at me, the way I looked at him. The way I catered to him, knowing what he wanted without him even having to ask; he'd raised me that way.

'Spite popular belief, I was all the woman Duke needed. Women who were out to get what was mine saw my age as a weakness for me and an advantage for them. They automatically assumed that Duke was only using me because I was some young and dumb little girl he knocked up and had to take in. They thought that just because I was young I was deaf to their little snide remarks and comments and blind to their actions.

"Baby, you ain't nothing but a baby." They would laugh. "How a baby gon' take care of a grown, fine-ass man like Duke?"

One bitch was even bold enough to throw the pussy at Duke right in front of my face. All night long she had been hitting on Duke, blowing out little sexual innuendos and shit, like I was too dumb to pick up on them.

This high yellow bitch with bright red hair straight from a box had *hood rat* stamped on her forehead. "So, Duke, can I have some too?" she asked, referring to the beer he had just asked me to go into the kitchen and get him. "Or do you need to check my ID to make sure that I'm *under* twenty-one."

Everyone started cackling like that shit was really that funny.

"Duke, honey, there ain't no more Miller longnecks." I came out of the kitchen, interrupting their little joke.

"Damn! Baby, you feel like running to the carry-out to get some more? I still got another game to play after this one, and I'ma need my buzz to keep whoopin' these sorry niggaz' asses."

"I'll be your buzz," the redhead said, making a noise like she was a bumblebee. "Besides, she ain't old enough to buy beer, is she?"

"No, I ain't old enough to buy beer."

"Muhammad know you my girl." Duke slammed the Ace of Spades down on the table. "Y'all niggaz goin' set. Shoulda went board, muthafuckas." He then pulled out his wallet and handed me his ID. "If them bitches ask to see your ID, just show them this bitch, and it's all good."

He talked with such a foul tongue around his peoples, but I guess every man acted different around his boyz.

"You don't let me drink it, but you'll let me go buy it?" I said, my hands on my hips. My intuition did not want me leaving my man alone with redbone.

"Here." Duke took a fifty-dollar bill off the pile of money that was sitting on the table.

"Nigga, what you doin'?—That's the pot," one of the dudes he was playing cards against said.

"Aw, mu'fucka, y'all niggaz 'bout to go set anyway, and that money gon' be me and my partner's. So shut the fuck up."

"I knew you'd understand," I said, taking a stab at honesty's heart.

"You knew I'd empathize and help save your ass," Penny corrected me. She was right. "I understand why you did it, Harlem. I understand why you killed those two men who did that to you and your best friend, but my understanding isn't enough to keep you from going to jail." She took a sip of her juice and composed herself. "How I see it, there's only one thing to prevent your going to jail for the rest of your life." Penny paused for a moment. "Well, two things."

I looked up at Penny. Her words, "Jail for the rest of your life," danced through my head. I couldn't go to jail. From what I'd heard, jail was worse than life out here in the free world, and if you ask me, sometimes it's a prison out here.

Up until just a few years ago, I had felt imprisoned my entire life. My life had been one big, dark, fucking pit. Finally pulled out, I could breathe again. Now all of a sudden I felt trapped all over again. I had had a taste of just how good life could be, and now there was a chance it could be taken away from me. Was God fucking with me again? *This is some bullshit.*

It was times like these when I asked myself, "Why didn't I just let the goddamn cops handle the shit?" Or like Penny told me that day in her office, I would have had a far better chance at getting away with it, had I not planned it out the way I did, tracking down their address and following them and shit, had I not threatened the two girls, had I not kept it to myself for so many years.

Penny informed me that it was the fact that her mother prepared two weeks to kill her boyfriend that she wasn't acquitted. Penny said had her mother left that doctor's office and went straight over his house and blew his brains out, she would have had a much better chance of not going to jail. But the fact that she premeditated his murder, and had a sit-down dinner with her daughter afterwards, made the jury see her as a cold-blooded killer. I believe telling them about Penny's pregnancy might have helped her too, but that was something that they'd both decided to take to their graves.

I ran my hand down the two teardrops that were tattooed on my face. *Oh, yes, they'd definitely see me as a cold-blooded killer. They'd send my black ass to jail for life for sure.*

"I can't go to jail, Penny. I won't spend my life in some hellhole. I won't."

"Then there's only one thing to do," Penny said with a cold face. "You killed once. Could you kill again?"

Chapter 9
The Ex-Factor

I entered the laundry room, located in a room off to the right at the foot of the basement stairs, I went to put a load of clothes in the washer, but it was already full of wet clothes. As I rummaged through the items, I saw that nothing in there belonged to Jazzy or me. It was all York's stuff. I sucked my teeth, tired of that nigga using our space as a flophouse. He was half there, so I never knew when he was coming or going. I dropped the load of clothes I had in my hands onto the floor, opened the dryer door, and started loading York's wet clothes into it.

As I bent over to pick up my load of clothes to put in the washer, I heard a noise. A smacking-like noise. I slowly crept out of the laundry room and was surprised by the fact that York actually was home, and had company. I hadn't noticed him and his lady friend when I came down the steps because they were on the floor. The laundry room was right there at the bottom of the steps, and I had just gone straight in it without even looking their way.

"Damn, I missed this pussy," I heard York whisper softly.

"It's always been yours; you know that," the female who was riding York said.

I couldn't tell who she was. York was lying on the floor with his feet up on the futon—nigga knew better than to be fuckin' on my futon—and she was on top of him just a-poppin' that pussy away. Her head was thrown back, sweat dripping down her neck.

From that point on, all I could hear was the sounds of their body's smacking and humping on each other. All I could see was York's hands gripped around her waist, steering her up and down on him. His body arched, and she began working them hips like the matrix.

After a couple of groans, she collapsed on him, resting her forehead against his, her long, black hair scattered about. I didn't deliberately stand there watching; I was just a little in shock.

Before I could back out of the room, the girl looked up and stared me dead in my eyes. A smile crossed her face, and she began to throw that ass like there was no tomorrow, going for round two strictly for my benefit. How in the fuck was York's ex up in my crib like that? I thought my ass was bold. But hell, the fact that she was fucking that nigga in my house was probably what really made her cum.

I knew she still had a thing for York. She tried to make some noise when he and I first start kickin' it, but I nipped that shit in the bud. In turn, to get back at York, she started fucking Jazzy.

I know all of this sounds like a bunch of ghetto talk show shit, but . . . well . . . fuck it. Who am I kidding? It is some ghetto talk show shit.

It had been a long day. I was supposed to go over to the other store and help Jazzy with inventory, but Reese said she would do it. We be at that store all fuckin' night when we do inventory; I was more than grateful to get a pass.

I pulled my Mustang into the garage and damn near tripped over my own feet, trying to get inside the door. I threw my Coach signature purse down on the kitchen table as I passed through the kitchen and headed straight for my bedroom. As I walked down the hallway, out of nowhere, York came out of the bathroom door and ran smack into me.

"Shit! You scared me." I put my hand over my heart. "You got my shit beatin' ninety miles per hour."

"I'm sorry, ma." York was right up on me, all in my personal space. Slowly, he raised his hand. "Let me feel it," he said, gently putting his hand on mine, his fingers in between mine, touching my chest. "You're right, your heart is beating fast." He stood there staring into my eyes.

I was frozen. I had to admit, I very much remembered his touch . . . and I liked it . . . too much.

"I miss your touch, Harlem."

"York, don't. Don't." I shook my head.

"My bad." He removed his hands from me and put them up in surrender. "I'm sorry. It's just hard, standing here this close to you. Damn!" He looked me over. "Why do you think I'm gone all of the time? It's hard as fuck staying here with you, under the same roof as my boy. This shit is crazy." He walked up on me, and this time with more authority in his tone and beating on his chest with each word he spoke. "I knew you first. Harlem Knew York—remember that shit?"

Oh God, did I remember. I had tried so hard to forget, and had been quite successful until now. Why was life so funny like that? When I had York, I craved Jazzy. Now that I had Jazzy, I had the nerve, at that moment, to be trying to crave York. But now with him standing right here in front of me, the memories and the feelings were starting to resurface. The difference was, though, what I was feeling for York at this moment was lust. I was in love with Jazzy.

"Then maybe you should just stay gone." I tried to be

strong and allow my love for Jazzy to overpower my resurfacing lust for York.

"Is that what you want? Do you want me gone? Why? What are you afraid of, Harlem?"

"You know me—I ain't afraid of shit."

"Still the same hard-ass tough girl, huh? That role is no longer becoming of you. You showed me another side of you, the one that's deep down right there. " He pointed to my heart, touching me again.

I could only hope that he didn't feel the sudden quiver that shot through my body.

"C'mere." He licked his lips.

I blinked. Hell, I couldn't get any closer. I could feel my guard, like London Bridge, slowly falling down.

York moved in as close as he could get and leaned to whisper in my ear, his hand still on my heart. "It's been so hard not touching you." He placed his lips against my ear. "It's killing me, Harlem. I sometimes hear you two, you and Jazzy. Ain't never wished that I was another nigga more than when I know he's up inside of you and it should be me." He softly touched my arm. "It's killing me."

Chills went throughout my body. I closed my eyes and reminisced about those times York had sexually pleased me, how he had brought out the woman in me. But then a scene from the most recent past flashed before my eyes, snapping me right the fuck back into reality.

"Was it killing you to keep from touching Zondra too?" I pulled away from him.

York gripped my hand, allowing me to separate myself from him only but so far. "Fuck Zondra—this here is about me and you."

"What are you doing, York? Let go of my hand."

He stood there momentarily, smiled this sexy little smile then released my hand.

I stood there for a few seconds before he spoke.

"It's killing you too, I can tell." York looked me up and down. "You know shit didn't end right between us, Harlem. Mu'fuckas can't just cut their feelings off like that with no closure, man. So I know you want me, ma. Stop playing."

"Oh, now I want you." I snapped my neck and sucked my teeth.

"Yeah, 'cause if you didn't, when I let go of your hand you would have marched your happy ass right on into your room and closed the door. Instead you just stood here, waiting for my next move, hoping I'd make one, hoping I'd do this—" York grabbed me by the back of my head in a rough but sensual way, looked into my eyes as I stood there breathing heavily, then allowed his tongue to hit every inch of my mouth. His tongue fiercely thrashed about.

I sucked up as much of it as I could.

York began to fondle my breasts, popping buttons off of my white button-up blouse, pulling out my breasts. "Remember when we used to make love, Harlem? Huh?"

His tongue grazed across the tip of my nipples and I almost melted. My head fell back, and I quickly repositioned it.

"Do you remember?"

"Yes," I said, panting like a dog, "I remember when we used to make love."

"That's good to know." He undid his belt and unzipped his pants. "But I don't wanna make love to you, Harlem." He pulled away from me and looked me up and down. "I wanna fuck."

I felt as though juices were running down my legs. It felt like this nigga had me bustin' nuts on just the thought of him being up inside me.

He pulled his dick out and went to pull down my pants.

"No." I placed my hands on his chest in an attempt to push him away.

He grabbed my wrists. "Don't fight me, Harlem; don't fight it."

What choo gon' do, nigga? I felt as though I was in the process of detonating a bomb and only had five seconds to decide whether to cut the blue wire or the red one. I could hear time ticking away. I could feel my wetness dripping. "Let go of me." I yanked my hands from York's grip. "You know I like to use my hands." I gave him a wicked smile, and then the shit was on.

Engulfed by York's tongue down my throat, I managed to kick off my pants. There I stood in the hallway, outside of the bedroom Jazzy and I shared, wearing a ripped-open blouse, a black thong and matching bra, my titties hanging out, and some Coach lace-up ankle boots. I was in straight hooker mode fo' real.

I wrapped my arms around York's neck as he lifted me up against the wall. My head bumped into the African mask I had hanging in the hallway, but that didn't stop my flow. I shook it off and started working my pelvis against York's. I felt like we had been born together. He was that much inside of me. My pussy wrapped itself around his dick for dear life and flexed on it.

"Harlem," he moaned in my ear.

"York," I moaned back.

"No matter what, I want you to know this shit right here is real." He slid deep inside of me. "The way I feel about you . . . this is real, girl."

I didn't think he could go any deeper, but with one more thrust he did.

"York . . ." I trembled.

Just then, he exploded inside of me. His dick jerking around inside of me, with the added sensation of him squeezing my ass and fucking me crazy as he came inside of me, I juiced all down his dick. I could feel the levee inside me break and the floodwaters pour out.

Then with one last hard ram, York was deeper inside of me than any man had ever been in my life. We just stood there, him using every muscle in his body to maintain the position until every ounce of cream in his body had run up in me.

I began to whimper from pure "secstasy," until I heard the garage door opening. I knew it was Jazzy. York and I couldn't get our shit together soon enough.

York pulled out of me.

Juices began to flow out of me like a waterfall.

Between him and myself, I don't know who'd come the hardest.

He grabbed his shirt then ducked away into the bathroom.

I nervously grabbed my pants to pull them on. The heel of my boot caught the cuff of my pants and ripped it. "Fuck!" I said to myself. I pulled up my pants and buttoned them.

Just then, I heard Jazzy come in the kitchen door. Still I stood there, titties hanging out of my pretty much buttonless blouse. I took my right hand and crossed it over, to make it look like a wrap shirt. Then I made a run for the bedroom.

Jazzy came out of the kitchen before I could disappear into the bedroom. "Harlem World."

"Hey," I said in a happy-go-lucky tone. I crossed both my arms over my shirt.

Jazzy came towards me. "Did I get any mail?"

"I don't know," I said nervously. "I didn't check."

Just then, Jazzy made a detour over to the front door. He opened it and stuck his arm out to get the mail.

I immediately looked down at my shirt and buttoned the two top buttons that hadn't been ripped off because I had left them unbuttoned in the first place. Then I buttoned another button that was hanging on by a thread. I tucked in my shirt and folded my arms again as Jazzy closed the front door with mail in hand.

At that moment, York came out of the bathroom. "Yo, Jazzy—oh shit, hold up." York went back into the bathroom and sprayed air freshener.

That was good lookin' out on his part, just in case there had been sex in the air. He managed to spray some in the hallway too, so Renuzit Rain was now in the air.

"Damn, man!" Jazzy walked up to York and gave him a five and a snap. "You stankin' up the place and shit."

"Oh, dawg, you know it takes months to completely clear your body of that shit they be serving in the joint," York joked. "You wanna play some NBA Live?"

"Oh, hell no, man." Jazzy yawned. "I'm 'bout to go take me a shower and go lay it down for the night."

"What are you doing home so early?" I asked Jazzy, trying desperately not to look like I had just had one of the best fucks of my life. A bitch had to be glowing. "I thought you and Reese were doing inventory; it usually takes us forever and a day."

"Yeah, well," Jazzy said, kissing me on the lips, "Pat, that new chick from Reese's church that she hired to intern, helped out too."

"Oh okay. I see. Well, that was nice," I said, searching for words. "Well, can I make you something to eat or anything before you knock out?"

"No, I'm good. We ordered pizza at the store. All I want is that bed." Jazzy leaned in and whispered into my ear, the same ear that only just moments ago York had whispered into, "And I want you in it." Jazzy ran his index finger across my lips then headed down the hall.

I let out a fake giggle. "Okay then. Well, you go ahead and jump in the shower. I'm gonna go grab me a nightcap." I wasn't going into that bedroom until I knew Jazzy was calling hogs—I couldn't risk him trying to unknowingly go for sloppy seconds.

All of a sudden, Jazzy stopped in his tracks. "Maybe it's just me, but is there something strange to y'all?" He examined the hallway.

"Uh-uh," York and I said in unison.

York looked at me, and I looked at him, shrugging my shoulders. My fuckin' heart stopped beating. *Did Jazzy notice my shirt? Did he spot one of the missing buttons laying on the ground? Did I put my panties back on, or were they lying on the hallway floor?* My mind started going wild.

"Then you two are crazy." Jazzy walked over to the African mask. "This mask is crooked as fuck." He straightened up the mask, headed into the bedroom, and closed the door behind him.

York and I let out a huge sigh of relief. We gave each other the "don't-you-ever-tell-even-if-a-muthafucka-is-pulling-your-fingernails-off-one-by-one" look.

Then he went his way, and I went mine.

Chapter 10
The Hood Life

"One glass of ginger ale, AKA sick pop, coming up." Reese whisked off to the kitchen of her two-bedroom apartment. "Thanks for coming to church with me today, baby girl, even though I know you aren't feeling well."

"That's okay, Ma." I lay down across Reese's couch.

My head was spinning, and my stomach wasn't feeling too hot. My guess was that it was that ulcer starting to act up again, something that sick pop definitely wouldn't cure. But I let Reese feel like she was doing something anyway. After all, in my opinion, she was always trying to make up for the years she was a shitty mother by being June Cleaver. I didn't want to piss on her parade.

"Church was nice," I offered as a conversation piece.

"Yeah, the pastor has a way of making you feel like he's preaching only to you, like the Lord gave him the message just for you to hear that day and nobody else."

Reese couldn't have been more right. When that pastor got to talking about running from man but not being able to hide from God, I thought I was going to fall out. He was talking about how God has a way of pulling the covers off people. If I didn't feel like I was sitting there butt-naked on the pew, then I don't know who did.

"Here you go, baby girl." Reese sat the glass of ginger ale down on the coffee table in front of me. She then lifted my head, sat down on the couch, and placed my head in her lap.

After she got nice and comfy, she began rubbing my head. "Do you want to talk about it?"

"What?" I lifted my head.

"Do you want to talk about it? It being whatever it is that's got you feeling this way."

"Ma, please . . ." I sat straight up and grabbed my drink off the table to take a sip.

"Come on now, you know the Lord blesses us with a spirit of discernment. Well, mine is telling me that what's got you feeling this way ain't physical at all, but mental. Now keepin' it real, I simply got the sick pop to entertain you. I know how you always liked that as a little girl; mentally it made you feel better. But now, pardon my French"—She looked up—"And God forgive me—But you's a grown-ass woman now, so spill it. Are you and Jazzy having problems?"

"Ma!" I said in shock. I couldn't believe she had just used God's name and a curse word in the same breath. Now I do the shit all the time, but it wasn't typical of her to do it.

"Don't *Ma* me. Harlem, you know I loved your daddy, Ray, to death, but living the life I lived, I met quite a few of Jazzy's kind. And again, although I loved your daddy to death, a sista craved a man with a little thug in him." Reese giggled and squirmed at the thought. "But at the end of the day, Ray was a good man, a damn good man. I could easily take him home to Mama. I knew the life that came along with them thugs, though, them hustlers and gangstas. I asked myself, 'How in the world would I look taking one of them home to Mama?' How would I have explained that to her? I mean, what was I supposed to say? 'Mama, I'm in love with a gangsta. I can't help it. I really love that nigga.'"

We both laughed at her failed attempt to re-enact Coolio's hit single.

"Ma, please save the story and the attempt to get in the rap game. Jazzy is not back into that lifestyle, if that's what you are trying to get at."

Reese let out a sigh of relief.

"Actually, Jazzy and I are just fine. Better than I expected even."

"What's that mean?"

I took a deep sigh. "I told him, Ma. I told him about my real father. I told him about you and Peanut."

Reese just sat there nodding her head at the blast from the past I had just brought up. She had the look of a bank robber who thought he had gotten away with a million dollars only to have the red dye pack explode. I could tell the subject was something she'd tried to forget. Christian folks got so caught up in the name of Jesus, they sometimes forgot that they weren't always saved.

"Oh, I see. And what did he say?"

"He was pissed. He wasn't pissed about the secret itself, he was pissed at the fact that I kept a secret from him."

"Keeping secrets can destroy a relationship. Trust me, I know better than anybody. They can eat you alive."

Trust me, I know.

"Well, then if you and Jazzy are fine, then what's had you moping around the stores these past couple of weeks? You've spent more time in the bathroom sulking than you have with the customers. And when I asked you to church, you didn't even try to make up not one excuse. Now that's not the Harlem I know. Not to say that I don't like her just a little better . . . 'cause she ain't got as fresh of a mouth and puts up less of a fight than that other Harlem." Reese chuckled. "But still . . . what gives? Does it have anything to do with that Detective Somore?"

My muscles tightened. I quickly tried to relax, hoping Reese hadn't noticed. "Huh?"

"Detective Somore. He stopped by the store and talked to Pat that day you left early because you were sick and we had to run your store."

"Oh," I said, more relaxed.

"Is that what's bothering you—bringing up old memories about Morgan? What happened to you two?"

"I guess you could say, something like that."

"Well, talk to me, baby girl; that's what I'm here for."

"Look," I said with a lightweight chuckle, amused by how Reese thought she could get me on that couch and play psychiatrist with me, "I am not one of them women at Mary Haven that you be counseling. I'm fine. Just an upset stomach is all I've been having." I drank some more of my drink.

After a couple more sips, I felt that ginger ale coming right back up, so I had to race to the bathroom real quick. I hadn't been able to keep anything on my stomach. As much as I hated to, I knew I was going to have to go back to the doctor to see about this ulcer business. I was worrying myself sick.

After rinsing my mouth out in the sink, I headed back to the living room and heard my cell phone ringing.

"I'm going to go fix us some ice cream, praline pecan."

I entered the living room, making a dash for my purse to get my cell phone. "I'll be right back."

"Hello," I answered. "Hello," I repeated when I got no reply. I could hear Jazzy's voice in the background. "Hello, Jazzy."

He still didn't respond; he just kept right on talking.

How dis nigga gon' call me and make me wait while he's talking to someone else? Again I shouted, "Jazzy," but still he just kept right on talking.

"Man, I did good hooking you up with Malibu and shit," I heard him say. "Do you know what the fuck you're asking me to do, man?"

"I know, Jazzy," I heard York's voice say. "I know, man, and you know I wouldn't be asking you this if I really didn't need you to do this for me."

At first I was going to hang up. I realized that Jazzy must have pressed up against his cell phone buttons or something and accidentally called me. However, when I heard Jazzy say, "You're asking me to get back in the game," I reconsidered. Curiosity kept the phone bonded to my ear.

"No, I'm not," York said. "I'm asking you to put me in the game with some real players, not some okey-doke bench-warmer like Malibu."

"I took a risk even hooking you up with Malibu. He might be college ball compared to the NBA players in New York, but it's a start. You can build your shit up from that. It's just going to take a little more time."

" 'College ball'? Try little league. That nigga be spoon-feedin' me and shit. Besides, I ain't got that kind of time to be fuckin' with that nigga. I'm ready to be drafted into the NBA right now, if you feel me. I'm like Lebron, nigga—fuck college, send my ass straight to the pros."

"I do feel you and shit, man, but do you know how long it's been since I've done business with them niggaz? I don't even get down like that. You see how much convincing I had to do to get Malibu to fuck with you; now you asking me to hook you up on a whole notha level? I can't just send you up to New York on my word to fuck with them. Them Island cats would send your ass back to Ohio in a FedEx box—four, five FedEx boxes, matter of fact."

"I know. That's why I need you to do it. I need you to go handle that shit for me. Make them think you the one that's gon' get rid of the work. All you got to do is let me work it, though. We'll do that shit a couple of times, let them cats see my face with you and shit, then they'll fuck with me, when they see how much loot I'll be cracking. I'll make the cut worth their while, no greed on my end as a sign of my gratitude, and willingness to work hard. All I need to do is get in a position to let these cats down here know who to come to in order to get double for their trouble. I'll have the shit on lock."

There was a moment of silence, and then I heard Jazzy say, "Damn, man, I can't believe you putting me in this position and shit. You my boy." Jazzy paused again.

My heart was racing.

Finally, I heard Jazzy say, "I can't. I have too much to lose."

"A couple of bookstores, nigga?"

"Is that all you think me and Harlem got going on, a couple of bookstores? Do you know how much hard work it took to get in the position we are in with those stores? Do you know all that Harlem has been through to make those stores a success?"

"All right, all right, all right. I'm sorry. I'm sorry, man. I didn't mean to downplay you and Harlem's hustle. I know it's more than just bookstores. I see how hard you two work. But remember how hard we used to work?"

There he went, trying to pull out his kryptonite and shit again.

"Jazzy, it's me, your boy, York. Don't tell me you done got soft on me while I been away. What's up, yo?"

"Do you know what Harlem would say if I told her I was going back to the hood of thangs?"

"Who said Harlem needs to know?"

"Me and my girl don't keep secrets, man."

"Oh, y'all don't?"

"No, nigga, we don't."

"All right, I feel you on that. But since when do you care what a broad thinks about what you do?" York's voice was now louder and more intense. He acted as though he had a bomb attached to him and that if he didn't get Jazzy to fold, then in a matter of minutes the bomb would explode.

"I don't even know who the fuck you are anymore," York

said, "painting and shit, like some black Picasso. In all our years of putting in work together, was there ever a time that you called on me and I didn't answer . . . ever?"

"Naw, man," Jazzy said, almost under his breath.

"What? What did you say? Speak up; I didn't hear you."

"Naw, nigga, damn! Clean your muthafuckin' ears out."

"Then what do you say?—One trip to the Big Apple—what's up?"

Jazzy was silent, as both York and my eavesdropping ass waited for his reply. My heart was beating so loud that I could hear it.

Before either him or York could say anything else, the phone cut off.

Chapter 11
The Ball's in Your Court

"Is it a national holiday? Did the store burn down or something?" York asked as I walked out of my bedroom and into the living room, where he was playing the game station.

"No, just not feeling well," I said before going to the kitchen. I went to the cabinet, grabbed a box of crackers, and headed back towards my room.

"Stay out here and keep me company," York suggested, his eyes glued to the game he was playing.

I paused at his invitation, only because it had caught me off guard. Ever since York's and my last encounter, we had been avoiding each other like the plague, so for him to deliberately want to keep company with me threw me off a little.

"No, I'm going to lay it back down for a minute. I have a doctor's appointment later on this afternoon, so I need to muster up some strength in order to get there."

"Do you want me to drive you? A nigga got a felony and can't vote, but I got a driver's license."

I chuckled. "No, I'm good."

"Well, just lay down out here on the couch or something."

"York," I whined, not in the mood to go back and forth with him.

"Okay, go 'head and lay down. But before you go back in your room, there's something I want to talk to you about real quick."

I sighed. I knew it was inevitable that eventually we'd have to talk about what happened between us. I was Jazzy's girl, he was Jazzy's best friend, and we had acted out a sex scene from *Basic Instinct* right under Jazzy's nose.

"Look, York, it was a mistake; we shouldn't have gone there."

"No, not that. I don't want to talk to you about us; I want to talk to you about me." He briefly looked up at me and then back at the game.

"Huh? What about you?"

"Well, let me just cut to the chase." York sighed. "I know you know I only got one way of life."

"Yeah, I know, York. It doesn't take a rocket scientist to figure out what you've been up to, but you need to watch your back. I mean, you ain't been out so long where they still ain't watchin' your ass."

He snickered as if he knew something I didn't know. "You're preaching to the choir. Besides, your boy done preached at me enough. But this is the life I know, Harlem. This is the life I live."

"But it doesn't have to be that way, York. I've always told you that . . . even back when you and I were—" I stopped myself and then tried to brush over it by continuing on. "Look at Jazzy, look at how he's living now—one hundred percent legit. Look at all we've got." I held my arms up and scanned the room with my eyes. "Look at the stores. Look at Jazzy's art career. Look—"

"Look what Jazzy has." York turned his attention away from the game to look at me. "He's got something I need."

He stared at me hard and then turned and continued playing the game.

"I know." I tried to not let it slip from my tongue that I'd heard part of his and Jazzy's conversation, that I knew that Jazzy had what he needed. A connect.

"Jazzy has something that I once had." He looked up at me. " He's got you."

My heart melted. I wasn't expecting that. I wasn't expecting that at all. *Damn, why do I keep letting him catch me with my guard down?*

"If I had a bad-ass bitch like yourself standing behind me—no offense, I meant *bitch* as in a strong black woman—I'd have a reason to live right too. But I don't, Harlem. Every time I'm laying down there on that futon, I can't help but think that I'm supposed to be that nigga upstairs with you. I'm supposed to be that gangsta gone legit. You were supposed to make me want to be that type of man for you. I could have become that type of man for you, ma. I could have been your man; I should be your man."

This nigga was hittin' me with some smooth shit, but I had to be strong. "Look, York, what we had—"

"What we had was the shit, and you know it. Then all that shit between you and my sister . . . I lost you over that bullshit. Now, look, not even my own fuckin' sister—my blood—has got my back." York pounded his fist down next to him.

I remained silent, allowing York to compose himself. He had already broken down in front of Jazzy before; I knew it would kill him to break down in front of me.

"I asked Jazzy to do something for me," York continued after regaining his composure, "something that would put me on big time. So big that I won't have shit to worry about no more. I won't have to worry about staying here with you . . . and my boy. I won't have to worry about shit. Not another bitch fuckin' over me."

Did he just call me a bitch without actually calling me a bitch? I made it up in my mind that regardless of the situation, I wasn't about to be one more bitch, and that was real.

"Jazzy and I were like brothers. We did shit for each other without even having to ask twice. It wasn't blood that made us brothers, but loyalty. So when I asked him to do me this one favor, when he told me no, you can imagine the feeling of betrayal I felt."

I sighed a sigh of relief. Now that was one less weight off my mind. My insides were jumping for joy, when I heard York's words. Jazzy stood his ground and stood by his word to me that he wasn't going to even get his feet wet in the game anymore, but I knew it must have been killing him inside. It was a double-edged sword. Trying to be loyal to two people sometimes meant that you had to betray one.

"I was hurt, no doubt. But I was even more hurt to find out that it was because of a broad." York chuckled. It was a wicked chuckle. He then looked up at me in a way he had never looked at me before. "Because of you, Harlem—that nigga let you come between us. How is that for irony? When that nigga came to visit me in jail to tell me that he was fuckin' the girl, the first girl who I ever even fixed my lips to tell I loved her, did I let that shit come between me and him? Hell no!"

I could tell he was getting a little frustrated, and I didn't have the energy to go toe-to-toe with him in an argument. "Look, York, that shit is between you and Jazzy. I don't want to get into this with you now."

"I'm sorry, Harlem—for once, it's not fucking about you; like I said when I started this conversation, I want to talk about me—it's all about me now."

I had been too nice, too long. It was time to dig down deep in my soul for that "old Harlem" muthafuckas kept talkin' about. And she wasn't too hard to grasp a hold of.

"Muthafucka, as long as you are in my goddamn house, it's gon' always be about me. I can't help it if my man made a decision on wanting to be an honest, hard-working brotha and live life right. You the one who got in the game, nigga. While in the game, you should have been handling your own shit instead of sniffin' up Jazzy's ass. You should have at least had something to fall back on. Jazzy might have been in the game, but he still had a college education to fall back on. Even me, growing up with all the obstacles and tragedies I had to face, I could have chosen so many other roads to travel than the ones I did, but I—"

"Don't do that!" York yelled. "Don't do that shit you do. That thing where you try to make people think that you are this righteous chick who had to work hard for everything she's got. You didn't make your come-up grindin'. Your granny died, for Pete's sake, and left you this house, a car and all kinds of loot and shit. Yeah, you were only eighteen and could have jerked it all off like the average eighteen-year-old, but you still didn't have to put your life on the line for that come-up—it was basically handed to you on a god-damn silver platter, and for that you think you special?"

"Don't you dare try to downplay all the shit I've been through to maintain what I got!" I screamed at the top of my lungs.

"Oh, Harlem, I'd never do that." York stood up, using his eyes like daggers to cut through me. "I'd never do that. I know exactly what you've been through, ma." He slowly walked over towards me. "And the fact that I know exactly what you've been through is the reason why you're going to give Jazzy a pass and let him do this favor for me that he needs to do."

"Nigga, what?"

"You're going to talk Jazzy into making this move Up Top that I need for him to make for me."

"Nigga, you done lost your mind." I threw my hands up and turned to go back into my room.

York grabbed my arm.

My instinct was to take my free arm and bust him upside his muthafuckin' head, but he grabbed it just as I had balled my fist. But not to worry, I had already made it up in my mind that I was gon' windmill his ass, like a faggot in a fight, just as soon as he let go.

"Maybe I have lost my mind." He held me by both my wrists. "You know, jail can drive a muthafucka crazy. I mean, imagine if you went to jail, Harlem. Imagine if you did something that could land you in jail. You'd go crazy too. Hell, you'd probably go crazy on just the thought alone of going to jail, wouldn't you, Harlem? Wouldn't just thinking about spending the rest of your life in jail make you sick to your stomach?"

There was something about that way York was talking to me, looking at me. His words seemed to have more meaning to them than what he was laying on the surface. Once again, I got this awful feeling in the pit of my stomach that didn't have shit to do with an ulcer.

"But you going to jail is the last thing I'd ever want to happen." York stared me dead in my eyes. He then looked down at my wrists, which he was still holding. "Oh, I'm sorry," he said, snapping out of his zone and releasing my wrists.

"Fuck you, York. I'm not telling Jazzy shit!" I pointed my finger at him hard, damn near touching his nose. "He's his own man; try being yours. Fuck you! And you can get the fuck out of my—"

"You wanna talk about being fucked?" He laughed. "You don't want me to fuck you, Harlem. Trust me, ma, you really don't want me to fuck you. Now my words might have confused you a little bit, but I wasn't *asking* you to have a talk with Jazzy, I was *telling* you."

York walked away as if he was that nigga. He went and picked up the game controller and started playing the game system again.

I didn't even have words. That was definitely not my York,

the York I had love for. Something about him was just so cold. It was as if he wasn't even hearing me. Had jail done this to him? Had sitting in jail made him this cold and bitter? This wasn't the York I thought we invited into our home to look out for. Whoever he was, friend or no friend, once Jazzy made it home, I was telling him that his boy had to go.

I made it to my bedroom, closing the door behind me. I leaned up against the door and replayed all of York's words over and over in my head. *What is that nigga trying to get at?* I thought. *I know he don't think he's going to hold that shit over my head about me cheating on Jazzy with him.* I began to pace. *He ain't gonna tell because, if he does, Jazzy definitely ain't gonna look out for him. No, it's got to be something else.*

I thought for a moment, and as if I had seen a ghost, a sudden chill came over me, followed by a sudden fear. "Please God, no." I opened up my bedroom door and made a beeline to the basement, creeping behind York, who was still playing the game station.

Once I made it to the basement, I went straight to the laundry room. I struggled to lift and scoot the washer out from against the wall. I didn't remember it being that heavy and hard to move the last time. Maybe it was because I was on an adrenaline high before. This time I broke a sweat.

Once I was finally able to move the washer, I kneeled down, only to be looking at nothing but a concrete floor. My heart almost stopped.

Where the fuck did they go? I panicked. *I know they have to be here. Nobody looks under the washer.* I huffed, puffed, and moved the washer out further. When I looked down, I was still simply looking at a concrete floor.

"Fuck!" I said in a low whisper. *Who the fuck moves a washer like it's an everyday piece of furniture?* "Okay, get it together, girl," I told myself. *Maybe I moved them somewhere else and just forgot about it.* "Think, Harlem. Damn it, think!" I closed my eyes and sat there for a moment.

"Looking for these?"

Startled by the voice, I opened my eyes and looked up, only to see York standing there, holding in his hands just what I had been looking for.

From that point on, life was in slow motion.

York just stood there in front of me, waving them in his hand, taunting me like I was a crack fiend and he had the last rock on earth. "You know, Harlem, I'm a strong believer that everything happens for a reason. So when I accidentally dropped my cell phone while I was doing a load of laundry and the fuckin' battery popped off and went under the washer, I was mad as hell. I mean, moving a washer ain't like moving an everyday piece of furniture. But once I moved it and found these, I was a little puzzled. But then as if life was all about timing, as I held these in my hand, the doorbell rang. I slipped them in my pocket and went to answer the door. You know, it could have been for me—Zondra or somebody—but it wasn't; it was a Detective Somore."

Just listening to York was like nails down a chalkboard. I knew shit was only about to get worse.

"I had a real fine chat with Detective Somore. I learned a lot about you through talking to him. But what I learned most was why these were under your washer machine—" Once again, York waved them in his hand. "Because at first I said to myself—" He then began to read the IDs that he had in his hand—" 'Who the fuck is Wendi Mosely and Tiana Everette?' But after my little chat with Detective Somore, I found out just who the fuck Ms. Tiana and Ms. Wendi were. Them the bitches you scared shitless to keep from IDin' your ass as the one who took out them two dudes over near Alumn Creek." He started laughing as he looked at the IDs. "You done watched *Set it Off* one too many times. Good try, though. From the sounds of it, I don't think them bitches gon' talk."

His laughter ceased and he glared at me. "Now me,

Harlem . . . well, I'm not going to talk either, that is if you do talk—to Jazzy that is. Get your boy to come through for me. So you have that little talk with Jazzy, you know. Tell him how he owes me and shit. You good at philosophizing and shit, so just do one of them spiels you do; I get what I want, you get what you want—which is these."

To be honest, I don't know how much of York's conversation I heard. Like I said, everything was in slow motion, including his speech. I was sweating, and the room was spinning. A huge lump formed in my stomach. I managed to get up off the ground. I hunched over, grabbed my stomach, and pushed past York. I barely made it to the upstairs bathroom in time to throw up. On the ground, hugging the toilet bowl, my head hanging over it, I heard footsteps entering the bathroom.

"Harlem, you all right?" I heard Jazzy ask.

I looked up into his concerned eyes.

"I was worried about you." Jazzy kneeled down and began rubbing my hair. "I know you gon' be pissed, but I closed down the East store to come see about you. I know how you hate going to the doctor and shit and I just wanted to make sure that you went, so I came to take you."

"I'm all right." I grabbed a piece of tissue and wiped the saliva from around my mouth. "It's nothing. Just that ulcer again."

Jazzy paused for a moment while he stared at me.

I looked up at him.

He started shaking his head. "Come, clean."

All I could do was throw my arms around him and hold back tears . . . right along with the truth.

"He can stay in the room, doctor," I said to Doctor Ferguson, my family doctor. "He knows everything about it already."

"So I take it this must be the father?" Doctor Ferguson asked. "Congratulations."

When it muthafuckin' rains, it pours.

"Hold up, Doc," Jazzy said. "So you saying Harlem is pregnant? She's going to have a baby? How did that happen?"

"Well, you'd know better than me, son." The doctor laughed.

"I mean, ever since the last scare, when she didn't end up being pregnant, but had an ulcer instead, which is what we thought it was in this case, the ulcer," Jazzy rambled on. "We've only had protected sex—condoms; none of that I'll-pull-out shit or nothing. Excuse my language, Doc. But on the real, we've used condoms every single time. You sure it's a baby and not that ulcer? I mean, they are probably the same size, right? What you think is a baby might be the ulcer."

Doctor Ferguson laughed. "There's no mistake. Both the urine test and the blood test say it's a baby. Pardon me for laughing because I can't tell whether this is good news or bad news for you, but condoms have been known to break." He turned his attention to me. "Aren't you still on your triphasal birth control?"

I was staring at the ground in a daze. "No, I stopped taking them after I started taking all that medication for the ulcer. I thought it was making me sick. I knew Jazzy and I were using condoms, so it wasn't a big deal."

"Well, like I said, there are cases when a condom was used during intercourse but broke, and a pregnancy results. Looks like this is one of those cases—that's the only explanation I can come up with."

I sat there in silence knowing that in my heart of hearts I could come up with a completely different explanation of my own.

Chapter 12
Marked Man

Convincing Jazzy to drive up to New York and set York up with his connects really wasn't hard at all. It was like I had lifted a weight off of his shoulders by making it seem like it was my idea to put York on so that he could get on his feet. I made it seem as though I was tired of a grown man living in our basement and how that must make York feel as a man. I whined about feeling sorry for York and how he had did time in the joint only to come out and have our relationship rubbed in his face, yada, yada, yada. It made me sick to my stomach to do it. I felt like I was now betraying Jazzy just to save my own ass. *How did my life get so fucked up? How?*

I picked up the ringing phone. "This is Harlem."

"Hey, it's Penny. What's going on?"

"You don't want to know, trust me." I sighed.

"What is it—Jazzy getting on your nerves or something?"

"No, he's not even here. He just left about an hour ago to take care of some out-of-town business."

"Have you thought anymore about that question I asked you a while back?"

"What question?" I asked curiously.

"About your options. About eliminating certain factors in your life in order to live freely, breathing fresh air twenty-four seven, if you like."

"Oh, that question." I remembered the discussion we had about what to do about the Wendi and Tiana situation. "No."

"No, you haven't thought any more about the question?"

"No is the answer to your question."

Penny sighed a huge sigh of relief.

"What's that about? You act like you were holding your breath for that answer."

"I was pretty much. I mean, if your answer was yes, then that means I would have had to have been the Jada to your Vivica."

I chuckled, even though in her serious tone I knew she wasn't joking. I knew it, and that was one of the reasons why I had truly gone to Penny in the first place. First off, with her legal knowledge, if at all possible, I wanted to tell her my story and see if she could figure out any one hundred percent guaranteed way to keep me from going to jail. Secondly, if she couldn't, if shit had to get grimy, with what she had been through with her own situation, never having avenged it herself, I knew she would be able to take all that bottled-up anger and resentment and use it for my own benefit. But the more I thought about it, about how I had fought so hard not to become someone I couldn't look at in the mirror, had Penny and I gone on some rampage chase to get those two witnesses, I wouldn't have been any better than the two men who killed Morgan. I was not going to allow her death to be in vain.

"But had my answer been yes, would you have . . . would you have helped me?" I just wanted confirmation on my intuition about her.

There was a long pause.

"Never mind. Don't answer that," I said, letting her off the hook. "But just so you know, I got love for you, Penny. If I was a pimp, I'd know who to count on to be my bottom bitch."

In the middle of her laughter, she stopped. "Oh yeah, I figured out where I know your boy from."

"Who?"

"Ol' dude. That guy that was at your house that day I first came over."

I thought for a moment. "Oh, York."

"Yeah, his brother is a client of one of the partners at the firm."

"Huh?" I asked confused. " 'Brother'?"

"Yeah, his sister hired the firm about a year ago to take on his deal. They didn't trust dealing with the feds alone."

"Wait a minute—what deal?—York copped a plea years ago."

"No, Ms. Hawkins was just in the office yesterday. That's what reminded me of where I knew him from. I went to get my messages from the receptionist's desk, and I saw her leaving out. I think York was even with her. I could hardly tell from the back. But it dawned on me then where I knew him from."

" 'Ms. Hawkins'?"

"Yes, Yvette Hawkins."

"It's a set-up. This whole thing has been one big goddamn set up."

"What?" Penny searched for an answer to no avail. "Harlem, you there?"

I started rambling, as all the pieces to the puzzle fell in place. "He knew that he had a better chance at working on Jazzy if he was right underneath the same roof; that's probably what the feds told him to do. 'Model inmate,' my ass—that nigga is turning over, and Jazzy is caught up in the crossfire."

"Working on him how?—'Crossfire'?—Harlem, what's going on?"

"You don't need to know all of that." I wasn't about to put Jazzy's shit out there like that. "I've already told you enough of too much shit as it is. All I know is that nigga planned this. He had it all planned out from day one—he's setting Jazzy and his peoples up."

Pissed the fuck off, I began pacing back and forth. I couldn't believe it. York had played Jazzy like a piano. And me too, for that matter. He had gotten us right where he wanted us and then got what he needed from the both of us. He knew damn well that Yvette wasn't going to be at that house the day we drove him there when he got out of jail. Her sheisty ass probably had them a big house on a hill somewhere. *That's probably where that nigga been laying his head when he's not staying at our place . . . son of a bitch!*

"I have to stop him. He's setting Jazzy up, and, Penny, I gave him the final ammunition he needed in order to pull it off. And just to think, I let him inside me." I put my head down in complete shame. Not only did I let him inside my head, I let him inside my body. Now I knew what the words he whispered in my ear while he was inside of me meant. 'No matter what, I want you to know this shit right here is real. The way I feel about you, this is real, girl.'

"What are you talking about?—I'm lost."

I took a deep breath and tried to take my time. "York found out about the two witnesses. He's blackmailing me."

"Blackmailing you for what?"

"To help set Jazzy up. He pretty much threatened that if I didn't convince Jazzy to do a not-so-legal favor for him, that he'd turn me in. I just turned Jazzy over to him on a silver platter. I have to call and stop Jazzy from going to New York. He needs to turn that fuckin' car around now!"

"No, Harlem, wait!" Penny shouted. "Think about what you're doing here. If you make that phone call, then you might as well make another one—right to Detective Somore."

As my body quivered, I thought about what Penny was saying. York had the card to send me to jail, directly to jail. If I stopped Jazzy, then that's exactly where I was going. If I didn't stop Jazzy, then that was exactly where Jazzy was going. One of us was going to jail. All I had to do now was figure out whose ass I was going to save—Jazzy's or my own.

The Final Chapter

Making that call to Detective Somore was the hardest thing I ever had to do in my life. It was even harder than when I was asked to read the eulogy at Morgan's funeral and had to stand up in front of a church full of folks and tell them that I couldn't read.

"You're doing the right thing," Detective Somore said, when I called him directly after hanging up with Penny.

There really wasn't much to think about. For the past months, I had felt imprisoned anyway. I may have been free to roam the earth, but my mind definitely wasn't free, running from the skeletons of my past. Whether literally or in the theological sense, my mind was imprisoned. Besides, I wouldn't have been able to live without Jazzy. If he went to jail, everything we built would have just crumbled. I may be a hard bitch sometimes, but 'spite popular belief, I still had a heart.

Just sitting there alone in my living room on the couch, I had to think of the words I needed to tell Jazzy about what I had done, why I was about to spend Lord knows how may years in jail for a double homicide. This was going to crush

Jazzy, especially with me being pregnant and all. There hadn't been any talk of an abortion. In fact, when we left the doctor's office, we drove straight to Babies "R" Us, where Jazzy got a cartload of blue stuff and baseballs and footballs. Something about knowing that a living human being was actually growing inside my belly changed his opinion about me being pregnant and wanting to have a child, preferably a man-child.

Detective Somore would be arriving soon to take me in, so for now I decided that I needed to quit wasting time on how to tell Jazzy all of the details as to why I was going to jail and just worry about keeping *him* from going to jail.

I picked up the phone and dialed Jazzy's cell phone number and it went straight to voicemail. My nerves started jumping. I quickly calmed myself down and dialed his number again. Once again, it went straight to voicemail. "Nooo!" I screamed. "God, noooo!"

All of a sudden, I found myself on my knees, bent over the couch with my hands folded. "Dear Heavenly Father," I began to pray, "I know you haven't heard from me in a long time, but I still hope that you recognize my voice. If ever in my life I have acknowledged how much I've needed you, it's now. I've done wrong, and I know I've done wrong by taking the lives of those two men, Lord. I fought a battle that was not mine. And I'm sorry. I've been running from you, thinking that I can hide what I've done from you, Lord, thinking if you couldn't find me, then I wouldn't have to be held accountable. But I'm tired of running, Lord. I'm tired. I've called the police, and they're on their way to take me in. First I have to get in touch with Jazzy. Please, Lord, allow me to reach out to him. Jazzy is a son that you have restored, and he never looked back to where he came from until I helped coerce him down that path. Please don't hold him accountable, Dear Lord, please. So, Father, I just ask that you let me get through to him, please. You can give me life in prison—I don't care—just spare Jazzy. I say this prayer in the name of Your Son and my Savior, Jesus Christ. Amen."

I stood up and sat back down on the couch. I took a deep breath and dialed Jazzy's cell phone. Once again, it went straight to voicemail. This time I decided to leave him a message telling him about York's scheme, and to turn the car around ASAP.

"Jazzy—" Just as I began I heard my other line click in. I immediately answered, hoping that by some chance it was Jazzy. "Hello," I said after clicking over.

"He's dead! Harlem, he's dead!"

"Hello. Who is this?"

"Harlem, it's me. He's dead. Some fuckin' semi came over into our lane and hit my truck. He's dead, Harlem! York is dead!"

Just as Jazzy's words fell into my ear, there was a knock on the door. It was Detective Somore. All I could do was look up to God and laugh to keep from crying. *He got me again,* I thought. *He got me again.*

Since I turned myself in, I didn't have to waste the state's time and money with a trial. I was quickly sentenced to seven years in the women's state prison.

Reese fainted, when they sentenced me. She'd had a couple of church members there with her for support, but when she came to, she didn't want anything to do with church, church folks, or God.

"After all those years I didn't have you in my life," Reese cried, "God restored our relationship. He gave you back to me, and now He's taking you again. You're my child; you're a part of me. How does God expect me to give up a part of me, the part that keeps me going?"

Once Reese found out that I was pregnant and that she'd have a part of me on the outside after all, she eventually repented, claiming that this was just another test God was giving her for an even greater testimony.

Penny was still Penny, and that was unfortunate. Because once I cleared up the mess I was in, I wanted to see her and Baby maybe try to get to where Reese and I had gotten. I told myself I was going to try to spend some time with Baby and—I don't know, do what Reese does with those women at Mary Haven—just talk to her.

I mean, mine and Reese's scenario was nowhere near Penny's and Baby's, but as bitter as I was towards Reese, as much hate as I had for her, if we could work things out, any mother and daughter could. I didn't know if they'd be working out anything anytime soon though.

Unfortunately, Baby ended up getting pregnant. All that did was give Penny a bona fide reason to put Baby out on the streets and sever their relationship altogether, something she'd been starving for. Now she didn't have to look at her any more.

She got the grandbaby, but she still wouldn't have anything to do with Baby to this day. For a minute there, Baby was living with some man who was taking care of her and her child. Then I heard she was about to get back with her child's father, and something happened with that. So that that didn't go down as planned. I felt bad for Baby. She had to be struggling, trying to make it. And that scared me.

Not tooting my own horn, but not every young girl from the hood who found herself in a bad situation, like myself, was able to be strong and endure the struggle. Some made quick, fast, and fucked-up decisions that they later regretted, or pretended not to regret. I just wished there was something I could've done for Baby to make sure that she didn't go down the wrong path.

With me being locked up, Jazzy and Reese needed help with running the stores. They'd been working poor Pat to death. It was just so hard to trust people with a business we'd worked so hard to build and maintain. I'd asked Jazzy to see what he could do about locating Baby so that he could maybe hire her. Reese will probably try to counsel her to death, but that might be just what she needed.

Jazzy visited me every week. He brought our son, York Jason Fields, with him. He insisted on naming him after York in his memory. Because Jazzy was driving, he felt so responsible for York's death, even though he had no control over that truck hitting them. Jazzy was torn apart. York died in his arms. I couldn't bear to crush him by telling him York's true intentions with him. *'Model inmate' my ass.* That nigga made a deal to get up out of there. And just to think, he had already served so much of his time. He really didn't have that long to go. I guess, looking at the big picture, it wasn't even about the time he was serving. It was about him getting back at Jazzy for living the life that he wanted to live. I guess he was living by my motto—when someone fucks you, you fuck them back . . . harder.

Jazzy said Yvette was at the funeral. He said she wanted him to know that she didn't blame him at all for York's death. Of course, she didn't. Jazzy ended up getting about $10,000 from the company the trucker worked for as compensation for his injuries, which included a broken leg. I was sure Yvette got way more than that, since her brother lost his life. Knowing her, she probably ran to her attorney's office to file a civil suit before she even went to identify the body. On top of that, I know she had a life insurance policy on his ass—that's just the type of person she was.

Yvette told Jazzy to tell me that she had no hard feelings against me, that she was willing to let bygones be bygones. "Yeah, bye, bitch. Begone, bitch, begone," was all I had to say to that.

I didn't tell Jazzy that though. I mainly let him do all of the talking anyway when he came to visit.

"Reese took our lil' guy to church today. That's why I didn't bring him with me," Jazzy explained when he saw the look on my face when he showed up without our son. "How you doing?"

I nodded. Like I said, I didn't say much. I had talked shit my entire life, it seemed. Listening wasn't so bad after all.

"You know, this doesn't get any easier, coming to visit you here." Jazzy touched my fingertips with his. Coming here just to sit at a table with you doesn't cure the pain of me wanting to hold you and caress you. And remember how we used to spend our Sundays?"

I smiled at the thought. But thinking about making love to Jazzy right then and there only reminded me that I couldn't make love to Jazzy right then and there, which led me to think about who was making love to him. He'd been doing a lot of talking about Yvette lately. *Maybe it was that bitch. Or maybe Zondra was playing on, and taking advantage of his weak moments of losing his best friend.* It seemed like all I thought about was who he was fuckin'. I ain't stupid—that nigga wasn't about to jack off, nor did I expect him to, for five more years.

"Damn, Harlem, why didn't you just tell me—" Jazzy stopped himself. He asked me that every time he came to visit. He asked me in every letter he wrote me. Every card.

"I just couldn't," was what I always told him. "I just couldn't."

"Look, Jazzy," I told him, "I know we never talk about this but . . . you're a man . . . and I know you have needs. So if you—"

"If you are even thinking about going there," Jazzy snapped, "then you need to turn around and bring your ass right back."

"Please, Jazzy, you don't have to pretend—"

" 'Pretend'? Is that what you think I've been doing for all these years . . . pretending?" Jazzy's forehead wrinkled as his bottom lip began to tremble. He took a couple of deep breaths and then looked at me with tearful eyes. "I love you, Harlem." Tears began to fall from his eyes. "You my mu'fuckin' world and ain't no woman"—He slammed his fist on the table—"no bitch, gon' ever replace you."

I closed my eyes as my jaws began to tighten. Seeing Jazzy cry just broke me down. It took me forever to try to regain my composure, but fighting back those tears was one fight I was not going to win. I lost it. I began bawling out of control. "I love you too, Jason Fields. I love you more than I love myself, more than you'll ever know. I'd trade my soul for you. If only you knew. I'm trying to be strong. I'm trying to stay focused and keep my head straight in here, but it's hard with everybody I love out there."

"Don't worry 'bout nothing. I got you. And our son—I'm gon' be the best daddy in the whole wide world to that boy. When I look into his eyes, I can't ever imagine not wanting a kid. And you know Reese gon' be there to help."

"I know, but it's still hard." I wiped my tears away, and my nose.

"Look at us." Jazzy chuckled and wiped a few of his own tears away. "Look at me anyhow. I feel like some ol' big bitch."

We both laughed.

"You know how normally it's the woman who gotta hold shit down while her man upstate? Well, not this time. I'ma hold this shit down for you. We gon' have three stores by the time you get out of here. Fuck that—we gon' have a chain of stores—that's my word."

Just as I had wiped my last tear away, he had to take me back there again. "Jazzy, I love you," I cried with an uncontrollable amount of tears. My body began to tremble. How could I live without him? He had been my air. How could I breathe now? How could I live without my son who, it seemed, was taken away the minute after they laid him on my chest?

"Look here, stop crying." Jazzy began to assist me in wiping my tears away. "As long as we stay strong, it's gon' make the time go by quick, you'll see. It's gon' be all right. You gotta feel me on this, or it ain't gonna work, Harlem. It's like praying to God, asking him to do something for you—you gotta believe; if you don't believe, it ain't gon' work." He stared at me for a second. "You ain't think a nigga was listening in church, did you?"

I smiled. "I do, baby," I said, sniffing, calming myself down. "I do believe."

I felt like a buster up in there. The CO was looking at me like I was her orgasmic letdown. I had come up in that joint like a hard dick, with my hard-ass attitude and cockiness about mine. I got mad respect, and now here I was sitting there, bawling like some ol' "Rudy Poo." I couldn't help it though. My heart was in pain. I suppose the CO had seen enough of this drama play out, so she informed me that my visiting time was up.

"Just one more minute, please," I begged. "Please?"

"Time," she said aggressively.

I turned to look at Jazzy. "I gotta go, baby."

"It's cool, 'cause you know I'm gon' be back; I ain't going nowhere. Never! All right? So you can erase those kinds of thoughts from your head, all right?"

I shook my head then stood up as the CO tugged on my arm, aiding me up from the chair.

"Don't cry, mama," Jazzy said. "I love you. I'ma make you my wife, Harlem. Me, you, and our son . . . happily ever after like that fairytale shit most broads want."

We laughed.

"Remember now," I said, recomposing myself, "I ain't 'most broads.'"

"That's what's up." He winked.

I took a deep breath and tried to "woman up" real quick. I exhaled as Jazzy blew me a kiss. The CO then whisked me away.

As I walked back to my cell, all I could think about was

how, once again, I had lied to Jazzy without saying a word. My poor Jazzy. I guess he ain't Superman after all. If he were, he would have seen right through me, that I was a living a lie and allowing him and our son to unknowingly live one as well. How could I continue to allow him to believe that York Jason Fields was his son? This was just one more skeleton I had to bury in my closet and hope that it wouldn't come back to haunt me. *Oh, God, when will I ever truly be free?*

I couldn't help thinking, *If only Jazzy had called me five minutes earlier to tell me that York had died I would've been free.* I, more than likely, would've never made that call to Detective Somore, turning myself in. Granted, those two witnesses may have eventually pointed me out. But maybe not. I guess I'll never know.

THE END

Baby Girl McCoy

**An urban novella
by JOY**

Dedication

This story is dedicated to my young Baby Gurls out there in search of that man just like Daddy. Think about it, ladies—He abandoned you, left you and your mother for dead, yet you search the streets high and low, trying to find him in some young, thugged-out gangsta. He moved on without you and probably started another family somewhere else. Do you really want a man just like Daddy? Well, if you keep searching for him in them streets, you will sure enough find him. Open your eyes.

—JOY

Prologue
The Night of Conception

I was out living on my own by the time I was seventeen. My mama couldn't handle the fact that her baby girl was in love with a gangsta. So, she'd rather see me gone than under her roof head over heels for some nigga who she thought wasn't shit, not to mention one minute I was sweet sixteen and never been fucked, and the next I was going on seventeen and pregnant. She put me out before I even started showing. I think all of my life my mother had been looking for a reason to rid herself of me, her only daughter, her only child. I don't know why she had me in the first goddamn place. If I had been her, I wouldn't have had me. What woman keeps a baby that's the product of a rape, a rape from her own mother's boyfriend nonetheless? I hate to say it, but thank God for a woman's right to an abortion. Not saying that abortion is right for everybody, but in situations like that, a bitch would have been the first one in line exercising my right to choose.

Any other seventeen-year-old girl probably would have been scared to death if they had been thrown out on the streets pregnant, with no job. Lucky for me, though, I had a man like Duke in my life. Contrary to my mother's opinion, he wasn't some nigga who wasn't shit. He was a good man. He was my king. Duke was more of a man than any one I'd ever known, and probably ever will know. I had never had a father figure in my life, so that's probably what attracted me to him in the first place. I was only going on seventeen and he was thirty. He was more like thirty going on forty. Duke had lived a hard-knock life, forced to be a man before ever knowing what the life of a little boy was supposed to be like.

At the age of nine, Duke's mom was killed during a robbery at the gas station she worked at. He never really knew his father, the man who abandoned him, his mother, and his little sister that was two years younger than him, right after his little sister was born. After that, Duke had to supposedly be the man of the family, left to watch over his little sister because his alcoholic auntie, the one they had to go live with after their mother died, damn sure didn't.

The only way Duke knew how to get money was to follow the lead of the boys in the neighborhood that had come before him, so he started hustling. Pretty soon, he got more wrapped up in the game than worrying about taking care of his little sister. So by the time she was fifteen, she was the single mother of a little boy. By the time she was sixteen she was a statistic, a high school dropout on welfare. By the time she was seventeen she was turning tricks with the neighborhood dope boys. By the time she was eighteen she was giving the dope boys their trick money right back to get high. Before she even made it to nineteen, she had given her little boy up for adoption without even telling the family, and three months after that she was found dead as a result of some bad dope.

Duke grew up real quick after that, becoming a passionate and caring man.

I was drawn to the nurturing maturity about him. To me,

he was just like a Daddy, until I turned eighteen, of course; then he became my lover. The king of the castle, he crowned me his princess.

Nobody could put anybody's love up against ours, not Whitney and Bobby's, not Bonnie and Clyde's, not Jay-Z and Beyoncé's, not nobody's. Nothing compared to Duke's and my love. My mama wouldn't accept him, though. But that didn't keep her from her grandchild. Believe it or not, she loved my little girl more than she loved her own little girl. Go figure. My baby got eyes like mine, so when she looked at her, she had to see me. So why didn't she hate her the same way she hated me? I probably sound jealous, right? As a matter of fact, I was. I don't sweat it though. I ain't on that shit. As long as I had Duke I knew I was gonna get all the love I needed. I didn't need no Mama's love or Daddy's love. All I needed was Duke's love, the love of a real man.

Duke gave me the nickname Baby *Gurl.* Well, my name was legally Baby Girl anyway, first name Baby, middle name Girl, but Duke always called me by my first and middle name. And the way my middle name rolled off of his tongue made it sound like he was saying *gurl.* Nobody said my name like him.

Baby was the name my mom put down on the birth certificate. After she gave birth to me at the hospital, the nurse put a little card on my bed that read: Baby Girl McCoy, McCoy being my mother's last name. My mother couldn't even stand to look at me, let alone give me a name.

Come to find out, my mama would have gotten an abortion if she could have, but she was prevented from doing so. I learned that one day, when I overheard her talking to one of her friends in the kitchen. I had left out of the house to go sit on the porch and wait for my ride. When I felt the raindrops, I decided to go back inside and just look out for my ride through the living room window. They didn't hear me come back in the house, so they continued the conversation they had started having, once they thought I was gone. That was the same day I found out who my daddy was.

Before that day, she had told me that my father was just some boy she had gotten pregnant by. They had broken up, and before she could even tell him that she was pregnant, he and his parents were all killed in a car accident. I had believed that story for thirteen years prior to that day.

My mother told her friend that when she was first pregnant with me she started getting sick and my grandma took her to the doctors to see what was going on with her. She tested positive for being pregnant. Her mother clowned and demanded to know who the father was. So sitting there in the doctor's office, butt-naked on the examining table wrapped in tissue paper, she was forced to tell her mother something she had been afraid to tell her for years. She had to tell her how the boogieman had come into her room at night and took something precious from her. She had to tell her how her boyfriend had been fucking her for four years. My grandma froze up with rage. She didn't say two words. Made my mother get dressed and took her home like the day hadn't even happened.

Later that same day she went to the gun store to purchase a piece. She didn't even think about the mandatory two-week waiting period before she could take her piece home. So, for two weeks my grandma waited patiently for her .22, acting as if shit between her and her boyfriend hadn't changed.

My grandma still allowed him to visit. Only, she inconspicuously made sure she kept an eye out that he didn't fuck with my moms. So for two weeks she didn't sleep. She sat up in bed all night reading John Grisham books, such as *A Time to Kill*. She even allowed him to fuck her, to keep him off of her daughter. But two weeks to the day, she went back to the gun store and picked up her merchandise.

My grandma invited him over for dinner that same night she picked up her .22 from the gun store. My mom said that for some strange reason my grandma actually prepared dinner and it was a feast. She had prepared all of my mom's favorite dishes—macaroni and cheese, roast with gravy, mashed potatoes, green beans, fried chicken, collard greens, yams, corn on the cob, buttered rolls, and chocolate cake with white icing. The two of them sat at the dinner table silently and waited for the guest of honor.

Just as soon as he knocked on the door, my grandma got up from the table, walked over to the side table drawer and opened it, pulled out her gun, opened the front door and emptied the bullets into his head. She pulled the trigger three more times just to make sure all of her bullets were in him. She closed the door then sat down at the dinner table, where she and my mom ate dinner together, with his bleeding corps outside on the doorstep. It was their last supper together before the police came and hauled my grandma away.

My mother was only fourteen and became a ward of the state, a pregnant ward of the state. She begged and pleaded for her pregnancy to be terminated, but the state wouldn't allow it. The state forced her to be a mother to me, making her attend classes to learn how to take care of me so that I could live with her when she was eighteen and on her own and no longer a ward of the state. She was emancipated at seventeen, so with nothing but Section 8 housing, food stamps, a monthly check, a health card and a baby that she didn't want, she was on her own.

I know this may sound crazy, but when I found all of this out, I was elated inside. I was happy because for all the years of my life I had wondered why my mother hated me so much and why she treated me so bad and talked to me like a dog on the street. But now I knew why. It wasn't me that she hated, it was him. I never mentioned anything about the conversation I had overheard to her. I just allowed her to deal with her pain however it was that she needed to, even if it was by taking all of her anger out on me. After all, forget about who the daddy was. Being a pregnant, single, teenage girl with no one there to help her was hard enough to deal with in itself.

I could have ended up just like that if it hadn't been for Duke. He made sure that I wasn't pregnant and alone. I don't know what I would have done without Duke. *Just saying that nigga's name makes a bitch's clit tingle.* Damn, I loved that nigga. And unless you knew my story from beginning to end, you could never understand why I'd always love him. And 'spite a lot of the bullshit we went through, I knew deep down inside he'd always love me. Thank God too . . . 'cause he was all I had. Knowing that I could be loved the way Duke loved me was what kept me breathing. I mean, Duke changed my life. It seemed as if one minute I went from being my mama's baby girl to being his Baby Gurl.

My mother did everything possible to keep me from turning into some little ghetto girl who didn't think about anything but dicks and nice cars. She moved us to the burbs and all. But I was a true believer that ghetto is hereditary; that shit runs in the veins like blood—it don't matter how far you try to move away from the ghetto, ghetto-ass shit will always manage to hunt you down. But fortunately for me, I used that ghetto mentality in my favor. Instead of becoming the average ghetto girl, I lucked out and became a ghetto princess. I'm Baby Girl McCoy, and this is my story.

Chapter 1
Not Gon' Cry

"**B**aby, if you don't hurry your black, nappy-headed ass down them steps, I'm gonna leave you up in this muthafucka," my mother yelled at me from downstairs.

One would have thought that she had been calling my name a hundred times, but she hadn't. That was my first notice that she was ready to head out the door for church. A woman who fills her Sunday's air with that much swearing needed Jesus all right.

"Coming, Ma." I ran down the steps while slipping my black pumps on.

"What did I tell you about wearing them hooker shoes to church? You go to church to hear the Word of the Lord, not to walk the runway like you some Victoria Secret model. And put on a goddamn sweater with that slinky-ass dress. Your arms hanging all out and shit."

"But, Ma, there ain't nothing wrong with th—"

"Are you about to talk back?" She raised her hand to strike me.

"No, ma'am." I sighed as my mother snatched her keys off the key hook and stormed out the door.

Back in the day, I would have started to cry. In fact, I would have cried all the way to church, then Penny, that's my mother's name, would have taken a tissue from her purse and wiped away my tears as hard as she could. That shit hurt like hell too. She would rub so hard with that tissue that she'd leave red marks underneath my eyes. So I learned early on to suck it up and not to cry.

After church, my best friend, Celeste, came and picked me up with her and her kids and took me back to their house. I always looked forward to going to kick it with her. I mean, that was my girl for real. I talked to Celeste on the phone all week, e-mailed her during library time at school, and went to her house every Sunday after church to hang out. I didn't even have to call her to come and get me on Sundays. She usually just pulled up in my driveway at the same time every Sunday, beeping her horn.

Before we moved to this part of town, I used to hang out with Celeste every single day. We used to live in the apartment next to Celeste before my mother uprooted us to live out here with all these white folks. I ain't got nothing against Caucasians, but I preferred being around my peeps. It seemed as though the longer you're around hunkies, the more accustomed you became to their ways. Then the next thing you know, you start acting like them, wearing shorts in the winter, coming outside with your hair wet and shit.

I think that was my mother's entire purpose for moving in the first place. She figured if she raised me around them, I'd end up having some class about myself—not to say that folks from the hood didn't have any class—instead of becoming one of those neck-snappin', gum-poppin', burgundy haired, micro-braid-wearin' chicks from my particular old neighborhood. But as the saying goes, you can take the girl up out of the ghetto . . . So, no, I didn't go outside with my hair wet, but I'd wear rollers outside in a heartbeat.

It wasn't too long ago that Celeste herself relocated from the hood. She didn't move way out like we did. She still lived around black folks, just not in the heart of the hood anymore. Her old man, Duke, didn't want their two kids, LD, short for Little Duke, their seven-year-old son, and Tara, their five-year-old daughter, to be bred in the hood any longer than they had to. He himself was a hustler, and as the kids got older, he found his lifestyle less easy to camouflage by still living in the hood. Every time they looked out the window, they saw a hustler, pimp, or baller. It didn't take them long to realize that the man lying in bed with Mommy looked just like the ones they saw when they looked out of the window. Kids are smart. Taking them away from the streets doesn't mean that they won't eventually find their way back. When will parents learn that?

Like Jay Z said, the hood has mental telepathy. From the moment we are birthed into the hood, there is a bond formed for life. The hood knows what we are capable of, just like God knows. The shit is already written. It's in our blood. Ain't no escape. But nonetheless, Celeste and Duke's move gave them peace of mind.

Celeste was older than me, closer to my mother's age than mine, but age ain't nothin' but a number. She understood me. I could share any and everything with her, and she could relate. She was the only person I'd ever told about the conversation I overheard between my mother and her friend about who my father was.

She never looked at my thoughts and opinions as just some dumb old teenage shit like my mother did. Any idea or thought I had, no matter how grown-up I thought it was, my moms deemed it stupid. She never half wanted to listen to anything I had to say in the first place. Celeste was always happy to listen. Sometimes I thought she lived vicariously through my youth. Me talking about cheerleading and high school crushes reminded her of her and Duke, who were high school sweethearts. Although Celeste and Duke referred to each other as husband and wife, they had never made it official on paper. But with a love as strong as theirs, there wasn't a damn thang a piece of paper from the courthouse could do to make it any stronger.

"Hey, Baby. How you doin'?" Duke said to me when we all entered the house. He then walked over to Celeste and planted a kiss on her lips. "Dinner is ready," he said to her.

"Thank you, sweetheart," Celeste said to him with a smile. She then turned to the kids and ordered them to go upstairs and wash their hands before they ate, which they did.

Duke walked over to the living room table and grabbed his wallet and keys.

"Where you goin'?" Celeste was all too quick to ask.

"I got business—now don't start." Duke gave Celeste the look.

She sighed and waved her hand. "Yeah, yeah. Business as usual," she said, brushing by him.

I plopped down on the couch and watched their minor lover's quarrel play out. Even when they were spattin', I still could see and admire the love they had for one another.

"I know you ain't even gon' act that way." Duke had a frisky smile on his face as he patted Celeste's ass. "Your husband done cooked you his specialty, your favorite, lasagna, and you wanna go start actin' fresh?"

"Don't touch me," Celeste said, even though the tiny grin that crept across her lips showed that she liked very much for him to touch her.

"What if I die out here tonight? You gon' regret you even acted like this."

"Not as long as you paid the life insurance policy up this month." Celeste winked.

"Come on now, Cee-Cee—you wrong for that."

"I know. It's just that dinner would taste so much better if you were here eating it with us."

I just sat there watching them. It was hard to believe that even when they called themselves arguing they were cute. Come to think of it, I had never seen them have a real argument before. It was like they were born for each other, like they were one and the same. What Duke and Celeste had is what I wanted some day.

"I knew you only loved me for my pimp juice." Duke kissed Celeste on the neck.

She playfully shooed him away. "Get on out of here, boy."

"I'll see you in a few hours, all right?"

"Yes, Duke, whatever you say."

"See you later, kids," Duke called upstairs.

"Bye, daddy," the kids responded.

How I envied their home, their relationship, their kids. Having a daddy, at least where I was from, was a rare gem. I think Duke saw this envy in my eyes.

"I almost forgot about Baby Gurl." Duke stopped in his tracks and dug down into his pockets. He pulled his wallet out. "Here." He handed me a twenty-dollar bill.

"What's this for?" I looked at it.

"That's for the other night when you watched the kids for us."

"Celeste already paid me." I held the money out to give it back to him.

"Then keep it until next time," he said with a wink.

"Okay, if you say so," I said with hesitation in my voice. "I guess I owe you one."

"Go on and keep it, Baby," Celeste said. "There have been many of times you done sat with them bad-ass kids for nothin'. I'm sure we owe you for one time or another."

"See there." Duke smiled at me. "We probably owe you anyway for one time or another." He winked at me again.

"Thanks, Duke." I smiled as I stuffed the bill into my pocket.

"Be good," Duke said, walking out of the door.

"I will," I shouted.

I was such a leech, sucking up all of Duke's kindness, like he owed it to me. I knew Duke was only that nice to me because he pitied me. I was sure he knew enough about my life through everything that I had told Celeste. I was sure she had probably told him some things about me during their pillow talk.

I remember telling myself that he probably could have cared less about me, that he probably only felt sorry for me and that's why he was so nice to me. But even if it wasn't genuine, I liked it. I wanted it. I needed it. Since I didn't have my own daddy around to be nice to me, I sure wasn't gonna reject somebody else's daddy being nice to me—even if it wasn't real.

Chapter 2
I Wanna Be Your Chick

"**W**e are the Bearcats. We can't be beat." I did a buck high into the air. I was notorious for being the girl on the school cheerleading team that could deliver the highest, most straight-legged bucks on the squad. This one in particular had to be one of my best bucks ever. That's because he was watching, Tonio Mackey, the hottest boy at our school, or should I say the hottest boy to ever drop out of our school.

He had a honeycomb complexion, green eyes, and slicked-black, shiny hair that he wore in a long ponytail down his back. Most of his features he got from his white mother. But that well-hung piece of meat that bulged even in his baggy pants, he had to have gotten from his black father. He had the black chicks and white girls alike on his dick. He was the best of both worlds. But I swear he only had eyes for me. Maybe it was just part of my fantasy, but I swore that when I wasn't watching him, he was watching me. But in all reality, I knew that was the furthest thing from the truth. I had been over at Celeste's a couple of times when he had come by to talk some business with Duke. He never even thought twice about looking my way, but that didn't keep me from fantasizing about him and I being a couple some day.

Tonio would have been a senior, if he had stayed in school. Instead, he decided to "sling them thangs." Initially, he used to do it before school, in-between classes, and after school. But like the average "entreprenigga," he realized sooner than later that if he dedicated even more time to slingin', he'd make more money than any high-school diploma could ever bring his way.

Like clockwork, every day he showed up at the school football field at 4:15 p.m. That gave him a few minutes to watch his little brother, Benzo, who was a sophomore, finish up football practice. In my head, though, I always pretended that he was there to see me. I knew I didn't have a chance in the world with him. He would have been a senior. I was only a junior, what they called an in-between borderline chick at my school, so he probably wouldn't have fucked with me even if he did still go to my school.

There was something about them rowdy boyz. They either liked dumb freshmen girls that they could talk out of their cherries, or the experienced senior girls who already knew how to throw that ass. Sophomores and juniors were last options. I was only a junior, almost a senior, but at the same time, I had little experience. Okay, I had no experience, but with a boy like Tonio Mackey, I was willing to learn.

I made myself comfortable on the couch as the kids sat on the floor in front of the television watching *Sponge Bob Square Pants*. Celeste and Duke hadn't been gone a good fifteen minutes, when there was a knock at the door. I got up and peeked out of the window. I couldn't make out who was at the door, but I saw a white Cutlass with shining twenty-inch rims parked in front of the apartment. A smile crept across my face just knowing who the owner was.

I walked over to the door and, clearing my throat, asked, "Who is it?"

"Ay, yo, it's Tonio."

"Hey." I opened the door, trying to hide my smile, but it was too forceful.

"Hey yourself," Tonio said.

There was a sudden spark in his eyes as he gave me the once over, peeping out the cute little cantaloupe-colored, cotton knit Ralph Lauren tennis skirt outfit I was sportin'. This was the first time he had ever been able to see my runner's legs this close up, and how toned they were.

"Is Duke around?" he asked, once able to take his attention off of my legs.

"No. Him and Celeste went to the movies. I'm here sitting with the kids until they get back."

"On a Friday night, you sitting around just baby sitting?" Tonio asked, as if I was supposed to have something better to do.

I just shrugged my shoulders.

Tonio poked his head in the door to check out the kids. "Hey, LD. Hey, Tara."

"Uncle T," the children said in unison. They got up from in front of the television, ran up, and hugged him.

"Come sit down and watch *Sponge Bob* with us, Uncle T," LD said.

"Yeah. C'mon, please." Tara pulled Tonio by the hand.

He looked at me for approval.

I nodded and shrugged my shoulders. I know I didn't mind his company, not one little bit.

Tonio had completely worn the kids out by wrestling, playing the claw, and carrying on with them. They fell out right there on the living room floor. Tonio and I just sat on the couch laughing and talking, watching back-to-back episodes of *Law and Order* on USA. It was unreal to me. Never in a million years did I imagine that I, Baby G. McCoy, would be spending a Friday night snuggled up next to Tonio Mackey.

"Can I ask you something, Baby?" Tonio said seductively during a commercial break.

"Sure," I said with that dumb, stupid, high-school-girl giggle trailing my words.

"How come you don't never say nothing to me when I be up at the school? I know you be seeing me; I be seeing you seeing me."

"What?" I asked, stunned.

"I know you be seeing me, girl. Don't even try to play me like that."

I blushed. "Yeah, I be seeing you, but you never pay me no never mind."

"Psstt." Tonio twisted up his lips. "You trippin' now. I always be checking you out. You be doin' them cartwheels, jumping up in the air all high and shit. Yeah, I be peepin' that."

"For real?" I giggled. "I never knew that you noticed. You usually over at your car surrounded by folks or hanging out on the bleachers, like you James Dean or something."

"A rebel, huh?" Tonio nodded his head and licked his lips. "So, you probably scared to fuck with a nigga like me, huh, a rebel? Ain't that right, Baby?"

As the mood became more intense and the sexual attraction between us thickened, I was quick to respond, "I ain't never scared."

Tonio leaned in close to me. "Oh yeah?" he said in a whisper, his lips almost touching mine. He put his hand on top of my leg. "Then why you trembling?—Seem scared to me."

Engrossed in his words, on fire by how close he was to me, I repeated, "I ain't never scared." I scooted my body towards his, to let him know that I really wasn't scared, but in fact, I was scared shitless. I couldn't back down though. It was too late now.

After a few seconds of looking into my eyes, Tonio pressed his lips against mine.

I closed my eyes and melted. My body literally went limp. His lips were so soft, like marshmallows. I just sat there taking in the gentle pressure his lips applied against mine. Then the next thing I knew, his tongue was working its way around the inside of my mouth, like a water hose on the loose.

I opened my eyes in shock. Tonio's eyes were closed as he continued thrashing his tongue in my mouth. I had never kissed before, so all I could do was go with the flow. It felt kind of weird, but at the same time, it felt good to be connecting with someone of the male species.

My heart was racing one hundred miles per hour. My palms were soaking wet. I wanted so badly to stop and ask, "Am I doing this right?"

Obviously I was, because as I proceeded to follow Tonio's lead by thrashing my tongue in and out of his mouth, he began moaning and rubbing my light, dusty-brown hair that I wore straight and that fell right below my shoulders.

After what seemed like forever, Tonio finally separated his lips from mine.

I just sat there, waiting for my cue as what to do next.

Tonio looked down at the sleeping kids on the floor. "Let's take this upstairs." Tonio grabbed me by my facc then kissed me again.

Then the words just slipped right out of my mouth. "Okay," I said, breathing heavily.

Tonio stood up.

I stood up behind him and followed him up the steps and into LD's bedroom. It was dark, but Tonio and I managed to stumble our way to the bed. We sat down like two first-graders waiting to play "you show me yours, and I'll show you mine."

Tonio began kissing me again. He pushed down on me so that I would end up lying down on my back. He opened my legs, climbed on top of me, and began grinding me. Even through my panties and his pants, I could feel his huge knot massaging my private area. It was an unfamiliar feeling to me, but I liked it.

"You're so sexy," Tonio whispered.

No one had ever even told me that I was pretty before, let alone sexy. Was I even old enough to be sexy? I always thought that grown women were sexy, not teenage girls.

"Thank you. So are you." I figured that I'd return the compliment just to be courteous. Hell, I thought Tonio was cute. Fine even. The word *sexy* just never danced in my mind about him.

Tonio stood up and lifted his shirt over his head. The bits and pieces of moonlight peeking in through the bedroom blinds gave me a silhouetted glimpse of his bare upper body. At that moment, I could honestly define him as sexy.

I bit down on my bottom lip and just lay there, trying to figure out what could possibly happen next. Then I heard it—Tonio's zipper being undone.

I sat up. "What are you doing?"

"What choo mean, what am I doing, girl?"

"Why are you taking your pants off?"

"Stop playing, Baby." Tonio took off his pants, his underwear going down with them. He stepped out of them and positioned himself back on top of me. Before I could say anything, he was back to kissing me again. The next thing I knew, he was tugging my panties down.

"Tonio." I playfully pushed his hand away.

"What, girl?"

"Stop, boy." I tried to giggle it off.

Tonio rolled over from off top of me and stared up at the ceiling. "You one of them teases, huh." He sighed.

"No, I'm not trying to tease you. I just don't—I mean, I've never . . ."

Tonio sat up and put his hand on my face. "You mean to tell me that a girl as pretty as you are ain't never been with a man before?"

All I heard was the word *pretty*. Tonio thought that I was sexy. Tonio thought that I was pretty. Hearing those words for the first time ever made me feel so special. To hear them from a man was priceless.

I shook my head no.

"Why not?"

I shrugged my shoulders. "I don't know. I guess I've just never been ready to do that kind of thing before, you know. I mean, I've never even kissed before." I sighed, realizing that I had really let the cat out of the bag about my inexperienced ass now.

"Word?" Tonio said, surprised.

I looked away into the dark.

"You mean all that tongue you were throwing me down there, it was your first time kissing?" Tonio turned my face towards him. " 'Never been ready,' huh?" Tonio kissed me softly on my lips.

I kissed him back, sticking my tongue in his mouth first. I wanted to show him that I could be a big girl if I wanted to. I grabbed him by the head and began kissing him wildly.

"Damn, girl." Tonio pulled back. "Seems like you're ready to me."

"I'm sorry," I said, acting coy.

"Naw, it's cool." Tonio sat there thinking for a moment. "Look, hold up." He jumped out of the bed.

"You mad?" I asked softly.

He chuckled. "Just hold up. I'll be right back." Tonio

slipped on his pants then exited the room barefoot. He ran down the steps then I heard the front door open.

What the hell is he doing?

After a few moments, he came back up the steps and entered the room. I could hear him fumbling around.

"What are you doing?"

"Shhh." He continued to fumble around. I heard some clicking. It was silent, and then Tonio made his way back over to the bed.

The next thing I know, I was being serenaded by the twelfth song on R. Kelly's 12-track CD. "Lay down," Tonio said, joining me back on the bed.

"But—"

"Please, Baby, just trust me. I'm not going to hurt you."

I lay down, closed my eyes, and braced myself for whatever was about to go down.

Tonio started tugging my skirt down.

I flinched.

"Relax," he whispered.

I took several deep breaths and then just lay there like a corpse, my eyes closed tight.

Slowly Tonio slid my skirt all the way off of me and gently spread my legs, placing his hands on my inner thighs. My muscles tightened, but I just lay there, still believing in his promise that he wasn't going to hurt me.

The next thing I know, through my panties I felt light pressure and warmth. It sent chills through my body. I could feel Tonio softly nibbling down on my private. The heat of his breath went through my panties like a raging fire. As he nibbled and put pressure on me, I began to croon. I had never even touched myself before, and yet here I was allowing someone else to become better acquainted with my body than I was.

My panties were soaking wet from Tonio's saliva and the wetness my pussy was producing. All of a sudden, Toni started putting harder pressure on me, sucking like crazy. It was so intense that I didn't even realize him moving my panties aside and placing his tongue inside me.

"Ohhh," I moaned. "Tonio, what are you doing to me?"

He didn't answer.

By now I had lifted my ass off of the bed, giving him full access to eat me out.

He sucked. He plunged his tongue in and out of me. He flicked at my clit with his tongue. He drove me crazy.

When I lost my strength and allowed my ass to fall back down onto the bed, I could feel the wetness underneath me.

"Ohhh. Ohhh." I began to moan harder as the feeling grew even more intense. I started calling out his name. "Tonio. Oh God, Tonio."

By now, R. Kelly's CD had started over and was well into the third song. It was a more upbeat tempo that Tonio seemed to be trying desperately to maintain a groove with as he ate me out. I hated hearing the song fade as Tonio's tongue began to slow its motion.

"It's time." Tonio sat up on his knees in front of me, my legs spread wide-open, welcoming him. He managed to take my panties off. Then there went the sound of his zipper again. He pushed his pants down to his knees, cupped his manhood then laid his body on top of mine. "Am I too heavy?" he asked with genuine concern.

I shook my head no as R. Kelly's words, "Coulda sworn you were ready to go all the way," frolicked through my head

"Don't worry," Tonio said. "Don't you worry, Baby."

My body was trembling uncontrollably as I felt the tip of Tonio's dick tango with my clit. Damn, it felt good. Had I known the shit could feel so good, I would have at least been grindin' on niggaz long before this, or touching myself even.

"Ohhh," Tonio moaned softly as he played peek-a-boo with the tip of his dick in my pussy. "Ohhh . . . shit, Baby."

He sped up his pace, still not sticking it all the way in. But

I could feel him slowly but surely trying to get more in, centimeter by centimeter.

"Tonio," I said in pleasurable agony.

"Just let it go in slow. Just get it over with."

"Tonio," I said. I wanted to tell him to stop, but the words wouldn't come out. I took my hands and tried to push him off of me by his chest, but before I knew it, my arms were wrapped around him pulling him to me.

"Tonio, Tonio." I felt more and more of him coming inside of me. All of a sudden it didn't feel so good anymore, but by then it was too late. It felt as though my shit had split wide open. "Oh, God!" I shouted, tears running down my face.

"Oh, Baby. Oh shit." Tonio stroked in and out of me. "Oh shit, Baby. Oh shit. I'm cummin', girl. Oh fuck, girl. Fuck!" Tonio stopped stroking and just began trembling inside of me.

I didn't know what the fuck was going on. I could feel every muscle in his body tightening up. Then as if he couldn't take it anymore, he just started fucking me really fast.

"Tonio," I said, scratching my nails down his back

"Ugh!" He roared like a beast as he pushed himself as far up inside of me as he could and just let it flow. He then collapsed on me, breathing heavily. "I'm sorry, Baby. I'm sorry."

I just lay there sobbing.

He began brushing my hair back with his hand. "I'm sorry, Baby. It's okay, beautiful." He then kissed me on the forehead, then my eyelids, then my nose, until he finally planted a soft kiss on my lips.

Sexy, pretty, and now beautiful. I began to cry even harder. *I think I could love this boy.*

As Tonio began to put on his clothes, I felt around for and grabbed my panties and my skirt. I then got up and went into the bathroom. I turned on the light, closed the door behind me, and then stood there with my back up against the door.

I can't believe I lost my virginity in the twin bed of the kid who I was baby-sitting. I put my hand over my mouth and began to giggle. *I just had sex.* I giggled again. I finally composed myself then walked over towards the toilet to take a pee. Walking towards the toilet I passed the medicine cabinet mirror. I stopped and looked at myself, wanting to see if there was anything different about me.

My eyes were still light brown, my hair was still long and straight, and my skin was still an almond brown. From what I could tell in the mirror, there was nothing different about me. But then all of a sudden I felt it. I felt the difference. I felt sexy. I felt pretty, beautiful even. There was something different about me after all. I wasn't a baby any more.

Chapter 3
Age Ain't Nothin'

By Monday morning I couldn't even think straight. I couldn't wait to see Tonio again. Now that I had given him the most precious thing that any girl could ever give a man, her cherry, I knew that I was now a part of him. I felt like he was carrying me around on his arm, without me even being in his presence. Because he had been my chosen one, the one I chose to share my temple with, he was now a part of me too. I could still feel him inside of me. I could still smell him. I could still smell the aroma that danced over us in the air as we made love. It wasn't sex. Plain old sex couldn't have had me feeling the way I was feeling. Plain old sex couldn't have made me feel so special. It had to be love.

I knew the moment I came out of the bathroom over Celeste's house, after Tonio and I had made love, and found him standing in the doorway waiting for me, that he was not only my first one, but he would be my only one, the last one.

"You okay, girl?" he said to me as I had come out of the bathroom. He looked deep into my eyes with those green gazers of his.

"Umm, hmm." I put my head down. I was embarrassed

about the glow about me that I knew was lighting up the dark hallway.

"Don't do that." He lifted my head back up by my chin. "Don't be ashamed. I don't think any differently of you. As a matter of fact, I think more of you." Tonio kissed me on the forehead. "Come on, let's go back downstairs."

He took my hand and led me back to the couch downstairs, where he sat next to me for about an hour. He sat close to me.

I remember taking the initiative, resting my head on his shoulder.

He then put his arm around me and ran his fingers through my hair, every now and then kissing me on the head.

Girls only dream of a first time like this. It wasn't a wham, bam, thank you, ma'am. He stayed with me to comfort me and let me know just how special he thought I was. Even before he left, he asked me for my phone number. But I knew that the only way I would be able to communicate with him was if I saw him after school or over Celeste's house. There was no way Penny was going to allow a boy to call the house for me. She would cuss him out so bad that I would be embarrassed for him. I didn't want to even put that boy through that.

So when he asked me for my digits to holler at me, I didn't even lie in telling him that I wasn't allowed to have boys call my house. There was no reason for me to start our relationship off with a lie. Anything that begins with a lie ends with a lie. Tonio was my first, and I knew that I had made the right decision by giving it up to him. He was going to be the man I married. I could just feel it.

The last bell of the school day couldn't have rung soon enough. I headed straight for the girls' locker room and changed into my gym clothes. Today I had especially packed my little yellow shorts that had blue lettering with the school name on the butt. I wore my little blue T-shirt that had the school name in yellow lettering on the shirt. They weren't supposed to be that little on me; they were actually last year's clothes. I wanted to wear something that I could fill out, something that would put a smile on Tonio's face when he saw me walk on that field. I wanted to look different for him—older, bold, and grown.

"Well, damn, mama." Tia smacked me on my ass as we headed onto the football field for cheerleading practice. "You been covering all this up underneath them baggy-ass sweat suits you usually practice in? No way I would have been hiding all that. You look good." She then brushed by me and did a light jog over to where the other members of the squad were already positioned and stretching.

"Girl, you silly." I blushed.

Getting a compliment from another female was the ultimate. Girls at my school, no matter how much they smiled in each other's faces, hated the shit out of each other. Jealousy was flagrant, a stench that couldn't be hidden with the sweet smell of perfume they tried to spray over it. So for Tia, the very feminine and very beautiful captain of the cheerleading squad, to compliment me, just took me to another level.

I hardly had time to wallow in her compliment before I noticed him. It wasn't hard to not notice him. He was over at the parking lot, standing against his car with a crowd around him. Wherever there was a crowd of hoochies trying to give their pussy away in hopes of money for an outfit or to get their hair done, and wannabe flunky thugs trying to ride on his coattail, there would be Tonio.

Pretending not to notice him, I joined the rest of my squad in stretching. I could feel Tonio's eyes burning through my skin and the heat was melting me. I wanted to feel him inside of me again. One time wasn't enough. Now my body was craving him. The first time was painful, but I knew now that he had broken me in, it would be nothing but pure pleasure. I hoped this was a natural feeling, because my wanting him so badly scared me. I had never wanted him as much as I did now. I mean, it was to the point that I didn't care if one of those white girls was over there sucking his dick, I would just thank the bitch for warming him up for me—that's how bad I wanted him.

I don't know how I managed to get through practice, but I did. As the girls started back towards the locker room to change clothes and head home on the activity bus, I faked stretching a little more, giving Tonio time to step to me. *I know that nigga ain't gon' make me walk up over to him in front of all those people.*

No sooner than the thought entered my mind, it exited, as Tonio, with his bowlegged walk, emerged from the crowd around him and headed my way. "Damn, yo," he said as he approached me and ran his index finger around the rim of my shorts, pulling it, then allowing it to snap back on my ass. "I call myself being a gentleman, but you make a nigga wanna get all up in that."

I bit down on my lip and smiled.

"You looked so damn sexy when you just did that," Tonio said in a serious tone. "Baby, I really do want you right now."

"I want you too."

The next thing I know, Tonio had me bent over under the bleachers.

"Oh, God, Tonio," I moaned, as he slowly slid his dick in and out of me.

The more I cried out his name, the faster and harder he pumped me.

"I love the way you make me feel, Baby." Tonio pulled me up so that he was whispering in my ear. He was inside of me, pushing me back and forth with the hand he had on my waist. His other hand was caressing my right breast.

"Tonio, I love the way you make me feel."

He now slowly bent his knees and then unbent them as he went in and out of me.

I felt wrapped up in Tonio. This second time was not quite like the first time—it was better. I was ready. There was no pain. I could take it.

Before I knew it, I found myself sliding up and down Tonio, as if I was doing squats. Everything started to come naturally, as I began to throw that ass back at him.

"Yeah, Baby. Just like that, girl. Do that shit."

"Tonio, I love you." I really tried to catch those words before they slid into his ear, but it was too late.

Immediately I was horrified. I did not want that boy thinking that he had me so sprung that I was already telling him that I loved him. I loved the idea of loving him, and I wanted him to know, but not now.

Tonio made it all better when he replied, "I love you too."

I don't know if it was his seven and a half inches banging against my walls that put me on the verge of cummin', or him telling me that he loved me, but all I knew was that my syrup gushed out like a waterfall onto Tonio's dick, making him squirt up inside of me.

"Oh, shit," he said as he trembled against me. "Oh, shit, Baby. Girl, you feel so good. You feel so good." Tonio was breathing heavily.

Words can't explain how good it felt to make Tonio feel so good. Never mind how good he made me feel. At that moment, at that time, I only wanted to live to please him. I know it might sound crazy, me talking like this being so young and all, but really, age ain't nothin' but a number. Feelings have no age. I was living proof.

"No disrespect," Tonio said, "but looking at you in those little-ass shorts and shit, I had to have you now, even if it meant taking it from behind under the school bleachers."

"Don't apologize." I placed my index finger over his lips.

"Don't take away from what just happened here with an apology—I liked it, I wanted it."

Tonio pulled me into his chest and put his arms around me. "I like you," he whispered in my ear.

His words were sweet, but bitter compared to *I love you.* All of a sudden a feeling of confusion came over me. *'I like you'—Did that mean that he didn't love me like he just claimed to have five minutes ago? Was that his dick talking before?*

"Look, I gotta go," Tonio said, releasing his embrace. "My brother is probably looking for me. When's the next time you going over Duke's and Celeste's house?"

"I don't know." I shrugged my shoulders, still stuck on the words 'I like you.' "Probably this weekend."

"I'm trying to figure out how we can get together, you know, besides on the school football field. I want to take you out or something."

Suddenly I perked up. He wanted to take me out. He wanted something more than just my pussy, which Penny had always warned me was the only thing all boys wanted from girls. But Tonio actually wanted to spend time with me.

"My mom would trip," I explained.

"That's why I asked when was the next time you would be at Duke's. I figured I could scoop you up from over there— your moms would never know."

"I'll probably go over there this weekend," I said eagerly, and more certain this time. "I'll tell my mom I have to baby-sit for Celeste or something."

"I need to give you my cell phone number then. Call me when you get over there, or if you can, you know, if your mom ain't home or something, hit me up sometime from the crib."

A bigger smile couldn't have covered my face. "Cool."

"Let me run to my car and write it down for you."

"All right." I watched him run off to his car. While he went to his car and wrote down his number, I crept from under the bleachers and waited for him to return.

"Make sure you call me whenever you get a chance, no matter what time it is." Tonio handed me the piece of paper with his number written down on it. "It don't matter what time it is. I keep late hours." He winked and then he was back off to his car, where Benzo was waiting on him, keeping the groupies and flunkies company.

"Damn!" I said to myself. "The activity bus." I immediately sprinted for the locker room. I knew I wasn't going to have time to shower and change back into my clothes, so I'd just have to put them on over my shorts and T-shirt on the bus. No way was I going to let Penny see me in this get-up. Besides, they weren't for her eyes; they were for Tonio's.

I quickly grabbed my stuff out of my locker and made it onto the activity bus just in the nick of time. I plopped down on the first empty seat I saw, which was next to Tia. Ordinarily her best friend and co-captain of the cheerleading team would have been sitting next to her, but she was home sick today.

"I thought you might have been getting a ride from ol' dude," Tia said as I slipped my jeans on over my shorts.

"Huh?"

"Child, please . . . Don't think I didn't notice you and Mr. Mackey make y'all's way under the bleachers."

"I don't know what you're talking about." I looked straight ahead.

"Sure you do." Tia leaned in close to me and began sniffing. "You smell like sex." She laughed.

"Oh, my God, do I?" I began sniffing the air.

"Girl, you stupid." She laughed again.

Little did she know, I was dead serious as I put on my blouse and buttoned it up over my T-shirt.

"So now that the cat's out of the bag, or should I say

panties, how was it?" Tia touched my private part. She was so bold and blunt that her actions weren't even surprising. Things that anybody else would have done and been questioned about, Tia got away with, because she was Tia.

"Tia." I turned away and looked out of the window as the bus headed for its first stop.

"Come on, you kissed, now tell."

Hesitantly, I gave in. It was killing me. I had to tell someone about my sexual experience with Tonio. I couldn't tell Celeste because no way was I going to tell her that my cherry got popped in her house, let alone her kid's bed. Celeste and I shared everything, so I had planned on telling her though, eventually. Now I'd just make it seem like our first time was under the bleachers.

"It was beautiful. He is such a gentleman too. I mean, he was just so gentle, smooth, and sexy as hell."

"Is he big?" Tia waited intensely for the answer.

"It's perfect!"

Then I proceeded to tell Tia every single detail about both our encounters, how good it felt, and how he had made me cum so much under the bleachers.

"Damn, girl." Tia fanned her pussy because my story had made her so hot. "He sounds like all that and then some."

"Even more than that," I said as the driver came to my stop. "Well, this is me. I'll see you tomorrow. And look . . . what I said . . . can we keep it between just me and you?"

"Cheerleader's honor." Tia held her right hand up and crossed her heart with the other.

"Thanks, Tia. See you tomorrow."

"Later, chick." She waved as I exited the bus.

When I walked in the door I ran straight up the stairs. If Tia smelled sex on me, then my mom damn sure would. I jumped in the shower to wash the smell of Tonio off of me. I slipped on a jogging suit then headed down to the kitchen table to do my homework.

I could hardly concentrate on my geometry, thinking about the encounter with Tonio earlier that day.

That night I tossed and turned, dreaming about me and Tonio. I hoped that he was thinking about me just as much as I was thinking about him. I wished that I had a cool mom that I could talk with, one who would understand my feelings. I couldn't wait to see what the future held for us.

The next day at school, I was glowing even more so than the day before. This new change in me must have been transparent because the fellas were checking a sista out. I must say that I had a new twitch in my ass that, I suppose, they couldn't help noticing. I wasn't some young, dumb virgin anymore. I now felt like I belonged, like I was a piece of the same puzzle the other girls were part of. I didn't mind the stares and googly eyes, but dem niggaz didn't have a chance in the world. This here pussy had been branded by Tonio—it was his for life.

After school I went to the field and noticed Tonio's car, but he was nowhere in sight. Puzzled, I made my way over to my team to stretch.

"Where's your cane, McCoy?" the coach yelled. "I told you guys we were going to be working on the cane segment of our routine for the local competition this weekend. Hit the shed."

"Yes, ma'am." I headed to the shed, which was what we called the equipment room where all the sports equipment and whatnot was stored.

As I turned the doorknob to the shed, I discovered it was locked. I tried turning it and pulling it a couple more times to be one hundred percent certain that it was locked. I then marched back out to the field.

"Coach, the shed is locked."

" 'Locked'?" A puzzled look crossed her face, but then she just dug into her sweat pants pocket and pulled out a key ring full of keys. "Here, McCoy. It's this one." Coach handed me the set of keys.

I headed straight back to the shed. With the key in hand I went to stick it in the door to unlock it, but just as I went to do so, the door slowly opened and Tia came out of the shed.

"Oh, Baby! You scared me." She grabbed her chest as if I had just given her a heart attack.

"I'm sor—" I started to aplogize, but then I noticed the figure behind her. "Tonio?"

Instantaneously I felt a wave of heat hit me. I could hear my heart thumping like a Caribbean drum beat. The room was spinning, and I just knew vomit would come up at any minute.

I looked at Tia who had a smirk on her face, and before I knew it, my arched hand was slapping her across the face, knocking the smirk right off of it. I knew that shit had to hurt her because my hand was stinging. I know if someone had hit me the way I had just hit her, it would have been on. Preppy school, 4.0 student, and on the cheerleading squad or not, I was still from the hood and I knew how to keep it street.

All she did was just look up at me.

At first her stare was as cold as ice, and I didn't know what to expect from her. But then she just smiled and started to back away. "Sorry, Baby." She looked at me and then looked over my shoulder at Tonio. "You didn't expect me to just take your word for it, did you? I had to find the shit out for myself." She then chuckled and began to walk away, but then stopped and turned to me to have one last say. "But if it's any consolation to you, for an experienced chick like myself, it was just . . . a'ight. So believe you me, after a couple more times under those bleachers, you'd come to see that he's no Ritz, just a regular, old cracker." She then put her hand on the cheek I had slapped on and walked away and laughed.

"Fuck you, bitch!" Tonio yelled to her.

Which only made her laugh harder as she vanished out of sight and sound.

I just stood there. I couldn't even bring myself to turn around and look Tonio in the face. I was so fucking stupid. I had fantasized about him so much that I made him something that he wasn't. I'd made him my fantasy. *But why did my body crave him and my heart love him like it was real?* Tears just began to stroll down my face, and then I felt his hand on my shoulder.

"Don't touch me!" I quickly turned to face him. "You raped me." I started crying uncontrollably.

"What the fuck?" he said, stunned. "Don't try to 'Mike Tyson' me."

"You raped me of something I believed in, something I thought could happen between the two of us."

Just then a look of remorse covered Tonio's face. "Baby, Tia's a 'ho'. That shit didn't mean—"

"Oh, my God, you are not about to give me that line. What do they do—teach boys that line when they circumcise y'all?"

He came towards me and tried to speak again but I just put my hand up, stopping him in his tracks. I didn't want to hear anything he had to say. I had been fooled once, and I wasn't about to fall prey to the "Please, Baby, please."

I stood there and stared at him for a minute, taking in everything about him, everything that had attracted me to him. Then it hit me. *What the fuck was I thinking?* Tonio Mackey was only the finest boy in the world who could get any girl he wanted, so what made me think that he would want me? What made me think that he would want me for anything more than I had given him?

Sniffling and wiping away the last of my tears, without saying a word, I turned and walked away from him for what I thought was forever, but little did I know, I was taking a part of him with me.

Chapter 4
My Best Friend's Man

"Hey, Duke," I said as he came in the door of their house. I was sitting on the couch, watching music videos.

"Hey, Baby Gurl." He winked. "Where's Celeste at?"

"She went to get the kids from her mom's house. The cable man is supposed to be coming to check out y'all's box, so I just stayed here and waited."

"What's up with the cable? Seems to be working fine to me." He walked over to the cable box and started fumbling with wires.

"Not this one," I said. "The one upstairs in you guys' bedroom."

"Ain't nothin' wrong with that damn television—it was probably just raining or something; you know how that satellite shit is."

"No, I think something is wrong with it," I said in Celeste's defense. "I was even trying to help her get it to work right. We tried everything, and it still wouldn't work."

"Why she just ain't call me or wait for me to get home?"

"You know how Celeste is. Besides, you know how you are.

She didn't want you tearing it up worse and then having to call the cable man anyway." I started laughing.

"See there . . . women, y'all always stick together when it comes to men."

"Hey, what can I say? No, but really, she said she didn't want to bother you, and that's what the cable guy gets paid for."

"Yeah, but it probably ain't nothin' serious and now them fools gon' probably make her pay a trip charge. What exactly is wrong with the box? Y'all sure it ain't the TV?"

"Here, let me show you." I got up off the couch and led Duke to their upstairs bedroom. I pointed to the main cable wire in the wall. "See right there." At the base it appeared to have a slit in it.

"Oh, yeah." Duke shook his head. "He gon' have to re-place that whole wire . . . unless . . ."

I could tell that Duke was having one of his bright ideas. One of those same bright ideas that was the reason behind Celeste not wanting him to fix it in the first place. He meant well, but for some reason, he always managed to make the problem worse.

Duke walked over to the television and turned it on. He then went behind the television and started undoing wires.

"Can you see the picture?" he asked.

"Nope," I replied, looking at a dark screen.

A few seconds went by. "Can you see the picture now?"

"Nope," I replied, looking into the dark screen once again.

In the screen I could see my own reflection. I began fixing my hair. I smiled. I wanted to see what Tonio saw in me that night he took my virginity. I wanted to see what, perhaps, he didn't see in me anymore.

My mama always told me that a young boy would say any-thing to get down a girl's pants. Perhaps that's what Tonio did, so I wanted to hear it from a man. "Duke, do you think I'm pretty?" I asked him out of the blue.

"What?"

"Do you think I'm pretty?"

"Sure you are." He continued to fumble around with the wires behind the television.

"*Beautiful*, maybe?"

"Yeah, that too," he replied nonchalantly.

I giggled. "How about *sexy*?—Do you think I'm sexy, Duke?"

"Ouch!" Duke hit his head on the television as he had suddenly lifted his head up.

"You okay?"

Duke went and sat down on the bed, in sort of a daze.

I followed and sat down next to him.

"Yeah, I think I'm straight."

I knew my running off at the mouth is what caused him to bump his head. I felt bad. "Sorry." I put my head down.

"No, no, it's not your fault, Baby. You cool." Duke rubbed his head then got back to the matter at hand. "Now what's this about you trying to be sexy?" Duke had this authoritative tone that I had heard him use only when he was scolding his children.

Suddenly I felt like a little girl. A little girl with a concerned father.

"Who you trying to be sexy for? One of them knucklehead boys at your school trying to—"

"No," I said, cutting him off. "Nobody. It's nothing. I was just asking. Never mind. Forget it."

"Look, Baby, if some boy got your head sprung—"

I looked away.

"Baby, look at me."

I didn't want to look at him. He would see it. I just knew he would. He would see that I wasn't innocent little Baby any more, that my cherry had been popped, and I was just as spoiled as Celie in *The Color Purple.*

"Look at me." Duke turned my face towards him. His hand warmed my face. This, too, was a feeling I had never felt before. It was the feeling of a man concerned about me for once in my life. Really, truly concerned about me. There was no mistaking this time.

I looked deep into Duke's eyes. He stared back into mine. I could see myself transforming in his eyes, going through the stages of life. He didn't see me the same any more. I could just tell.

The next thing, Duke leaned in and allowed his lips to touch mine. He pecked me once. He pecked me a second time. Then he all out French-kissed me.

Duke was a six feet five inches to my five feet six inches. His nice bulky physique towered over my petite frame. I could fit two of my almond colored hands in his huge dark mahogany one. Even though we sat on the bed like "beauty and the beast," I wasn't scared or intimidated. After all, I was a woman now.

Not taking his eyes from mine, Duke slowly began to caress my legs, slowly allowing his hand to go up my jean skirt. Once I felt his fingers make their way past my panties, I closed my eyes. It had been over a month since Tonio fucked me behind the bleachers after cheerleading practice that I had felt this kind of touch. I needed to be touched. If no one was going to tell me how beautiful, pretty, and sexy I was, I needed to feel it. I wasn't addicted to sex, but I was addicted to that feeling it brought about for me.

I threw my head back in ecstasy and allowed my little pussy to fuck Duke's fingers. I sat on the bed, crooning and poppin' my pussy, allowing it to eat up his fingers one by one.

My crooning, moaning, and groaning got the best of Duke. He quickly stood up and pulled his dick out.

"Oh my God! That's what a dick looks like. I had never looked

at Tonio's. But here Duke's was pointing right at me. It was big, black, and looked as though it could do some damage to my little cunt. What can I say? A bitch was scared. I wish I had never seen it; it was better not knowing what the thing going up inside of me looked like.

"Hold up." Duke made his way over to the closet. He dug around for a few seconds and then walked over towards me with a condom.

After watching him place it on his erect penis, I lay back and allowed him to slip my panties off. He sat down on the bed and pulled me on top of him in a sitting position, allowing me to take in as much or as little dick at a time as I wanted.

Slowly I went up and down over him, laying my chest on his. I took in an inch or two at a time as Duke breathed heavily in my ear. I was soaking wet, dripping juices down his tall order.

He grabbed me by my ass and started controlling me.

I felt like the hand on a joystick—back and forth, up and down, sideways, I went. I was workin' it out like nobody's business. I wasn't scared no more. It felt too damn good to be scared. I rode him back and forth as he controlled me by my waist.

Duke finally rolled me off of him and got on top of me. Looking into my eyes, he began to stroke in and out of me.

"Am I sexy?" I asked, still wanting to hear the answer to my question.

"Oh, Baby Gurl." Duke closed his eyes.

"No. Open your eyes." I began fucking him back hard. "Am I sexy? Am I sexy?" I repeated in a sexy moan. All I could hear was the headboard beating up against the wall and Duke's and my skin slappin'.

"What the fuck is going on here?" Celeste yelled, startling both Duke and me.

Duke pulled himself from inside of me just as he was

about to cum. He couldn't hold back the feeling, so he exploded right then and there. His dick was jerking around, as nut filled the tip of the condom.

I quickly pushed down my skirt, which had been lifted above my waist, to cover my exposed pussy.

"What's going on?" Celeste looked back and forth from Duke to me and began to cry hysterically.

For a minute, I thought she was going to come running at me and windmill me, beat my ass to a pulp. She didn't though. She just stood there crying. Her body trembled, but her feet stayed planted into the dark brown carpet. She was in far too much shock to even move a muscle.

I'll never forget that devastating look in her eyes as she pierced me with them. And although she wasn't saying a word with her lips, her eyes were saying it all. They kept asking me, "Why, Baby? Why did you do this to me? Why?"

I started to cry. I felt humiliated, embarrassed, and ashamed. I could tell that Duke felt bad. Celeste, the mother of his children, the love of his life, was the woman who had stood by him through thick and thin.

Duke jumped up and put his dick back where it belonged, in his pants.

I pulled my panties up and straightened out my skirt.

"I'm sorry, mommy." Duke walked over to Celeste and hugged her tight. "I'm sorry." He kissed her on the forehead as tears poured from her eyes. He just hugged her tight and started kissing her all over.

I could tell that Celeste wanted to take in the comfort of Duke's loving arms. I, too, knew how it felt to have his arms wrapped around me. It was a feeling that you never wanted to live without. Duke's arms were strong and provided a sense of security from the mean world. They were protection from anyone who dared to hurt you.

Then all of a sudden Celeste wiggled herself from his clutch then peered over at me. "Baby, how could you? I loved you, Baby. The kids love you. Why you wanna go do this to us? Please . . . I gotta know—is it something I did to you? What? How long, Baby? How long has this been going on? Oh, God!"

I just stood there with my hand over my mouth crying, looking like some silly young bitch. Not less than ten minutes ago I was lying there with my legs in the air, trying to be grown. Now here I was, bawling like a baby. I couldn't help it though. I was hurt too. It hurt even more looking into Celeste's eyes and seeing how much I had hurt her. If I wasn't mistaken, I had the same look on my face that Tonio had on his that day in the equipment shed.

Celeste had done so much for me. She had been so good to me. I couldn't have asked for a better best friend. I mean, she had actually looked out for me and treated me better than my own mother had. And now here I was fucking her man, in her bed. I couldn't help worrying: did I lose my best friend forever?

Chapter 5
Mama, I'm in Love
With A Gangsta

"How come every time I come in from working all day your ass is laid up in the bed?" My mother burst through my bedroom door. "You didn't even do the goddamn dishes last night. Now here I have to come home to a filthy-ass kitchen that you expect me to cook in . . . 'cause I know your lazy, black ass ain't started dinner. I told your lazy ass I was working late tonight."

"Ma, I'm sorry." I sat up, holding my stomach. I kept forgetting that the dishwasher was on the blink and that I had dish duty until the repairman could make it out to fix it. "I'll do the dishes now."

"Damn right, you will!"

Penny exited the doorway and went into her room, slamming the door behind her. It seemed as though the older I got, the meaner she got. I couldn't wait until I was the fuck up out of her house so that I didn't have to hear her mouth. Little did I know, it would be sooner than I thought.

Feeling queasy and lightheaded, I got up from my bed and headed downstairs. I had only made it to the hallway, when I felt a lump come up from my stomach and through my throat. I ran across the hall to the bathroom. Just in the nick of time, I lifted the toilet seat and began to vomit. Every time I moved I got dizzy and sick. I hadn't been able to keep anything down, so I hadn't even eaten all day. I was throwing up the lining of my stomach.

After cleaning myself up, in a full sweat, I went downstairs to do the dishes. I could barely stand up at the sink. All I could think about was hurrying back to my bed to lay down and rest. I had no energy whatsoever, so I ate some crackers and sipped on some 7 Up, while I washed dishes.

After I put the last plate into the dish rack I was ready to go lay it down, but then my mom start bugging the shit out of me to help her with dinner.

"Baby, peel some potatoes." She handed me the five-pound bag of potatoes from beside the refrigerator.

I took the bag and got the paring knife from the silver-ware drawer. I then grabbed a bowl from the cabinet and headed to the kitchen table to sit down.

"Where are you going?"

"To the table to go peel these potatoes."

"Just stand there and peel them over the garbage can."

I sighed.

She gave me an evil look.

"Okay." I sloshed over to the garbage pail. I could feel the beads of sweat dancing on my forehead. Then I felt that knot again. "Blahhh . . ." Puke splashed into the garbage pail and against the wall. "Blahhh . . ." There went the 7 Up and crackers.

"What's wrong with you, child?" my mother scolded.

"I don't know." I wiped drool from my mouth with the back of my hand.

"You ain't out there fucking, are you?"

I lied, "No, Ma."

"Better not be . . . 'cause if you come 'round here poppin' up pregnant, you out of here just as quick as you came. Now hurry up and finish peeling those potatoes."

The next day at school was awful. I could barely make it through the day. This was my second day in a row missing cheerleading practice. I hadn't really been into cheerleading anyway, since the captain fucked Tonio. Seeing her every day had made me sick long before now, but I couldn't let that bitch know I was pressed.

The coach told me if I missed one more day I couldn't cheer in the game Friday. *Fuck it! Who cares?* The thought of jumping around out there made me sick to my stomach. It was times like this that I needed Celeste. She had been the only person I could confide in. Here I was, sick as a dog, weeks late on my period, and no one to talk to. Times like this a girl should be able to go to her mother for help, but I wouldn't go to my mother if life depended on it. I feared her reaction more than I feared a baby busting out of my pussy. Why did I fuck things up with Celeste? Why now, when I needed her so much? I thought about that the entire bus ride home from school.

My bus stop was on the corner, three houses down from where my house sat. When the bus pulled up, I saw Celeste walking down my walkway, with my mother standing in the door. I swear, my heartbeat tripled its pace. I couldn't breathe. My stomach began to turn, and it had nothing to do with the possibility of being pregnant and everything to do with the content of the conversation Celeste had probably just had with my mother.

As the bus came to a complete stop, I just sat there staring out of the window, watching Celeste get into her car. As the other people filed off the bus, I just sat there dazed. I didn't want to get off. I wanted to go to the next stop in order to gather my thoughts and think of some lie to tell my mother about anything Celeste might have told her.

Some girl named Ronnie, who lived a couple houses down from me, tapped me on the shoulder. "Baby, this is our stop."

Still, I just sat there, my brain begging my feet to move, my feet turning a deaf ear.

"Baby, this is us, yo."

"Oh, yeah, my bad." I picked up my book bag and exited the bus.

My mother was standing in the door like a bull that had just had a hot poker shoved up its ass.

Slowly I walked. I just happened to have worn a red velour jogging suit that day. I was that bull's official target. I could tell that my mother was on the verge of coming out of the door and snatching my ass up, but she patiently waited as I took the smallest and slowest baby steps possible.

Once I was halfway up the walkway, I decided to get a feel for where my mother's head was at. "Hey, Ma," I said with a half-bait smile.

"Don't 'Hey Ma' me, you little whore," she said through clenched teeth.

"What? What did I do now?" I asked as I approached her, my legs almost giving out on me. I walked past her, and she just stood there.

She closed the door behind me.

I turned around. Before I could even do a complete 360, I felt a sting across the left side of my face. I didn't know what hit me. I made an attempt to turn again to face my mother, but yet again I received a blow to the left side of my face.

"Do you want to tell me what you've been doing with Celeste's husband?" my mother said, holding back tears of anger.

"Nothing," I said, failing miserably at holding back my tears. "Celeste doesn't have a husband."

"You know what the fuck I mean." She grabbed me by the throat. "Don't get cute with me."

I clutched her hands and peeled them from around my neck. "Ma, stop it, Ma!"

No matter how many names my mother had called me or how bad she had treated me, nothing was worse than when she put her hands on me. It wasn't often, but whenever she did, I just felt like some bitch on the street, rather than her child.

"God, Baby!" She threw her hands up in the air and walked by me. "Why does somebody have to walk up to my doorstep to tell me that my sixteen-year-old daughter is fucking a grown-ass man? I moved out to the suburbs and am paying an obscene amount of property taxes to stay away from that ol' ghetto shit, and yet here it seems to have followed us all the way here." My mother sat down on the couch and began to sob.

I had never seen my mother cry before. I heard her cry the day she was telling her friend about my father, but I had never seen her cry. For a minute I didn't even think she had tears in her.

She looked up at me, as if expecting an answer. She had this look in her eye, that same look in Celeste's eyes the day she caught me with Duke. It wasn't a look of hate or anger; it was a look of disappointment. I don't know if I had ever made my mother proud in the first place, but there was one thing I did know at that very moment—I knew she hadn't been that disappointed since the day I was born.

Chapter 6
Just Like Daddy

As I stood outside on my doorstep, shirt ripped open, bra-covered titties hanging out, I didn't know which way to turn. My mother was out of control. One minute I'm standing there while she's cursing me, calling me every whore in the book, and the next minute she's attacking me. I couldn't believe she was fighting me like that. I couldn't believe she had physically thrown me out of the house with nothing but the ripped-up clothes on my back.

I started walking in any direction the wind blew me. I had nowhere to go and no one to turn to. The only person who ever looked out for me in my time of need was Celeste. In church I learned that one must forgive in order to move on in life. Well, I hoped Celeste was ready to move on because I needed her to forgive me, and I needed her to forgive me now as I made the decision to go to her house.

When I finally arrived at Celeste and Duke's house, with nothing but the clothes on my back, I had already thrown up twice. Two different men pulled over and offered to give me a ride. The first offer I declined, but by the time the second man rolled around, I couldn't take another step. He looked like I could trust him, so I accepted his act of kindness. For all I knew he could have been a serial killer. In a sick sort of way, I was almost hoping that he was. That way I wouldn't have to worry about living long enough to worry about what I was going to do with this goddamn baby growing inside me, or myself for that matter. I was probably better off dead anyway.

"I wish I had a couple of dollars to give you for gas or something," I said to the gentleman who had driven me to my destination.

"Oh, no sweetheart," he said, tilting his hat; "it was my pleasure. You just promise me you'll take care of yourself, all right?"

I smiled a kind smile. "Okay." I stood there and watched him pull off. I turned around and faced Celeste's and Duke's front door. I took a deep breath and hesitated with each step towards the door. Right when I got to the porch I stopped.

What the fuck am I doing?

What audacity for me to show up, begging for help from the very best friend whose life I ruined by sleeping with her man, the father of her children.

I can't do this. I turned back around.

Again, I stopped in my tracks. *But I have to do it. I don't have anywhere else to turn.*

Before I could change my mind again I ran up the four steps leading to their small porch and knocked on the door. I closed my eyes and waited for it to open. When it finally did, Duke was standing there with nothing but some jeans on. I could see the trimming of his CK briefs. He didn't have a six-pack or anything like that, but his body was tight. Even his bare feet were sexy.

"Is Celeste here?" I asked softy, holding my shirt closed.

Duke sadly shook his head no then looked to the ground. We hadn't seen each other since Celeste caught us together. We really didn't seem to know what to say to each other.

"When do you expect her back? I really need to talk to her."

Duke looked up at me. "I don't expect her back—Celeste doesn't live here anymore."

"Oh," I said, not knowing what else to say. "Sorry to hear that."

Duke just shook his head.

"And the kids?"

"They're with her too. When she left me she took them with her. I can't even blame her, you know."

"Umm-hmm. Duke, I'm sorry I messed up everything for you."

"Baby, you didn't mess up shit. I'm a grown man and you're just a . . . no one is to blame but myself. Celeste and I tried to make it work, but it was too heavy on Celeste's mind. We were walking on eggshells until today, when she just finally blew up. Maybe Celeste and I need this time apart. Maybe we weren't meant to be together after all."

I shrugged my shoulders. *Maybe.* "Well, you take care of yourself." I turned to walk away.

"Yeah, you too," Duke said as he began to close the door. "Baby?"

"Yes," I said with the quickness.

"Is everything okay?" Duke asked, now that he had stopped feeling sorry for himself long enough to notice how fucked up I was.

I had scratches on my arms, bruises on my neck and a busted lip. And that was in addition to my torn up clothing. I turned around and fixed my mouth to say all of the things to him that I had prepared to say to Celeste, like how sorry I was and how I needed a place to stay. But instead, nothing but a wailing sound fluttered from my mouth as I began to cry.

Duke stepped outside. "Baby, what is it?" He walked down the steps and came over to me.

I just stood there with my face buried in my hands, crying my eyes out. "She put me out," I blurted out. "My mom, she put me out. Celeste came to my house and told her about us, me and you, and she threw me out. I don't know what I'm going to do. I don't have nowhere else to go, and I'm pregnant."

Duke backed away from me. He had each hand on my shoulder, and he was looking at me as if he could have fallen over dead any minute.

"It's not yours," I said, answering his question before he could even ask. Thank God he had worn a condom, or I would have had to take him and Tonio on *Maury*, the Maury Povich Show.

He let out a huge sigh that could have blown up a balloon. Then he pulled me back close to him. "Come on inside." Duke's led me into the house in the comfort of his arms and closed the door behind us.

Duke made sure I got to all of my prenatal appointments. He even paid for all of my doctor visits out of his own pocket. I told him that I could probably go down to the Franklin County Department of Human Services and get a medical card for me and the baby, but Duke wouldn't hear of it.

"You wanna be a statistic?" Duke asked me, almost with a hint of frustration in his tone. "You young girls kill me—you get knocked up, and then the first thing you want to do is run downtown to let Uncle Sam take care of you and your baby. Don't you know the welfare system is designed to do nothing more than enable you? You're going to finish school. You're going to go to college. You're not going to get a job, you're going to start a career."

" 'College,' Duke?—How do you expect me to pay for college if I don't get a job?" I sat on the bed, listening to his tantrum. "A career after college is all well and fine, but I need a job first in order to be able to pay for college. I know

I can probably get some loans and grants, but that's Uncle Sam too. So at some point in this life of mine, I'm going to need Uncle Sam. I'm not going to become dependent on—"

"No, listen to me, Baby. All you need in this lifetime is me. I'm going to make sure that you don't turn out to be some project chick who's a grandmother by the time she's thirty-five years old. I'll pay for you and the baby. I'll pay for you to go to college."

"But then won't I just become dependent on you?" I stood up from the bed and approached him.

He looked down at me. "No, Baby Gurl, you won't." He touched the side of my face with the back of his hand and I just thought I'd melt. "You'll be like my little bird. I'll take care of you; then once you are able to fly on your own, I'll set you free. I won't hold you back."

Now breathing deeply, engulfed by the tenderness of Duke's words, I walked in close to him, pressing my body against his. "But I don't wanna fly away from you, Duke. I wanna stay right here, in this nest with you . . . forever."

Duke lowered his head.

I closed my eyes and prepared my lips for meeting his.

He just brushed my hair back with his hands and softly said, "Oh, Baby Gurl." He then kissed me on the forehead like he was my daddy, instead of on my lonely lips like he was my lover. He then exited the room, leaving me standing there alone, wondering why.

"Hello," I said, answering the phone.

"Bitch, put Duke on the phone," Celeste yelled through the receiver.

I sucked my teeth. I was good and tired of allowing Celeste to call me out of my name. Every time she called the house I was "bitch, this" or "whore, that." I had made a mistake. I had done her wrong indeed. But she needed to get over it. I now had her man, the father of her children. I planned on being in his life the rest of mine, so Celeste needed to learn to have a civil tongue with me. I was going to be the stepmother to her children, and we needed to be able to communicate for the sake of the kids.

"Look, Celeste," I said in a calm tone, "all that ain't even necessary. Calling me out of my name isn't going to get you Duke back."

"Open your eyes," Celeste said. "Baby, you are just what your name says you are—a baby. Duke is a man, and if you think a little girl like yourself can take care of all of his needs, take care of all of his business, then you got another think coming."

If Celeste was trying to piss me off, it was working. Still trying not to go there with her, I remained calm. "Obviously I'm meeting the right needs—I'm here and you're not."

Celeste laughed. "Where are you, Baby? You in the kitchen? You in the basement?—You sure ain't in Duke's bed, so obviously you're not meeting the right needs."

Celeste's comment pushed a button with me, not because she was, in fact, right, but because she had no business knowing my damn business. Duke and I weren't sharing a bed together. I was getting pissed because I was wondering how in the hell she would know that. Duke must have been telling her our business. I took a moment to reflect then realized that it was possible that the kids might have told her that Duke and I didn't sleep in the same bedroom together.

"I have more respect than to sleep up under Duke in front of his kids. Our living arrangements are because we care about the kids."

"Then if you care so much about the kids, Baby," Celeste asked in a sincere tone, "then why did you destroy their home?"

I could hear her voice crack as my emotions began to stir inside of me.

"Celeste, I'm—"

"Don't say it, Baby."

I could tell by her tone that now she really was crying.

"Baby, I know what you've been through in your life. I know what you're looking for, but you're not going to find it in Duke, trust me. Wake up, girl."

"Celeste, you don't understand—Duke and I are in love."

" 'In love'? You're about to turn seventeen—what do you know about being in love, Baby? Duke will never truly be yours; he just feels sorry for you. He feels responsible for you. When all that wears off, how long do you think you two will last?"

"I know you're upset, Celeste, because I've replaced you."

"Oh, listen up, Miss Thing," Celeste said, "you will never replace me. You will never be the woman that I am; I know it, and Duke knows it."

Right before slamming the phone down in my ear she said, "And one day you'll know it too, but unfortunately you're going to have to learn it the hard way. But don't say that I didn't warn you."

Chapter 7
Baby Mama Drama

Giving birth wasn't anything like I expected. I thought it would be like in the movies, the doctor forcing me to push while I shouted obscenities at Duke. Unfortunately I had to get a caesarean. The baby wouldn't turn headfirst so the doctor had to do what he had to do to get the baby out healthy. I should have known then that it was going to be a girl. *Typical stubborn little bitch.* She must take after her grandma.

"I just need for you to fill out these papers so that the baby's birth certificate can be processed," the woman said, handing me a clipboard of papers and a pen to fill them out with. "When you finish you can just lay them on your tray, and I'll be back around to get them." She then exited the room.

"What are they asking?" Duke asked as he sat in the chair next to my hospital bed.

"Stuff to go on the birth certificate," I replied. I sat there staring at the papers. I filled out the first few lines then I stopped to look over at my new baby daughter for a few moments, watching her lie there with a head full of curly, jet-black locks. I then went back to filling out the papers.

"Brandy," I said as a smile covered my face. "She looks like a Brandy, don't you think?"

Duke had the biggest smile on his face. His given name was Brandon, so he felt honored that I was naming my baby daughter the closest name to his that I could think of.

"Yeah, she does." Duke walked over to touch her. He softly stroked her stomach through the blanket that she was wrapped so tightly in.

"I think so too."

I continued filling out the paperwork until I was stumped by one line.

Duke must have noticed. He leaned over me. "What?" He read down the paper to see what question I was stuck on—the line that asked me to list the father's information.

I never doubted Duke's word. When he assured me that he considered the baby in my belly as one of his own no matter if it didn't have the same blood as him, I knew he meant it. When he said he'd claim the baby as his own, I knew he meant that as well. But we had never discussed the matter of putting his name on the baby's birth certificate.

"Oh," Duke said, realizing my dilemma. He took a deep breath then took the clipboard from me. He scribbled down something then handed it back, kissing me on the forehead. "Here you go, Baby Gurl."

The tears falling from my eyes almost ruined the ink where Duke had signed his name on the birth certificate as Brandy's father.

As if he had a nine-to-five and had requested a leave of absence, when I came home with the baby, Duke spent more time at home than in the streets. He was still doin' his thang, but he made sure that he cut hanging out to a minimum. This was the most sensitive side of Duke I had ever seen.

Back in the old neighborhood, Duke was known for how hardcore he was coming up. His father, before he went MIA, had been a well-known local boxer. Duke's mother used to take him up to the gym to watch his father train. Duke didn't admire the man, but admired the stories about his father and wanted to grow up to be the heavyweight champion of the world. He thought that would make his daddy proud. Proud enough to have him back in his life. But then after Duke's mother was killed, he became angry and took everything he learned in the gym to the streets. He was constantly fighting and getting kicked out of school, always had his dukes up ready to fight, which is how he got the nickname Duke.

But after his sister died, and once he met Celeste and she got pregnant, he knew that he couldn't run around fighting and acting a fool, so he let that side of him go. But he could still be gangsta if he had to be, and only if he had to be. Otherwise, he was a good man, a good friend, and a good daddy.

"I made the baby's bottles." Duke came and sat down next to me on the couch.

Brandy was upstairs in her crib sleeping, and I was laying down on the couch. The pain pills had me buzzing. I was feeling good as hell, and Duke being there by my side made me feel even better. No drug had shit on the high he gave me.

"Thank you."

"How you feeling?"

I looked up at Duke and smiled. "Like a princess."

"That's how you're supposed to feel." Duke leaned over and kissed me on the forehead. Although his touches were never sexual, they still made me tingle.

Just as Duke was about to sit down, there was a loud hard knock on the door, like it was the police.

"Who da fuck?" Duke walked over to the window.

"It's me, damn it," I heard a voice yell. It was none other than the voice of Celeste. "Open up, Duke."

"Oh shit." Duke sighed and put his head down. He looked over at me. "Baby, why don't you go on upstairs while I talk to this girl?"

I could tell by the look in his eyes that he hated asking me to leave the room, but he needed to take care of Celeste all the same.

"Okay." I slowly got up, with Duke's help.

"Open up!" Celeste knocked even harder this time.

"Hold the fuck on," Duke shouted.

The tone of his voice made my insides quiver. That was the first time I had ever heard Duke lightweight lose his cool. *That Celeste is gonna get it now.*

I made my way upstairs. Instead of going into the baby's room, I went into Duke's room. His bedroom faced the street, and I knew I would be able to see what was going on outside. With the window cracked, I could hear what was going on too.

I walked over to the window, peeked through the blinds. I saw Celeste standing on the porch, and began watching this baby mama drama unfold.

"So you wanna play daddy to Baby's little bastard?"

At that point I wanted to run down the steps and fuck her up.

"Fine then. Then let that bitch play mommy to your kids . . . permanently." At that point Celeste stormed off to her car. She opened the door and LD and Tara got out. She started unloading suitcases and plastic trash bags.

"Celeste, what are you doing?" Duke turned his attention to LD and Tara. "Kids, go on upstairs to y'all's room."

Slowly the kids headed up the walkway.

"What the fuck it look like I'm doing, *R. Kelly?* You like kids so much that you had to fuck one. Well, don't forget you made a couple of your own. I be damned if that bitch and her baby gon' live up in here and try to take from mine. Fuck that! You ain't just gon' be sending me no check every month while you taking care of them twenty-four seven. No, my kids gon' get theirs. I wish I might let them see some other child livin' up in they daddy's house gettin' special treatment."

Celeste was on a rampage, throwing bag after suitcase out of the car and into the yard.

"Now calm down, woman." Duke grabbed hold of Celeste's arms. "You know I take care of my kids and you. I don't even know why you trippin' on me like that. I've always taken care of my business. For as long as I can help it, y'all ain't gon' never want for nothing."

I hated how Duke kept including her in the scenario. I mean, I could see him taking care of his kids, but fuck her. Let her starve. But I guess that was one of the things I adored about him—he wasn't spiteful at all. He never really cut people off. If things went sour, he didn't waste his energy hating; instead, he stayed levelheaded and upped his game even stronger. Kind of killed 'em with kindness. That's why Duke was so well loved by the streets. That's why Duke was so well loved by me.

I couldn't believe Celeste was abandoning her kids like that. Who the fuck did she think I was—Anna Mae Bullock? I had my own baby I was still learning to take care of. How did she expect me to take care of hers as well?

When I turned around and saw LD and Tara standing in the bedroom doorway, my thoughts immediately changed. Their little faces were filled with so much confusion. Had I done this to them? Was I being selfish by loving Duke so much? I don't know, but I just couldn't let him go. He was too good to me, too good to my daughter. So perhaps it was time for me to return the favor by being equally good to his children.

Looking into LD and Tara's eyes, I hoped they didn't blame me. I stood up from the window and opened my arms to them. My worst fear of them hating me was put to rest when they each made their way into my arms. I pulled them close to me and rubbed their little heads as they each wrapped their arms around my waist.

Each day my life seemed to take a turn in an unexpected direction. Just yesterday I was Mommy to one and now I was Mommy to two more. I was considered to be a baby myself, but I knew that as long as I had Duke to lean on, I would never fall.

"How's my babies?" Celeste said as LD and Tara ran from my side into her arms. She had come to pick them up to take them out to dinner.

It had been a couple of weeks since she had dropped them off to live with us, but it seemed as though every day she was either calling or coming over to the house. In my opinion, I had discovered the real reason behind her giving the kids up to Duke. As long as they were here, she felt she had a right to invade our space. As long as she was constantly invading our space, she would constantly know what was going on in our household. She was constantly in Duke's face. I guess in her opinion, if she stayed all up in his face, he wouldn't forget about her. If she only knew that what Duke and I had was a bond that could not be broken. Baby mama or not, if she wanted to bring the drama, I was 'bout that. And it was only a matter of time before I knew the drama would definitely come full force.

Chapter 8
Gon' Party Like It's
My Birthday

I was so pumped up leaving the doctor's office after my six weeks check-up that I could barely drive home. The stitches were healed. The coochie was ripe. It was on. I knew Duke had to be all backed up if he hadn't been jerking his shit off. He sure hadn't been getting any pussy from me. At first, I would try to set the atmosphere. I would say things and do little things to make him want to get intimate with me. But it seemed like right before we reached that point where one thing would definitely lead to another, he would turn cold on me, brush me away, or find an excuse why he had to leave or something.

I always heard that pregnant pussy was the best, but Duke didn't make love to me, not one time while I was carrying Brandy. I guess to some men it's a turn-off and Duke must have fell into that percentage of men. But tonight, that would no longer be an issue. I had given birth, I had gotten the green light from the doctor to resume sexual activity, and I was on birth control. The evening I was about to prepare wouldn't soon be forgotten by either Duke or myself.

* * *

"Baby," Duke yelled as he came through the front door.

"Shhh." I put my index finger over my lips as I lay sprawled out on the sofa. "It's after midnight. The kids are asleep." I then sat up and patted the spot next to me for Duke to come sit down.

He took off his leather jacket, hung it on the closet doorknob, and then walked over and sat down next to me.

"How was your day?"

I know that sounded corny, but I wanted the evening to be clichéd on purpose. I went through all the typical acts that took place in romantic movies and on soap operas. I had a bowl of strawberries, some whipped cream, and some chocolate sauce on a glass platter on the living room table. I had a candle lit at each end of the table and a bottle of wine chilling in a bowl of ice.

"It was fine." Duke chuckled lightly as he checked out the atmosphere. "What's all this?"

"This"—I reached over to get a strawberry, dipped it in the chocolate sauce, and then placed it at Duke's lips—"is to show my appreciation for all you have done for me."

His stuck out his long, thick tongue underneath the strawberry and then inhaled it. I watched his tight lips go in circles as he chewed the strawberry. He watched me watching him.

At that moment I just went for it. I pushed him back and climbed on top of him, lifting my dark wine-colored gown so that the matching panties showed just briefly. "I want to taste the strawberry too," I whined.

Duke reached his arm out towards the strawberries and tried to sit up.

I forcefully, but playfully, pushed him back. "From your mouth—I want to taste it on your tongue."

"Girl, you silly." Duke playfully pushed me off of him. "This is nice, though, Baby Gurl. You watch too much television, though, but it's nice. Thank you." He stood up, grabbed a strawberry, popped it into his mouth, and then headed up the steps. "I'm tired. I gotta go take a shower and then hit the hay."

I sat on the couch dumbfounded as I watched Duke head up the steps. *This nigga must be playing.* But then I heard the shower water start to run and I knew that he was so sincere. I sighed, but right when I was about to get up and clean everything up, with a towel wrapped around his waist, Duke returned downstairs.

I knew he couldn't resist me.

Duke walked over to the table and picked up the bottle of wine and one of the two glasses that was sitting next to it. "You're too young to drink." He winked as he headed back up the steps and into his shower.

For the life of me I couldn't figure out why Duke didn't want to touch me. We hadn't been intimate since that first time in his and Celeste's bed. I was sure that after six weeks, once the stitches healed and the doctor gave me the okay to resume sexual activity, he would be all over me. But here I sat in the most sexiest get-up I could piece together, surrounded by strawberries, chocolate, and whipped cream and I was alone, while Duke, the person I put on this show for, was upstairs taking a shower, and probably a cold one.

I was only seventeen and had only experienced the likes of two men, one who wanted me for sex and one who just wanted me. I guess I should have just felt blessed that Duke didn't want to use me as just some PYT to do what he wanted with. But I wanted him. I wanted him so badly.

Maybe he felt that it was still too soon after the baby; at least that's what I thought at first. But then almost a year later, when Duke still hadn't had sex with me, that theory went right out the window.

The nighttime was the worst. I would lay there in bed looking up at the dark ceiling, thinking about Duke, wanting him to be inside of me. Just wanting his large protecting arms to be around me. He didn't even have to make love to me, just hold me and show me some kind of affection. Lying there I often wondered how he handled the night, but I guess not sleeping in the same bed with me made it easy for him.

When Brandy was born Duke put a twin bed in her room so that I could tend to her easier during the night. Well, we had just celebrated her first birthday, and I was still sharing a room with her. Duke and I never even just plain ol' slept in the same bed together, unless Brandy and I had just happened to fall asleep in his room while watching television or something. But other than that, I slept in the twin bed that sat across from Brandy's crib, just waiting for the night Duke would come in and invite me back into his room, back into his bed, back into his body.

When I got home from school I was worn out. With senior final exams, it had been a long week, and I had been waiting for Friday to roll around since Monday. Duke took care of Brandy while I went to school. LD and Tara were in school as well, but on Fridays Celeste picked them up from school to stay with her for the weekend. When I got home I was surprised to find an empty house, no Duke and no Brandy. On the coffee table was a single red rose lying on top of a pink envelope. With a huge smile on my face, I picked up the card and read it. It was the sweetest eighteenth birthday card ever, and inside it was a folded up note from Duke.

The note instructed me to immediately make my way to the address that was on the note, so that is exactly what I did. My birthday wasn't until the next day, but I guess Duke couldn't wait to celebrate it.

I hopped in my five-year-old used Lexus that Duke had bought for me after I had the baby. He had gotten me the Lexus for a small lump sum of cash from some crackhead.

He had also paid for my driver's education class and even took me on a few driving lessons himself. He wanted to make sure that I had transportation to transport the kids and myself. I wanted for nothing. Duke provided everything I needed . . . well, almost everything.

When I arrived at the address, I found it to be the Embassy Suites Hotel on Corporate Exchange Drive. Using common sense I went to the front desk and gave them Duke's name. As if the clerk was expecting me, she handed me a room key and wished me a happy birthday.

I took the clear glass elevator that overlooked the dining area of the hotel all the way to the top floor. I exited the elevator and headed for the hotel room. I used the electronic keycard to let myself in.

The hotel room was laid out with roses, balloons, candles, and boxes of chocolate from Chocolates and Stilettos. The bed was covered with Victoria's Secret bags, Macy boxes, and Nordstrom shoeboxes. And lying next to them was Duke.

"Model for me." He took a sip from the bottle of Dom that he was holding in his hand. "Take off all of your clothes and model for me."

"Duke," I said, my eyes sparkling, "what's going on?"

"It's my Baby Gurl's eighteenth birthday. What do you mean, 'What's going on?' It's a party . . . a private party."

The way Duke looked at me melted me down to a puddle of chocolate. He looked at me like he longed for me, like he wanted to take me right then and there. I wanted to be excited, but at the same time I was confused. All this time Duke acted like my pussy was the plague, and now here he was ready to dive right into it.

"But, Duke, I don't understand."

Duke picked up on the look of confusion on my face. He could see something was wrong. He sat up and placed the bottle of Dom on the nightstand next to the king-sized bed. He patted a spot on the bed for me to come sit next to him. "Come here. Talk to Daddy."

I half-smiled then walked over and sat down next to him.

"What's on you mind, love?"

"Nothing, Duke. I mean, I guess I'm just confused." I looked down. "I thought you didn't want me anymore. I mean, you haven't been wanting me, if you know what I mean."

Duke chuckled.

"What's so funny? You think not being wanted is funny?" I was dead serious now.

Duke pulled me close to him, still chuckling. "Baby, I wanted you. God, you don't know how bad I wanted you, but I couldn't have you." Duke turned me towards him by my shoulders. "You were just a baby. You were a little girl. The shit wouldn't have been right. It would have been illegal as hell. But you're eighteen now. You're grown. You're a woman now." He kissed me softly on the lips once, and then twice, before using his tongue to separate my lips.

I pulled back.

Now Duke was the one with the confused look on his face.

I still wasn't feeling his answer. "I don't understand. We had already done it before I turned eighteen. We might as well have kept doing it."

"But it was wrong the first time too. You and me, we're not wrong. But me continuing to have sex with you underage would have been. Just because I made a mistake that first time didn't mean I had to keep making the same mistake. I never stopped loving you, though, you know that, Baby Gurl."

Every day, every minute, Duke gave me a reason to love him even more. All those months I kept thinking he didn't want me anymore, that maybe he had started looking at me like a kid. I even thought that he was appalled at the fact that

I had another man's baby growing inside of me, and the thought of touching me made him sick. Never in my life had I been so glad to be wrong about something.

That night, on my eighteenth birthday, Duke made love to me, taking me in his arms and kissing me slowly and passionately. He undressed me like I was his baby doll, unbuttoning my soul. Staring into my eyes, he laid me down and played with my body. After a couple of kisses on my neck, he moved down, and I giggled at the funny feeling of his tongue fishing deep in my belly button.

Soon after, that same tongue plucked at my clit like it was the only string on his guitar.

DAMN!

Duke's mouth was the cup in which I poured my special blend of juices. He drank every last drop and demanded a refill. Of course, I hadn't cum since forever, except on the nights my fingers found their way down my panties upon just the mere thought of Duke fucking me. But that didn't count.

As I lay there on the bed naked, cumming for the second time as the result of Duke's tongue work, I was greedy for more. I wanted him to make me cum again, but this time I wanted to feel him inside of me. I grabbed him by his head and lifted it from between my legs, pulling him to come towards me.

He smiled and allowed me to lead him. He dressed me with his body, laying on top of me and entering my wetness.

After three strokes, he moaned. After six strokes, I moaned.

Faster and harder, he thrust in and out of me, our pelvises banging against one another. I wrapped my legs around his waist and my arms around his shoulders and held him tight against me as we wildly fucked, banging our bodies against each other like we were angry, angry that we had stayed away from each other for so long.

We moaned. We came. We came together. It was an inde-

Chapter 9
Just Be Good to Me

No longer did Duke make me sleep in the room with Brandy. After my eighteenth birthday, he allowed me to sleep in the bedroom with him. Matter of fact, the very next day he moved all of my things from Brandy's room into his room—I mean *our* room.

Once I became a woman in Duke's eyes, he made sure that it was known that I was "that bitch." He even started introducing me to some of his peoples. Everybody knew that I was Duke's woman, that Celeste was nothing more than his babies' mama.

Even Tonio, who still did business with Duke every now and again, knew. One time he even came over to the house. I stayed upstairs, though, in order to avoid an awkward situation. But I knew that Tonio knew that I was Duke's girl, from word on the street, and that Brandy was his little girl.

High-school dropout or not, he was smart enough to do the math. He knew that Brandy had to be his. I knew he knew because of the questions I heard him asking Duke one time when he came over.

scribable feeling. I didn't even feel like the same person anymore. Here I was, this ripe lil' mama, and here Duke was this old school-style *G*, not one of them young bling-bling niggaz from the old hood, always broadcasting and bragging about their shit. Nuh, huh. Duke was a man. My man. And that night, on my eighteenth birthday, Duke made me a woman. His woman.

"Y'all crazy." I took the money from Duke's hand, grabbed the keys, and headed for the door. "I'll be right back, baby."

"Hurry back before I start to miss you," Duke said as I made my way out of the door.

I couldn't get to and from that fuckin' store fast enough. I didn't have no problem getting the beer, once they carded me and I pulled out Duke's ID, just like he told me to do. When I got back home and walked in the door, Duke wasn't sitting at the table playing cards anymore, and that loud-mouth redbone wasn't anywhere in sight either.

"Hey, Baby, you back?" his card partner yelled.

I might have been young, but I wasn't dumb. I knew he was yelling just loud enough to forewarn Duke that I was back. I quickly stomped by the card table and into the kitchen to put the beer in the fridge, but what I saw was Duke leaning against the fridge getting his dick sucked by Redbone.

From that point on, everything was a blur. I heard a loud crashing sound, which was the sound of the Miller bottles crashing to the floor. I snatched Red up by the hair and just started drilling her. The next thing I remember, I was on top of her, and Duke was behind me, holding me by my wrist so that I didn't cut her fuckin' throat with the piece of broken beer bottle I had in my hand.

"Baby, no!" he yelled. "Don't!"

I looked down at Red, who had a look on her face as though her life was flashing before her eyes. I then looked up at my hand holding the broken glass, with Duke's hand around my wrist. Red managed to squirm out from underneath me and run for her life.

One of Duke's boys came in the kitchen. "Y'all okay?"

"Yeah, man. We good." Duke was breathing heavily. "I'll check y'all later, a'ight?"

"Yeah, man. We holler at cha." Duke's boy exited the kitchen and led all of the guests out of the house.

We heard the door close behind them.

I let the broken glass drop from my hand and just broke down in tears. On my knees, I hunched over, buried my head in my hands, and just shivered in tears. I then looked up at Duke and yelled, "Why, Duke? Why you do this to me, baby? I've been nothing but good to you. What's wrong with me? Why does this happen to me? What's wrong with me, Duke?"

He tried to hug me, but I pushed him away and stood up.

He stood up with me and grabbed me from behind as I tried to leave out of the kitchen. He took me in his arms.

I tried to pull away, but he wrapped his arms tightly around me and wouldn't let me go.

"Nothing's wrong with you, Baby Gurl," Duke said as he held me from behind. "It's me. I'm just a man. Sometimes men think with the wrong head. I fucked up. I'm sorry. I know you don't understand. But she can't give me what you can give me. She wanted to fuck, but that's why I was only letting her suck my dick. I only want to be inside of you. I just want to be inside of you." Duke started kissing me on my neck and caressing my breasts. "Only you," he whispered.

Tears flowed down my face. "Duke, you hurt me."

"I know and I'm sorry. I'm so sorry. Please believe me. I just want you, Baby, just you." Duke turned me around and shoved his tongue down my throat. He pulled me down to the ground and unbuttoned my pants.

"No, Duke," I cried. "No, Duke." I clawed my nails down his hands, which were yanking my pants down.

For Duke it was pain before pleasure. He pulled his dick out of his pants and managed to slide my panties to the side and ram himself inside of me. "Baby Gurl, I love you. I love the way you make me feel," Duke said, sliding in and out of me.

I wanted to fight him. I wanted to push him off of me, but I couldn't. It felt too good. The next thing I knew, I was throwing my hips back at him, and we were making love. We were making love like it was "Armaghetto" and it would be our last time ever making love.

"Don't ever hurt me again, Duke," I cried on the verge of cumming.

He thrust his hips wildly. "I won't,"

"Just promise me one thing, Duke—Just be good to me. I don't care about the other girls. Do whatever it is a man does. Just be good to me."

And with that we came. Even though he had just hurt me. I guess for me it was pain before pleasure too.

Chapter 10
Locked Up, Won't Let
Me Out

I was in the bathroom bathing Brandy, when the phone rang. "Tara, sweetie, get that for Mommie Baby," I called out.

Yep, that's right, she called me Mommie, Mommie Baby to be exact. LD called me Mommie Baby too. It wasn't my doing; it was Duke's. But the kids didn't seem to mind. When he first told them to start calling me Mommie Baby, they said it a hundred times a day just because they liked the sound of it. I liked it too. In my heart, LD and Tara were no different from Brandy. I loved them all the same. LD and Tara were a part of Duke. I loved him so much, how could I not love them?

"Hello," I heard Tara answer the phone as I continued to wash up Brandy. "I don't know what the lady is saying." Tara entered the bathroom with the phone in her hand.

"Here, give it to me." I took the phone from her hand.

"Press one," I heard the operator say. "If you do not want to accept this call, press two."

My heart dropped. Although I had never had to get one

personally, I knew what kind of phone call this was—a call from jail.

I immediately pressed one before it was too late. "Duke! Baby, what happened? What's wrong?" I was frantic.

"No, Baby, this isn't Duke," I heard an all-too-familiar voice say through the phone receiver. "It's Tonio."

"Tonio?" I was even more shocked. "Tonio, you're in jail? Duke's not here. He's—"

"Good. I'm not really calling for Duke anyway, I'm calling for you."

I paused while we both marinated in the moment of silence.

"You there?"

"Uh, yeah, . . . I'm here."

"Can you come see me?"

"Tonio, do you know what you're asking me to do?"

"Yeah, I'm asking you to come see me, to bring my little girl to see her daddy, her real daddy."

I completely froze. A huge lump got stuck right in the pit of my throat. "Tonio, I—"

"Look, I know why you did what you did. It's done, girl. But just let me see my little girl. You ain't even gotta tell her I'm her real daddy. I just want to see my little girl, Baby."

"Why, Tonio, why now?"

"Man, sitting in the county these last couple weeks, I've had time to think about a lot of shit, a lot of shit I could have done differently. I could have done you differently, Baby."

"Look, Tonio, I don't think this is a good idea."

"Just this one time. Let me just see her this one time, and I promise, Baby, I promise, I'm out of your life for good. Can you just do that for me, please?"

"Tonio," I whined, not wanting to hurt his feelings.

"Baby, anything can happen to me in here. Knowing I never got to see my baby girl—"

"Okay, Tonio, I'll do it."

Hearing Tonio talk like that was pressing the buttons in my heart, as well as the guilty buttons in my soul, knowing that never even giving him a chance to be a father to Brandy was wrong. It was the wrong thing to do to him, but I felt it was the right thing to do for Brandy.

"You'll bring my daughter to see me?"

"I'll bring Brandy to see you."

I don't know what the hell I was thinking by telling that man that I'd come to see him and bring Brandy with me, the daughter Duke had claimed as his own and had been taking care of since she was inside my womb. Being a woman of my words, I did it.

"So do she call him *Daddy*?" Tonio asked me through the glass.

I looked down without saying a word.

Then Tonio repeated himself. "Do Brandy call that nigga *Daddy*?"

I wasn't expecting to see such emotion in Tonio's eyes. I wasn't expecting his emotions to break me down. Out of nowhere tears just started streaming down my face. He had me doubting my decision to allow Brandy to know Duke as her father and not him.

"Look, girl, it's cool." Tonio sighed, taking the phone away from his ear and looking up at the ceiling. After regaining his composure, he placed the phone back up to his ear. "She's beautiful."

"Yeah, she is." I looked down at Brandy, who was on my lap, stretching her hands up against the glass that separated us from Tonio.

Tonio took his index finger and traced her hands with it. "Look at those tiny little hands," he said with a smile. It was the first time he smiled since we had gotten there.

"How long you in here for?"

"I don't know." He sighed. "They trying to get a nigga to roll over and shit. They know I ain't nobody big in the game, but I ain't scared of them pussies."

There was a moment of silence as he watched Brandy play against the glass. She looked so cute with her six little curly twists in little bows. She looked like a miniature me. She was my exact complexion and everything. She was so loving; probably because she got so much love from me, Duke, and her brother and sister, not to mention her Grandma Penny.

Brandy spent more time with my mom than I ever thought she would. As disgusted as my mom was at the fact that I got pregnant, I was certain that she wouldn't want to have anything to do with my baby. But it was just the opposite—she spoiled Brandy rotten. She still hated the shit out of me and always ridiculed my parenting skills. If Brandy got a rash, I wasn't wiping her good enough. If Brandy got a runny nose, I wasn't keeping her warm enough. It was always something, but I just let her words roll right off of my shoulder and tried to be the best mother I could be.

"You do a good job with her, Baby," Tonio told me.

"Thank—"

"Yo, Mackey, time!" the female guard shouted.

"See how they trippin' on me? It ain't been but a minute." He then looked at Brandy again and smiled. "Baby, if I get up out of here . . . can I maybe—"

"Tonio, don't." I shook my head. I knew what he was going to ask me. No way could I let him form a relationship with Brandy. It was too late. If keeping Brandy from Tonio was a mistake, it was already a mistake that I had made and one that I would live with. Unfortunately, so would he.

"I feel that."

The guard shouted his name again.

"Well, I gotta go. But thanks for bringing her up here."

"You're welcome."

"Baby, you're a good girl; Duke's a lucky man." Tonio hung up the phone, winked, and then disappeared behind a door.

"Wake the fuck up!" Duke burst through the bedroom door and turned on the light.

It was two o'clock in the morning, and I was in a deep sleep.

"Duke, what's wrong?" I said, blinded by the light. I closed my eyes real quick.

When I opened them up, Duke was charging at me.

"Duke!" I managed to scream before his hands wrapped around my throat.

"You took my daughter to a fuckin' jail, huh, Baby Gurl? Is that what you did?"

I wanted to answer Duke. I wanted to explain the situation to him, but I couldn't breathe, let alone talk. His hands got tighter and tighter around my throat. I swear to God, death was just about to introduce himself to me before LD came into the room.

"Daddy! Daddy!" LD yelled as he jumped on his father's back. "Get off of her! Get off Mommie Baby! You said, 'Never hit a girl.' You told me never to hit a girl. You wouldn't even let me hit Tara back that day she kicked me. Get off! Get off of her."

LD's words were like a wake-up call to Duke. A look of confusion came across his face. He looked down at me like he couldn't even remember how he had gotten on top of me with his hands around my throat. He quickly removed his hands and stared at them like he only had three fingers or something.

I kicked Duke off of me and gasped for air. For a moment I wanted to die. I didn't even want to catch my breath. Every decision I had made for Brandy I thought was the right one, but now both Tonio and Duke were making me believe otherwise. I was in a catch-22, between a rock and hard place, and every other saying my mom used to walk around the house quoting.

LD came over and put his arms around me. And when I heard his little voice, if I never wanted to live before in my life, I did then. "Mommie Baby, don't die," he whispered in my ear as he hugged me around my neck. "Don't die, Mommie Baby."

I coughed, hacked, and cried. Finally I caught my breath and was able to breathe again.

Duke came back into the room with a cup of water in his hand. "Go back to bed, LD."

LD followed his father's orders and headed back to his room.

"Here, drink some water." Duke began to feed me the water.

I drank the water and felt stabilized again.

Duke placed the water on the nightstand then hugged me. "Baby Gurl, I'm sorry. I'm so sorry." His voice cracked as he fought back tears. "When Razor got to talking about how that punk-ass Tonio's girl came to see him a couple of weeks ago with his little girl, I lost it."

" 'Razor'?"

Duke got up off the bed and started pacing. "Yeah, he was Tonio's cellmate down at the county. Just got out a couple days ago."

Just my fuckin' luck.

" 'So I'm locked up in this bitch, while that nigga playing daddy to my kid,' " Duke began to mock the words that Razor said Tonio had told him. "That's what Razor said that nigga was ranting and raving back and forth in the jail cell. Razor thought that shit was funny, telling me in front of everybody while we playing cards."

Duke continued to mock Razor. " 'Y'all niggaz know good and well once y'all get locked up Jody gon' creep up from behind. Didn't you see the movie *Baby Boy*?' Then Razor started laughing, like this shit was some joke. All them niggaz was laughing at me, Baby Gurl—until I showed that nigga a real razor. Bastard probably up at Riverside now getting stitched up."

I swear I could see smoke coming out of Duke's nose and ears. He was on fire inside.

"Fuck!"

"Duke, I'm sorry. I'm sorry. I wasn't trying to make you look stupid."

"Why didn't you tell me?" He sat back down next to me on the bed. "Why didn't you just tell me? I shouldn't have found out like that, Baby Gurl."

Duke was right. He shouldn't have found out from the streets. I should have been woman enough to tell him. But I had no intentions of ever going to see Tonio, or letting him be a part of Brandy's or my life again. I wish I had never gone to that damn jail in the first place.

I wanted to make things right with Duke, but the words 'I'm sorry' just didn't seem like enough. Then I thought about something else my mom used to say, "Actions speak louder than words."

I slowly sat up on the bed in front of where Duke was standing. I unzipped his jeans while staring into his eyes, making sure that I had his approval. I then placed his dick in my mouth. With it entering back and forth, hitting the back of my throat, I apologized until Duke came in my mouth.

Apology accepted.

Chapter 11
The Lord Giveth . . .

I hated that I hadn't been to church in a month of Sundays. Didn't mean I didn't love God, though, or that I wasn't grateful for all the blessing he had given me. Church was in my heart. Every time I looked at Duke and every time I looked at Brandy and the kids, I thanked God. If God gave me nothing else in life, with them, I had everything.

Not many men wanted to take care of their own kids, let alone anotha nigga's kid. But looking at the way Duke treated Brandy, no one could tell that her veins didn't pump the same blood as LD's and Tara's. She had adopted a lot of their habits. Duke treated them all the same, too. Even spoiled Brandy a little extra, 'cause she was the baby.

Sometimes I would lie in bed next to Duke and watch him sleep. For some reason a fear would flow through my heart. I would start feeling like he was too good to be true and that I was offering pretty much of nothin'. I mean, I didn't contribute shit to the household. Yeah, I kept it clean, cooked when he didn't, and took care of the kids, but outside of that I had nothing to offer him. I had a high school diploma, but where could that get me nowadays?

I kept promising Duke I would start community college, but who had time for that? The day classes were so scattered. There was always evening classes, but Duke put in work during those hours and no way was Penny gonna keep all three of the kids. Hell, she probably wouldn't even keep Brandy if she knew it was to help me better my life. So that was out the window, for now anyway, 'til I could come up with something else. Duke would mention college every now and then, even bring home brochures and applications sometimes, but he never gave me ultimatums or pressured me.

I thought about asking him to loan me some money to start my own business, a hair salon or something, but that shit was so typical of a gangster's girl or a hustler's wife. Besides, once again, I'd be taking from him, instead of giving. For now, the only thing I could do was continue being his princess, making him feel like the king he was. Maybe my being so dependent upon him was exactly what he liked about me the most. Maybe it was that one thing that enabled him to feel more like a man; that would allow me to close my eyes to surviving in the real world, and continue dreaming.

If having a life with Duke was a dream, I wanted to overdose on sleeping pills and never wake up. Once he got over the fact that I had taken Brandy to see Tonio, for the next few months our relationship got rock-solid. He even stopped allowing Celeste to use the kids as an excuse to call and come over to the house whenever she wanted. I did start seeing less and less of him, though, but that was because he was putting in work to buy us a bigger house, one with an extra bedroom, where he could hire a nanny so I could go to college as planned.

"Baby Gurl, I'm gonna get you one of them homes up in New Albany, you know, one in those gated communities," Duke said as we sat in the tub together that was overflowing with bubbles. "We gon' have one of them corner Jacuzzis in the master suite bath. That way when we take baths together like now, we'll have more leg room.

"Umm, but I like wrapping my legs around you." I tightened my legs around Duke's waist.

He grabbed my ankles and began to massage them. "And I like your legs wrapped around me too."

"I love you, Duke."

Duke moved my legs from around him and turned around to face me. "I love you too, Baby Gurl."

There was something about the way he said it. It was almost as if he wanted to say, "But—" and then hit me with a whammy, but he didn't. Instead he just took a deep breath and then dipped his head under the water and between my legs. Who knew he could hold his breath that long? Long enough to make me cum?

"Duke, it's beautiful." I spun around in the great room of our new home that Duke had just closed on in New Albany, one of the most high-priced and classiest suburbs ever.

It was a huge 4,500 square-foot, five-level split, with a full finished basement. It had a built-in pool and a pool house damn near the size of our old house. Duke had always made me feel like a princess, but now he had even provided the castle to go along with the fairytale.

"You deserve it." He walked over to me and placed a soft kiss on my lips. "Really, Baby Gurl. You've come a long way. Instead of doing the expected, what most people expected someone like you to do, a young girl who got pregnant too soon—drop out of school, get on welfare, and become the neighborhood chickenhead and start having more babies, you did just the opposite."

"But, Duke, I didn't become that statistic because of you. You saved my life." I buried my head in Duke's chest, with watered eyes.

LD came up the steps from the fourth-level entertainment room, holding Brandy in his arms, Tara close on his heels. "Dad, there's enough room down there for you to get me that air hockey table I been wanting that you said we didn't have room for at the old house."

"And we can make the upstairs loft my Barbie's house," Tara added, her hands on her hips."

"Not to worry, this house is big enough to make every-body's dreams come true."

Duke was right—moving into that house was a dream come true. Whoever thought that me, Baby Girl McCoy, a bastard from birth, a product of rape and whose granny blew her daddy's brains out before she was even born, would ever live in a gated community in the 'burbs with three beautiful children and the most wonderful man in the world? Surely not my mom.

The first time Penny came to pick up Brandy from the new crib, she was so heated with envy, she wouldn't even step foot in the door.

"Put grandma's baby's coat on and bring her and her stuff out to the car," she said when I opened the door after she had rung the bell.

"Ma, don't you want to come in and see our new house?" I asked her, a little hurt that she didn't even want to come in and see the place where her daughter and granddaughter laid their heads.

"What for? The minute that thug finds another little girl, you'll be up out of here, and don't come knockin' on my door when it happens—mark my words. Anyway, like I said, bring Brandy on out to the car. I'll be waiting."

I swear to God, when she turned her back to head out to her car I wanted to stick a knife in it. I know that's an awful thing for a girl to say about her mother, but I swear that's how she made me feel sometimes. I think it would be more pleasing to her if I had turned out like one of those young girls Duke was talking about, the type of girl that he didn't want me to turn out to be. But pleasing her was the last thing I wanted to do, and I would see to it that I never did, no matter what I had to do. No matter what.

I finally managed to start taking some college courses. I could only take two classes for the semester, but it was a start. Duke paid this girl named Harmony to sit with the kids while I went to school. Harmony was some wannabe white girl that was the girlfriend of this guy he did business with named Nikko. Once upon a time she had lived the kind of lifestyle with her parents that I was now living with Duke, until one summer she just straight fiended out. But that was a few years ago. Nikko got her cleaned up. Word was that it was his fault she got hooked on drugs in the first place. She ended up getting herself together, went to college for childcare development, got an associate degree, and had been making real good money as a private childcare provider. Her and Nikko were doing pretty good for themselves.

They lived a modest lifestyle, but everybody knew they could be living better. Hell, Nikko was the son of a hood legend, so he definitely had bank. But he wasn't a flashy cat. He wasn't into anything that drew attention to him. Harmony was low-key too; that's why she was perfect. She didn't run her mouth about what Duke and I had or what was going on in our house. And the kids loved her.

It's amazing how hard times can make a person soft. I felt bad that Harmony had to go through what she did in order to make her the person she is today, but she was just living proof that anyone could turn their life around. And let Duke tell it, I was too. The same way Harmony had Nikko to thank for making her get her life together, I had Duke to thank. Ironic how they both focused so much on making our lives right, yet they lived a life of doing wrong.

"Thanks, Harmony." I handed her a fifty-dollar bill.

"That's okay." She put her hand up. "Duke took care of it. He stopped in for a minute to take a shower and paid me, so it's all good. I'll see you Thursday."

"All right, girl. Take care." I closed the door behind her.

After Harmony left, I followed the sound of the kids' voices down to the entertainment room.

"Game point," I heard LD say to Tara. "I spanked that ass again."

"Oooh, I'm telling," Tara sang.

"Snitches get stitches," LD said through his teeth, like he was some gangster off the street.

"LD, what did you just say to your sister?" Before he could answer, I grabbed his arm and spanked his behind. Of course, it didn't hurt his behind none, but it hurt his feelings.

"I'm sorry, Mommie Baby," he said, putting his head down.

"I don't ever want to hear you talking like that, do you understand?"

"Yes, ma'am."

"Now get upstairs and get showered. You're going to bed early." As he moped away, I turned to Tara. "Did Grandma Penny call and say when she was bringing Brandy back?"

"Yeah. She said she'd bring her home in the morning. She has a runny nose and she said since you ain't doing nothing to make it better, she's going to keep her and take care of her until she's not sick anymore."

"She's not sick; she just has a runny nose."

"Well, she's your mama." Tara threw her hands up and walked up the steps.

I just shook my head and smiled. One thing I could say about Celeste, she raised some fine kids. *Now if I could only rid LD of that thug mentality he's starting to pick up.* It was critical that his attitude got nipped right in the bud, because everybody knows, once a thug, always a thug.

Chapter 12
The Lord Taketh

"LD, grab Brandy's diaper bag," I said as me and the kids got out of the car after an afternoon of shopping with some money Duke had given us to go on a shopping spree.

"I already got it," he said with a smile.

That boy was just like his daddy—he knew what to do without even being asked to do it.

Tara got out of the car and headed towards the house. "Somebody broke the door." She walked up onto the porch and reached for the doorknob.

"No!" I screamed, waking up Brandy, who had fallen asleep on the ride. "Get back, Tara. Let me check it out first."

I sat Brandy's car seat on the sidewalk next to where LD was standing. "Watch her," I told him. I slowly approached the door. "Get back," I said to Tara, shooing her down the walkway with my hand. I immediately could see that the door had been kicked in. There were dents in the door, the hinges were broken and wood from the frame was splintered. My heart began to race.

"What is it?" LD asked.

"Shhh." I pushed the door open. "Hello," I shouted, hoping that if someone was in there, my return would convince them to make their exit. If a muthafucka in a movie had done that shit, I would have been in the theater cussing that screen out. Here I was, doing the same dumb type of shit—that was the hood in me—ghetto broads think they invincible.

As the broken door screeched open, I almost fell to my knees at what I saw. The couch was turned over and some of the cushioning looked as though it had been cut out. The drawers to the side tables were pulled out and their contents scattered about. Pictures and mirrors were off the walls and in broken pieces on the ground.

I started to quiver as I began walking around. It was a disaster. Every kitchen drawer had been rummaged through. All of the coats had been yanked out of the closet in the foyer.

"Oh, my God," I said in a low tone. Then I went into panic mode. "Duke! Duke!" I ran towards the basement. "Duke, where are you, baby?"

I made my way to the basement steps, where the light was on. The basement light was never left on.

"Oh my God!" My body started to tremble. "Duke! Oh, my God!"

"What is it, Mommie Baby?" LD said, walking up behind me and scaring the holy shit out of me.

"Goddamn it, LD! Didn't I tell you to stay out there and watch Brandy?"

"Tara's watching her," he said, not the least bit moved by my words. "I heard you yelling. You expect me to stand out there and do nothing with a woman in here yelling?"

I looked at LD, who was nothing but a miniature Duke. *My little soldier.* My eyes began to water.

"Okay, LD, you wait right here for me."

"Okay, but if you scream again, I'm going to bust a cap in somebody's ass."

"LD!"

"I mean, I'm going to call 911."

"You do that."

I headed down the basement steps, scared to death.

Once I reached the bottom of the basement steps, I gasped at what I saw. The entire basement was turned upside down. The air hockey table was turned over, as was the big-screen television.

"Oh my God!" I put my hand over my mouth. The first thought that came to my mind was that we had been robbed, but on second thought, nothing looked like it had been taken. "Duke!" I dashed up the steps with my heart racing ninety miles per hour.

"What? What is it? What's wrong, Mommie Baby?" LD asked as I brushed past him. "What is it?"

I ignored him and headed up the steps. The upstairs had been ransacked too, right down to Brandy's crib being turned over. Mattresses were flipped and looked as if they had been cut open. When I went into the private bathroom of Duke's and my bedroom, I almost fainted when I saw the blood on the toilet bowl.

"Duke!" I yelled at the top of my lungs. "Duke!" I ran down the stairs with the intention of getting LD, who was already halfway up the steps, out of the house.

"Mommie Baby, please tell me what's wrong," LD begged with tears in his eyes. "Where's my daddy?"

"Come on, baby," I said to him.

Just then my cell phone rang. I took it out of my pocket and answered it. "Hello."

"Baby? It's me, Nikko."

" 'Nikko'?" I asked, wondering why in the world he would be calling me on my cell phone.

"Yeah, it's me, Nikko. Baby, it's about Duke . . ."

* * *

Although I had never planned on going back to the
county jailhouse again, there I was, walking the walk up the
stairwell that led to the visiting room. I stood at window
number three and waited. I didn't wait long before I saw him
come through the door wearing the Sunkist suit, the felony
orange, handcuffed, and led by a guard.

"Duke," I said, putting my hand over my mouth as my eyes
welled up with tears. Seeing him like this just broke my
heart. This was my Duke, my man, my king, my protector, my
lover, the only father figure I'd ever had in my life. He was
every man I ever needed all rolled into one. He took me in
off the streets and made me his gurl. He molded me and
then made me his woman. I made him my world. And now
here he was before me, separated by glass, chained like a
beast. With a bandage over his right eye, he looked like he
hadn't even been able to protect himself, let alone me.

Duke picked up the phone and then signaled for me to
pick up mine.

"Oh, my God!" I began to cry. "What happened to you?"

"Baby, don't," he said. "You fuckin' me up with those tears
right now. Please don't cry, Baby."

In an attempt to be strong, I wiped my tears and straightened myself up.

"The police fuckin' busted my head on the damn toilet
bowl when they arrested me."

"What were you doing over the toilet bowl?"

Duke looked at me like I was stupid. "Where's the kids?"

"They're all with my mom," I answered, sniffling.

"What? My kids too?"

"I know. Figure that. I couldn't get in touch with Celeste,
and I didn't want to bring all the kids down here with me. I
needed to find out what the hell was going on first and I
knew you wouldn't be able to really talk in front of them."

"Did you tell Penny why you needed to drop them off, where you had to go?"

"No, I just told her that it was an emergency. She probably thought it was school or something."

There was a few seconds of dead, awkward silence before Duke spoke. "It ain't looking good, Baby Gurl." Duke looked me in the eyes and shook his head.

I gulped and held back my tears. "What's going on, Duke?"

"Trafficking, possession, tax evasion, money laundering—"

"What?" I said, not knowing what in the hell all those charges Duke was rattling off was about.

"Baby, them muthafuckas probably even charged me with jaywalking."

I was too scared to find humor in anything. "Duke, be serious here—how much time are we talking? When are you coming home? How do I get you out of here?"

Duke looked at me as I waited for him to tell me something that would ease my fears. I could tell by the look on his face that he didn't have anything good to say. He just looked away.

The next thing I knew, I heard this helpless cry, this screeching yelp. It was me.

"Baby! Baby!" Duke yelled through the phone. "Damn it, stop it. Don't do this. Come on, you my Baby Gurl. Be strong. Be strong."

I know it was selfish, but all of my thoughts were of me and the kids. Although Duke would be the one doing the time, he would be doing it without us. He would be leaving us out in the world alone to fend for ourselves. Just the fear of living and breathing without him suffocated me as I fought an anxiety attack.

"Duke, no!" I cried through the phone, trying to catch my breath. "No, don't . . . don't leave us."

"Baby, stop it! Get it together and just listen to me—it's going to be all right, it's going to be all right."

I snorted and sniffed, then caught my breath. I looked up at the girl who was on the phone next to me.

"It's your first time?" the half-black, half-Latino girl said to me. "Don't worry, ma, you'll get used to it. That's what happens when you fall in love with a gangsta."

I took a deep breath and turned my attention back to Duke. "I'm sorry. I'm sorry," I said to Duke, regaining my composure. "I'm sorry, Duke. I don't want to upset you."

"It's okay. But, Baby, I'm really going to need you to be strong and hold it down."

"I just don't understand what's going on here."

I truly couldn't comprehend what was going on around me. Duke never told me his business; I never asked. I knew he wasn't doing good things, but he was a good man. He was good to me, and he was good to his children. And that's all I cared about.

"I know you don't understand, and I don't expect you to. But what I do know is that it's going to be a while before I'm a free man again, so you're going to have to learn how to hold things down without me, Baby Gurl."

"Duke, no. Don't say that, Duke." I put my head down. I couldn't stand to look at him if I couldn't touch him. If I couldn't hold him. If he couldn't hold me.

"When you leave here, get in touch with Nikko. He's going to help you get everything out of the house before they start seizing shit."

" 'Seizing'?"

"Just do what I said, Baby. Have him put it in storage or something until you can get a place."

" 'Get a place'? I have a place; we have a place."

"Trust me, Baby, I know the drill—they're going to take everything, so get what you can and then don't go back to the house ever again. Don't talk to anybody. Don't tell anybody anything. Trust no one, Baby, no one. Things are about to change; as a matter of fact, *everything* is about to change."

Duke was right. My world, overnight, turned upside down. After I left from visiting him in jail, I called Nikko the minute I got to my car. He met me at the house in a U-Haul and helped me move everything I could into a storage unit. And thank goodness too because, that very next morning, when I tried to go back and get a few more items, the house was already taped off with police officers carrying things out into a truck of their own.

I stayed in a hotel with the kids for a couple of days, per Duke's orders, until he was able to see to it that he got the kids and me a place. One of his boys who ran a strip club and owned a few rental properties hooked us up with a vacant double-family unit that he had available. Celeste eventually came and got Tara and LD to live with her, so it was just Brandy and me.

Several people on the streets owed Duke money. He had Nikko collect, and give every cent to me. Duke wouldn't even let me put any of it on his books. It was crazy, but somehow he still managed to take care of us from behind bars. For a minute there, I felt like everything was going to be okay.

Altogether, Nikko had dropped at least twenty-five grand on me. We were living rent-free. All I had to pay for was the utilities. For a nineteen-year-old going on twenty like myself, that was a lot of money. But once it came down to it, that was what a lot of people made in a year, which meant that's what they spent in a year. So when Duke accepted a ten-year plea bargain, I knew that for nine of those years I was fucked! But the same way Duke had waited on me, waited on me to become a woman, I would wait on him.

Chapter 13
My Favorite Uncle

Just as I had predicted, I managed to take care of Brandy and me for a little over a year with the money Nikko had brought over to me. But as the money dissolved, so did my spirit. And not even Duke could lift it.

"I don't know what to tell you, Baby Gurl," Duke said as we sat in the visiting room at Orient Prison, Brandy bouncing up and down on her daddy's knee. "I had Nikko give you all I had coming to me on the streets. I can't do nothing from this side of these bars. That's why I kept telling you that finishing school and finding a career was so important. I tried to teach you these things, Baby, but no, instead, you wanted to stay up under me."

"I did start school, Duke. You saying that like it's my fault we're in this situation." I really felt like Duke was trying to tell me that I should have seen this shit coming.

"It's not your fault; I know it's not your fault." Duke sighed and put his head down. He then looked up at Brandy. "I'm sorry," he said to her. "Daddy's so sorry."

I looked away. I couldn't take it. I'd never pictured in a million years Duke in such a helpless predicament. I knew it had to be eating him up inside, not being able to provide for us the way he always had.

"Duke, just tell me what to do," I asked in a desperate tone. "I'm out of money. I—"

"Have you tried to get a job?"

"Doing what?"

"Doing what ever it was you go to school for."

"What I *was* going to school for you mean. I couldn't finish school; I barely have money to buy Brandy clothes, let alone pay for college. Duke, please, just tell me what to do." I looked deep into his eyes.

He remained silent. There was nothing he could say and nothing he could do.

I sat there for about another half-hour or so, watching him play with Brandy, but say nothing to me. He could barely look me in the eyes. I guess he didn't want to see how I might look at him. But little did he know, I didn't look at him any differently; I didn't think any less of him. I still loved him and always would, no matter what. But right now, love wasn't going to pay the bills, so I had to think of something. Only one thing came to mind, though, and I knew Duke wouldn't approve.

"May I help you?" the woman sitting behind the huge oval desk at the Franklin County Department of Human Services asked.

She asked me like I was getting on her last nerve just by standing there, like I had been there all day just bothering her. I suppose, in her eyes, I had been. I was every other girl that had stood before her begging Uncle Sam for some money and food stamps. Begging like I was his favorite niece and knew that he couldn't resist saying no to me. She didn't see a different face, just another black girl, begging for a handout.

"Yes, uh, uh, I wanted to sign up for some assistance."

I had to force those words out of my mouth. All I could think about was what in the world Duke would think of me if he knew I was at the welfare office, turning myself into what he called a statistic. But I had no other choice. I was flat busted broke. I had even sold the car and had resorted to public transportation. I had no other choice, besides begging my mom to let me move back in with her, and there was no way in hell I was going to do that. There was no way in hell she would let me come back anyhow.

"Have you ever received benefits before in this county or any other county?"

"No."

She handed me a clipboard with several pieces of paper on it. "Fill these out. Bring them back up to me when you're done and then sit back down until your name is called."

"Thank you." I took the clipboard. "Come on, Brandy." I walked over to the waiting area, where tons of other folks were waiting to sign up for benefits, or to see their caseworkers about their already existing cases. I sat down, sat Brandy down next to me, and began filling out all of the papers.

It took me forever. Once I completed the paperwork, I returned them to the desk and sat back down.

A full hour went by, and my name still had not been called. Brandy started getting whiny and restless.

"Just relax, Mommy's baby," I said. "We won't be here long."

"Shiiit," a girl sitting behind me said. "You definitely a virgin to this system. Uncle Sam ain't molested you yet?"

I turned around and looked at her. She had her lips twisted up in the air, and her legs were crossed, her foot swinging. She was sportin' a navy blue and pink Nike jogging suit and wore her hair in a slicked-back ponytail that dangled down her back. Her huge hoop earrings were larger than any I would have chosen for myself, but they were cute on her. A pair of pink knock-off Gucci shades sat on the top of her head. She looked black, but had to be mixed with Latino or something. She was one of those chicks that was beautiful—as long as she kept her mouth shut.

There was a little girl sitting next to her that looked about three or four years old that was her "mini me"; it had to be her daughter, because they looked so much alike.

"You supposed to pack a lunch when you come up in this muthafucka," she said.

There was something familiar about her, like I knew her from somewhere. I just couldn't' put my finger on it. "Yeah, I see that now."

"Whatever you do, just don't lose your food stamp card once you get it. You gon' be waiting all day again to get a new one, and then you gon' have to wait 72 hours for it to get re-activated."

"Thanks."

"No problem, ma." She uncrossed her legs and leaned in to me. "I'm Coa-Coa." She extended her hand.

"Baby." I shook her hand. "This is my daughter, Brandy."

"Baby, like for real your name is Baby like that girl on *Dirty Dancing*?"

"Yes." I shook my head and giggled. "And the name Coa-Coa?" I said, turning the name game table on her.

"Oh, shit, girl," she said, shooing the air with her hand. "That was the name I used when I used to dance back in the day. I don't know, it just stuck with me. Hell, I liked the way it used to roll off them ballers' tongues while they was stickin' dead presidents in my thong. But after having this one right here"—She pointed to the little girl sitting next to her—"the body I used to dance with didn't stick with me."

"I hear you," I said, patting my stomach. I thought I'd make her feel better by suggesting that giving birth to Brandy had torn my body down too, even though my body was still on point. I just knew how misery loves company, so I decided to be its guest.

"Girl, please . . . you know damn well your ass can still shop in the junior's department, so don't even try to join my pity party without an invitation."

I chuckled. It was the first time I had laughed in a minute. This chick had seen right through me. And she was right on point about everything, including the fact that I wouldn't be getting out of that welfare office no time soon.

My name didn't get called for about another hour and a half. But for an hour of it, before Coa-Coa's name was called, we sat and talked about all kinds of stuff, right down to our men.

"So your dude is locked up too, huh?" Coa-Coa asked, right before her name was called.

"Yep, Orient. He was at the county for a minute, until he took a plea."

"Oh, shit! The county was my baby daddy's second home. The county?" She squinted her eyes and went into deep thought. "Oh, hell naw. Hell naw." She snapped her fingers and then pointed at me. "You ol' girl from the county that day. You was coming to see your dude and shit."

Bam! It hit me. That's where I knew her from. She was the girl who was sitting at the phone next to me when I went to visit Duke in jail that first time. I knew I had seen her face somewhere before. "Yeah, I remember you; you were right next to me."

"Isis Scales," a caseworker announced.

"All right then, ma." Coa-Coa scooped up her daughter. "You take it easy."

"Take care," I said and watched her disappear around the partitions. I was almost sad to see her go. I had enjoyed our little bit of time together.

Although loud, and perhaps a little obnoxious, I kind of got a kick out of Coa-Coa. Besides, the only girlfriend I ever really had was Celeste. With Duke being locked up, I didn't have anybody to talk to now. He never even called me collect anymore; said he knew I wouldn't be able to afford the phone bill.

After my name was called, I went back with my assigned caseworker and presented her with the items she needed in order to get the ball rolling on my case. There were several things that I still needed to present to her before I could start receiving benefits, but all I had to do was make copies of the documents she still needed to see and drop them off at the desk for her. I wasn't going to have to wait again.

Once I finished up with my caseworker, I headed to the bus stop. To my surprise, Coa-Coa was at the bus stop too.

"Hey, girl," she said, when she spotted me. "You handle your business? They gon' hook you up with a check?"

"I have to turn in a couple more things first."

"Well, they upped my food stamps, so holla at a sista if you need a few groceries to get by until they get you together. We family; we related now. We both got the same Uncle, so I guess that makes us, at least, cousins." She then dug down into her purse, pulled out a scrap piece of paper and a pen, and began writing. "Here's my phone number." She handed me the piece of paper and put the pen back down in her purse. "I put my cell phone number on there too. It's turned off now, but I'ma get it turned back on the first of the month."

"Cool." I tucked it in my purse. "Write down mine."

She pulled her pen back out and another piece of paper and proceeded to write my phone number down. No sooner did she do that, than the bus came.

"Come on, Naya," Coa-Coa said to her little girl.

I scooped up Brandy by the hand, and we all got on the bus.

"Show Rosa Parks some respect," Coa-Coa shouted to me as I headed for the back of the bus.

"Huh?" I stopped and turned around to face her.

"You done passed up a hundred empty seats to move to

the back of the bus. If white folks still made y'all's ass sit back there, the shit would hit the fan." Coa-Coa then sat down at an empty seat in the front of the bus.

I sat down next to her, and we put the kids in the empty seat across from us.

"Where you stay at anyway?" Coa-Coa asked.

"Over on Norwood, off of Oakland Park."

"Get the fuck outta here!—I stay on Karl, off of Oakland; we neighbors and shit."

I couldn't help noticing how every other word out of Coa-Coa's mouth was a curse word. I knew I cursed a lot, but not around Brandy. People on the bus were looking at her like she was crazy.

Thank God Rosa Parks ain't on this bus to hear your mouth.

"Yeah, but I don't know how long we gon' be neighbors."

"Why you say that?"

"Well, the place I'm staying at, one of Duke's boys owns it. I don't see him letting me stay there until Duke gets out."

"Oh you best believe that nigga gon' be knocking on your door any day now for some pussy."

"Huh?"

"Girl, please . . . that nigga can't wait to tell other niggaz he fuckin' Duke's girl. He gon' fuck you for two years, get tired of the pussy, and put yo' ass out anyway so he can make room for the next nigga's girl who gets snatched up by the feds."

Coa-Coa was spittin' too much for me. I thought I knew the streets, but I didn't know shit. It was just too much, and as hard as I tried to cope, I couldn't any more. I started sniffing back the snot running out of my nose as the tears fell from my eyes. My chest started to jerk from me holding back the squeals that I wanted to let out of my throat, but I fought. I fought like hell. But I was already a mess.

"Oh, I know you ain't about to cry," Coa-Coa snapped.

"Girl!" she snatched me by my arm. "Look at her! Look at her!" She pointed at Brandy, who was sitting in the seat across from us, playing with Naya. "You got how many more years to take care of her? How many years to see to it that she grows up to be a strong black woman? A strong black independent woman so that she don't feel the need to get caught up with some nigga and swallow his nut and a dream, thinking he's always gon' be there to take care of her and end up like us? Huh? And you sittin' here looking as weak as they come, as weak as they come, girl." She released my arm with a jerk. "You better get it together 'cause this is only the beginning."

I looked over at her. She was staring out the window, her bottom lip trembling. I could tell she wanted to cry too, but not for the same reason I was crying. She wanted to cry because she was angry. She was angry at the hand she had been dealt. She was angry at the hand I had been dealt and every other girl just like us. But 'spite that, she was living as best she could and believed in better days. I could see the hope in her eyes; she wasn't about to let somebody like me, anybody, steal her gleam of hope with tears of defeat for a battle she had her heart set on winning.

"If you was gonna fuck with somebody like Duke, you should have prepared your heart for this shit right here; you gotta know the odds of a hustler in the streets—your mama never taught you that?" Coa-Coa snapped her head back in disbelief, waiting on my response.

"My mom did everything she could to see to it that I didn't even get caught up with anybody like Duke. And now look at me. I can't even go to her for help. I had to go to Uncle Sam before I could go to my own mother."

"So Duke just left you and your little *chiquita* over there for dead, huh?"

"Oh no. When he got locked up, he had his boy collect

every dime that was owed to him off of the street and give it all to me. It was like twenty-five grand. But, hell, how long was that supposed to last?"

" 'Twenty-five grand'?" Coa-Coa laughed. " 'Twenty-five grand'?" She laughed even harder.

"What?" I waited impatiently for her to catch her breath and tell me what she was laughing at.

"Umm, umm, girl." Coa-Coa sucked her teeth. "Twenty-five *G*'s?—that ain't no stash—that ain't shit. Niggaz like Duke gamble that shit away in a night of dice and card games. Niggaz like Duke always got a stash. And believe me when I tell you that twenty-five thousand dollars was not that nigga's stash—I don' give a fuck what that nigga telling you. Oh, he got a stash, though. Question is—who sittin' on it?"

Before I could even respond, Coa-Coa shouted, "Oh, shit, this is our stop coming up." She rang the bell for the bus driver to stop the bus, grabbed Naya by the hand, and went and waited by the door for the bus to stop. "All right then, Baby. You take it easy and, like I said, we cousins now. Holla at your girl."

I smiled and nodded as Coa-Coa and Naya got off the bus. I went over and sat with Brandy until we got to our stop a few blocks down, thinking about Coa-Coa's words the entire time—*'He got a stash. Question is—who sittin' on it?'*

Chapter 14

AND IT, TOO, SHALL COME TO PASS

When Coa-Coa showed me the newspaper, I thought I was going to fall out. Then I did fall out; I completely lost all bearings.

"Baby!" Coa-Coa said, catching my fall. She held on to me until she could prop me onto the couch. "Baby, you okay?"

Coa-Coa and I had become inseparable, since I called her the next day after our bus ride from the welfare office. That girl really kept my spirits up. My relationship with her was nothing like my relationship with Celeste, who knew me inside and out. Coa-Coa and I still had a lot to learn about each other and to get to learn each other's ways, but I wouldn't have traded it for the world.

"Baby?"

I could hear air coming out of my throat, as if gasping for my last breath. At that moment, I didn't know if I wanted any air. Without Duke, I didn't know if I ever wanted to breathe again. Then I heard Brandy doing that whining thing she does when she finds herself alone in a room after waking from a nap. The more Brandy whined, the more I cried.

I wasn't crying because of what I didn't have any more,

which was Duke; I was crying because of what I did have—
Brandy. How in the hell was I going to raise her alone for the
rest of my life? Ten years had just turned into forever.

Just knowing that one day Duke would get out of jail and
come back and save us, like a knight in shining armor, is
what kept me moving. Just that hope and dream alone gave
me the strength to make it on to the next day. But the morning newspaper shattered that dream into a million little
pieces, right along with my heart.

I don't know what made me think that Duke would be
mine forever. I had gone to church with my mother enough
to know that God wasn't going to take a good man from one
woman—a good woman at that—and give him to me.

"I can't believe it, Coa-Coa. I just can't believe it."

"Hold on." Coa-Coa patted my shoulder. "Let me go get
Brandy."

Coa-Coa headed up the stairs and returned with Brandy.
"It's okay," she told Brandy, who was rubbing her eyes.

"What am I going to do?"

"I don't know, ma." Coa-Coa shook her head. "I mean, the
kids ain't say nothing to you about it?"

"Celeste hasn't let me see the kids since Duke got locked
up." I looked down at Brandy. "My baby don't even get to see
her brother and sister no more. I loved those kids. They
loved me too, Coa-Coa."

"I know, I know."

I started crying even harder.

"Married? How could he have gotten married? I'm the
one who visits him all of the time. I make sure during mail
call that nigga's name gets shouted out. I have even put
money from my welfare check on that nigga's books, Coa-
Coa. And he marries her? And on top of that, I got to find
out in the fuckin' newspaper? That nigga ain't even have the
balls to tell me to my face." I picked up the paper, balled it
up, and threw it across the room. "All them years they were

together, and he never married her before. Why now? How could he do this to me? Why would he do this to me?"

"I don't know." Coa-Coa took a deep breath. "But there's only one way to find out."

Coa-Coa was right. There was only one way I could find out why Duke had hurt me the way he had, and that was by asking him. As I walked towards the prison door, I knew this was going to be my last visit to Duke. Rather than get an answer to the question that was eating away at me, I'd almost rather just never see him again for as long as I lived and continue living my life just not knowing. But there was a part of me that just would not rest until I heard it from the horse's mouth.

As I entered the prison, preparing for my body search, exiting was a face I hadn't seen in some time. I didn't know whether to stop or to just keep walking, but upon seeing me, when she stopped, I followed suit. The first thing I noticed was the blinding gleam of the bling on her ring finger. I tried to be subtle with my glances at the ring, but I couldn't.

"Oh this"—Celeste held up her hand and admired what was obviously her wedding ring—"it's nothing. Just a little somethin'-somethin' to let bitches know who the real wifey is and will always be."

I had no words. I knew Celeste was expecting me to say some ol' slick shit, but I just didn't have it in me. Whether she knew it or not, I still loved her. She had been so good to me, so very good, but I was young, stupid, and just wanted to be loved. I wanted to be loved by a man. Because I wanted it so badly, when Duke showed me the love I had longed for, I didn't even stop to think about Celeste and her feelings, or her children. I had just finally found that void in my life, and I wanted to fill it at all cost, even our friendship.

"Believe it or not, Celeste," I found the strength to say, "I'm happy for you, but I'm not going to lie, I'm sad for me.

But, again, I'm happy for you. I'm older now, and I know what all this means to you, to marry the man you've loved all of your life."

Celeste looked me into my eyes. "I hope you really are sincere, Baby, 'cause you hurt me. When all I ever did was love you, you turned around and hurt me. I was so pissed off at you. But then the anger turned to understanding, and my understanding turned to pity. I understood you and your circumstances, and I pitied you for that. That's why that day I went to your mother's house, I didn't go to rat you out. I went to protect Duke. I went to protect my children. I went to beg Penny not to report Duke to the police. I didn't want my children to have to pay for the sins of their father by carrying that cross with them the rest of their lives. I explained to her that if it hadn't been Duke, it would have been any man. That's just how desperate you were to find Daddy. The world is full of girls like you, Baby. Only, some of them aren't lucky enough to get a man like Duke."

" 'Lucky'?"

"Don't even go there—Duke could have left you a long time ago; as a matter of fact, he wanted to."

A huge knot formed in my throat. At first I thought Celeste was just saying that to hurt me, but the more she talked, the more I knew she was being nothing less than honest with me.

"Oh, he tried to crawl back in my bed a thousand times, and I'll be honest with you, yeah, I used to let him; used to fuck his brains out, thinking I was getting back at you. But the truth was, I really loved that nigga. My mama used to always ask me, 'All your daddy and I did to raise you right so that you could find yourself a good husband, a doctor, or a lawyer, or something, and you run off and shack up with that thug, wannabe gangsta—Why?' " Celeste chuckled. "Even then all I could say was, 'I really love that nigga.' Duke is like an over-the-counter drug—if you're not careful and take too much of it, you can easily become addicted, or even worse, overdose. Well, I'm addicted; and he's addicted to me, Baby. Yeah, he loved you. I mean, he really did love you. I know when a man loves a woman. But at first it was the kind of love a man has for his daughter, but then you changed all that. He's a man, but at the end of the day, you're just a baby to him. He knew this day was coming, the day he'd get a temporary layoff and end up in this place. He couldn't count on you to hold things down, handle his business, his money. I bet you cried like a baby the first time you ever visited him in jail, didn't you?"

I took a deep breath. I didn't want to give her the pleasure of telling her that she was right.

"Thought so," she snickered. "That's why he wanted to walk away a long time ago. But I knew that you had already swallowed way more of Duke than you could handle. You had overdosed. You would have died, had he walked away from you. You would have turned out to be just like his little sister, and that's what he was afraid of." Celeste put her head down and shook it. When she looked up again, her eyes were full of tears. "And something inside of me still cared about you, Baby. I loved you so much. As bad as I wanted to see the look on your face when he walked out of your life and back into mine, I just couldn't imagine allowing anyone to hurt you like that. Not again."

It was at that point Celeste broke down, causing me to break down too.

"I loved you." She began to cry. "You were my friend. You were like this little bratty sister or something that I wanted to protect. I didn't want to see you hurt. I would have given you the clothes off my back; I would have shared my last meal with you; I would have shared anything with you, even my man. And for that reason, for that reason only, I wouldn't let Duke back in my life."

Tears began to fall from my eyes like a waterfall.

"You had been hurt enough," Celeste continued, "not that it doesn't hurt any less for you now. But this way you've had a chance to wean yourself from him so that it doesn't hurt as much. I know it still hurts, but not as much." She paused. "Baby, this is the best thing that could have happened to you, trust me. You're young. You have a future ahead of you. You have plenty of time to do something with yourself. You don't know nothing about this life. I mean, do you really think he had one of his boys collect all that money off the streets and give it to you? I told Duke, 'I figured that was the least we could do for you and your kid.' Hopefully it was enough to tide you over. Anyway," she said, straightening herself up and wiping her tears away, "the kids ask about you. They ask about Brandy too. I'll tell them you send your love. Bye, baby." Celeste proceeded to walk past me and towards the exit door.

I turned and called to her, tears filling my eyes. "Celeste."

She stopped walking but didn't turn around to face me. She just held her hand up and said, "I know you are, Baby, and I accept," and she kept it moving.

"I'm sorry," I mumbled under my breath anyway, knowing she couldn't hear me. "I'm sorry." I just stood there with tears rolling down my face as Celeste walked out of the door.

Every question I had when I walked through that door had just been answered, but by her instead of Duke. I stood there contemplating whether or not I was still going to go through with my visit to Duke. What difference would it make hearing it come from his mouth? The only difference was that it would probably hurt far more.

I guess I was hoping that he'd probably just tell me what I wanted to hear, something that would make it all better. I'd take his word as truth, knowing it was a lie, forgive him, and continue to live life as his Baby Gurl. But it was clear when I read in the paper that he had married Celeste that I wasn't his Baby Gurl anymore. I had been forced to become a woman, and if I hadn't been forced, I probably would have stayed in the cocoon he had provided for me. So since I had truly been forced to become a woman, it was fine time that I started acting like one.

As I headed right back out of the prison door, I came to the conclusion that there was no better time than now to start acting like the woman I was destined to be. In order to do so, I had to cut the umbilical cord between Duke and I, which meant putting an end to that chapter of my life. So I did the womanly thing and closed the book. I walked away, hoping that Duke, Celeste, and their children would live happily ever after.

Chapter 15
Knight on Shining Rims

It was Monday afternoon, and I sat there going through the want ads from that Sunday's paper. I was frustrated that so many of the positions that sounded interesting required college degrees. My mom was on vacation for a week and decided to keep Brandy. That gave me plenty of time to go job hunting. With the reality that Duke was never going to take care of me again, I had to start making moves in the right direction. I was sitting on the couch at the living room table, when there was a knock on the door. I got up and looked out of the peephole.

"Fuck!" I said to myself. It was Hallow, Duke's boy who owned the property I was living at.

He had started dropping by lately, unannounced, talking about, he was "just checking up on me." Ever since Duke had married Celeste, Hallow was coming by more and more often to "check" on me. Just like Coa-Coa said he would, that nigga was working on me, letting me know that it was time to start checking in the pussy.

I grabbed the remote and turned down the television. I

stood still and silent by the door, while Hallow knocked again. I didn't feel like entertaining his lame advances.

After knocking one more time, he caught the hint and left.

I sighed as I walked back over to the couch and sat down. "I gotta find me a fucking job. I just have to." I knew my days were numbered, and I needed to start paying Hallow's ass rent until I could just up and move somewhere else altogether.

Five minutes hadn't gone by, when there was a knock on the door again.

"Not again," I said to myself. I tiptoed over to the window and saw a powder-blue Cutlass sitting on some phat-ass rims. I went to the door and looked through the peephole and standing there was Tonio. I was absolutely shocked. I no idea he had gotten out of jail.

"Just a minute." I ran over to the mirror hanging at the foot of the steps. I took my hand and ran my fingers through my hair. I quickly scrambled through my purse, pulled out a tube of honey-bronze lip-gloss and smeared it on. After a couple of puckers, I opened the door to see Tonio standing there with a huge pink basket full of pink girly accessories.

"Tonio, what are you doing here? How'd you know where I stayed?"

"Hello to you too, Ms. McCoy." He smiled. "This is for my baby girl." He handed me the basket. "Where is she?" He knew that with Duke being locked up, nothing stood in the way of him having a relationship with his daughter now.

"With her grandmother, but Tonio—"

"Shhh." He put his index finger over my lips. "Can I just come in?"

"Sure. Yeah." I stepped out of the way to let him in and closed the door behind him. "You can have a seat if you want."

"Thank you." He walked over to the couch and sat down, noticing the want ad section spread out across the table. "Bob Evans, Staples, Cashier." He pointed at some of the positions I had circled.

I shrugged my shoulders.

"You better than that. That nigga know you better than that."

Tonio stood up, almost as if he was angry, and walked over to me. He rubbed his hand down the side of my face. His touch felt so good; it felt better than good. No man had touched me since Duke. I almost forgot how good it felt to be touched by a man.

"Tonio, don't," I said. "Don't go there." I was not about to let him start bad-mouthing Duke, the man that took care of his child. Yeah, I might have played a huge role in his not being in Brandy's life, but a real man would have fought for the right to raise his child.

"Oh, my fault—how dare I talk about your baby daddy like that!

"Why are you here?" I said, copping an attitude. "What do you want?"

"Do you really not know the answer to that? Do you truly not know why I'm here? I'm here to get what's mine."

"Look, Tonio, I think you might have the wrong idea here."

"Don't deny me, Baby. Don't deny me this time. Brandy is mine. Before, I let you have your way because you was wit' dat nigga. He was taking good care of you and shit, but now look at you, struggling and shit while his bitch and his other kids living on two acres in Pickerington and shit. She driving around in a Mercedes, wrist, neck, fingers, and ears on ice." Tonio noticed the look of surprise on my face. "Oh, you didn't know that shit, huh?"

He was absolutely right—I didn't know that shit. I guess now I knew who was sittin' on the stash: Celeste. She probably thought she was doing me a big favor dropping that twenty-five thousand dollars on me. All the while it was nothing but a drop in the bucket compared to how much loot she was probably sitting on.

Tonio walked over to me and grabbed my hands. "Look, Baby, I'm not trying to hurt you. The last thing I want to do is hurt you . . . again. I was young and dumb back when we hooked up and—"

"Tonio, that was high school," I said, removing my hands from his. "Let's not even go there."

"I want to go there. I was your first." He walked up closer to me, purposely invading my space. "I was the first one to kiss you. I was the first one to make love to you," he whispered. "I was the first to hurt you, and I'm sorry. Just say you forgive me, and let's try to work this shit out. Let's try to make this ending what it should have been in the first place."

"Tonio," I said, pretending that I wanted to fight him off.

"Let me just try to do right by you and my baby." He looked over my shoulder. "Where did you say my baby was at?"

"She's with her grandmother; she won't be back for a few days."

Tonio paused for a minute. "Then I have an idea. You and me never did get to go on any dates. Let's just take these next couple of days to talk, just me and you. I'll court you and shit, you know what I'm saying?"

"Court me?" I laughed at the idea. "No, I don't know what you saying." I turned to walk away.

"Stop playing," he said, grabbing me by the arms. "I don't want to play games. You right, that was back in high school. This is different. We're grown now—no games. I wanna do you right. Man, being locked up was crazy. So much shit goes through your head that it's crazy. And the one thing that kept going through my head was you and my baby. You know how once niggaz go to jail they always making promises to God if He gets them out?"

I chuckled. "Yeah."

"Well, I promised God that if He gave me another chance, I'd right my wrongs. Don't make me break my promise to God."

I gave him a little smile.

"You're so beautiful." He spoke softly, as if he was whispering to me the biggest secret in the world.

I looked him up and down, searching for some kind of vibe. His body was screaming. That little bit of time in jail had done him some justice. He wasn't all huge and buff, but he was cut like I don't know what.

He pressed his body against mine. I heard it calling me, and I listened.

The next thing I know, I was answering—the kiss Tonio suddenly planted on me turned into me riding him right there on the couch.

Needless to say, I agreed to give Tonio a chance to be the man in me and Brandy's life.

For the next few days, while Brandy was with my mom, Tonio and I spent every waking moment together. I can't describe how amazingly special it felt. It was as if we didn't even have a past, and that it was love at first sight. We were acting like two crazy people in love. We took time to talk and get to know each other, to really get to know each other. I shared with him some of the same things I had shared with Celeste when I used to confide in her; some of the same things I shared with Coa-Coa when I confided in her. We did what we should have done before we ever even got intimate in the first place—get to know each other.

He opened up a little bit with me too. He told me how he planned on going legit once he finished putting his brother through college. His brother was on a college football scholarship, but got put on probation when he failed two of his classes. Tonio was paying for his tutors and for his schooling until he brought his grades back up so his scholarship would kick back in.

Coa-Coa said all hustlers tell chicks they're going to get out of the game after they handle the excuse they made for getting in the game in the first place. But she said one could bet the farm that they'd sure enough come up with another reason to stay in the game. But I don't know, I thought Tonio was sincere about getting out of the game. He just seemed tired, like living an illegal lifestyle was harder work than any legitimate job he could ever have.

I told him, "No way would I put all of my eggs in the basket of a hustler. Not never again."

But he promised me his word was bond, and we continued to talk about our plans to make Brandy proud of her parents.

Penny brought Brandy home Sunday at 1:00 p.m., right after church, just like she had told me she would. Tonio had spent Saturday night but had left out first thing in the morning to go take care of some business. He was coming to pick us up at 2:00 p.m. to take us to dinner, so I was all dressed and made up, when my mom knocked on the door with Brandy.

"Hey, Ma," I said, opening the door.

She just stood there looking me up and down before saying anything. "Look at you, all dressed up." She rolled her eyes and walked in the house after taking her index finger and thumb and rubbing the fabric of the red sundress that I had on. "Wearing the devil's color . . . you must be up to something devilish."

"I'm just going to dinner, Mom, that's all." I sucked my teeth. I was bound and determined to not even let Penny fuck up my newfound attitude, working with the hand I had been dealt after all.

"And where is grandma's baby going while you're out to dinner?"

"She's going with me . . . with us. It will be just me, her and . . ." I looked at Brandy, who had made herself comfortable in front of the television. I leaned in and whispered to Penny, "And her daddy, her real daddy."

"Oh, so you take Brandy out trickin' with you now?"

I couldn't believe my mom went there. For years she had talked to me crazy, like I didn't have feelings, and treated me like I was some kind of pussin' wart on her left tit that was driving her crazy. She talked to me like I wasn't shit growing up, and there was nothing I could do about it. Back then I was living in her house and eating her food, but this was now. I was grown. Now she was in my house, and I wasn't going to let her steal my joy.

"Why do you do that?"

"Do what?" she said nonchalantly. "Come give Granny a kiss goodbye." She walked right past me and went over and gave Brandy a kiss.

"Say nasty things to me, that's what," I said as she made her way back over to the door. "Ever since I can remember, you've always treated me like shit, saying all kinds of slick shit to me." My eyes watered as I thought back to every whore she had called me. Every bitch. Every bastard.

"Watch your muthafuckin' mouth!" She tightened her lips.

"No, this is my house, and I don't have to watch my mouth—you watch yours."

"Oh." She began to circle me, wearing this smirk on her face. "So you grown now, huh, Miss Thang? I bet you couldn't wait for the day you could disrespect me."

"Disrespect you? Disrespect you? All you've ever done my entire life is disrespect me. You might be a different person to those white folks you clock in for from nine to five at the law firm you work at, but other than that, you just a regular ol' ghetto girl just like the ones you tried so hard to keep me from turning into, moving us out to the 'burbs for show. It didn't matter, Ma; look how you act, look how you treated me, look how you raised me—embarrassing me every chance you could get. I hated even going outside to play when I was little. I never knew when you would snap and just come out of the door yelling, fussing, and cussing about something as minor as not putting a new roll of toilet paper on the roll. Then I'd have to hear about it and get teased from all the kids in the neighborhood. Do you know how humiliating that was for me?"

" 'Humiliating,' huh? You want to talk about humiliating?" my mom spat, spit flying literally. "Humiliating is being fourteen years old and pregnant by your . . ."

"Say it, Ma, go ahead and say it." I wasn't about to let her bail out now. She had been holding it in for so many years; for so long. I hit a nerve, and it burst. It was time she let that shit go. "Say it—fourteen and pregnant by . . ."

At that moment, she knew I knew. I could tell by the look in her eyes. And the thing about it was, she was pissed off at me for knowing.

"Who told you?"

"You did—I overheard you talking to Harlem that day in the kitchen."

I wanted so badly for my mother to take this moment to make it the turning point in our relationship; the point where we put everything on the table so we could move on in our lives and live the life a mother and daughter are supposed to live.

"So you've known all this time?"

"Yes, Ma. And I'm not mad at you; I don't hold anything against you."

"Psstt," she spat. "And you just ought not to."

"Why are you acting like this is my fault?"

"Because it is your fault!" she screamed at the top of her

lungs. "Had you never been conceived, I'd have grown up with my mother, instead of a constant reminder of why I didn't get to grow up with her."

"Had I never had been conceived, you would have continued living in hell while your mother's boyfriend—"

Before I could finish I felt a whack across my left eye. I stumbled backwards, but caught myself from falling.

"Mommy." Brandy ran over and wrapped her arms around my leg.

"Go to hell, Baby!" Penny said.

"It's not me you hate, Penny, it's him . . . and I forgive you."

Penny put her head down and sighed. And just when I thought this was it, the moment of redemption, she looked up at me and said, "Go to hell," and she started to storm out of the house.

"You can't keep torturing yourself like this, Ma. You gotta let it go."

She stopped and turned to me. "Bitch, you don't know what torture is." She walked up on me like she would have cut my throat if she had a knife in her hand. "Torture is some fat-ass, nasty bastard coming into your room every night, putting one hand over your mouth so you can't scream, while using his other hand to ram his dick inside of you."

"Ma!" I grabbed Brandy and covered her ears as Penny continued to relay the graphic details of years of being molested, which not even I wanted to hear.

"No, she needs to hear this. She needs to know, just in case one of these so-called gangsta thugs you have around her that you think wants your ass is really after hers."

"Is that what this is about? Is that why you take to Brandy the way you do? You're afraid that I'm going to let something happen to her?"

"You let something happen to you. You let a grown-ass

man fuck you with your hot ass. No telling what you'd let him do to her."

"Fuck you! Fuck you! Get the fuck out! Just get the fuck out! Don't ever come around here again! You'll never see her again! I won't let you poison her! Never. You'll never see either one of us again. Why didn't you just give me up for adoption if you hated me so much?"

By now Brandy was in tears, crying hysterically.

"You think I give a shit about not seeing your ass again?" She walked over to the door and snatched it open. "I'm glad to finally know I never have to see you again. I'm glad to finally get rid of you and never have to see your face again." My mom looked down at Brandy, and then she just stormed out of the door. She hadn't taken two steps before she stuck her head back in the door. "You wanna know why? You wanna know why I didn't just give you away?" She snickered, and before walking away and letting the door close behind her, she said, "I figured, hell, I don't even want her, her own mother. Why the fuck would anybody else want her? And, look, I was right—you're all alone living like you're living now because Duke didn't even want your ass. Used you for the little young piece of pussy that you were and left you for dead. Your so-called gangsta, your nigga, your ruff neck, your baller, your thug and whatever else you stupid broads run around singing songs about. He left your ass for dead, which is exactly what I should have done."

I stood trembling and stunned. Penny's words were like ice. They froze me. I was frostbitten, my body in pain. I don't know how long I stood there unable to move before I heard Coa-Coa.

"Damn, I just passed your moms and shit," Coa-Coa said, walking in the door with Naya. "I tried to be nice, but ole' girl was stomping like Miss Sophia and you had told Harpo to beat her." Coa-Coa chuckled. "You ready for your little family outing?"

Coa-Coa looked at me trembling, ready to burst with emotion, and quickly ceased her laughter and conversation. She looked down at Brandy who was still clutching my leg in fear. "Baby?" She walked over to me. "Baby, you okay?"

I know Coa-Coa hated when I cried. I had only cried in front of her that day on the bus and when I found out that Duke had married Celeste. I knew I was about to let her down, and there was nothing I could do about it. Before I knew it, I had fallen to my knees and cried out. I held my fist up to the sky and just began to cry out to God in confusion.

"Why?" I screamed. "God, why? Why?"

Coa-Coa then said, "Naya, go upstairs and play with Brandy," and the two of them headed up the stairs.

Coa-Coa didn't say anything to me at first. She just stood there like she didn't know what to do with me, while I sat there on my knees, crying out at the top of my lungs.

"He could have put me in anybody's womb, anybody's! Why did God choose her? Why?"

Coa-Coa walked over to me. She kneeled down and put my head on her lap and started rocking me and humming.

I closed my eyes and wished that I was a child and that I was being held against my mother's bosom, a mother who loved me. I think Coa-Coa could sense how I felt by the way I clung to her. I think that might've been because, at one point or another in her life, she had felt the same way too.

She'd never really talked about her mom much, other than mentioning the fact that she died when she was only ten years old. I sometimes wanted to ask, but I could sense it was something she'd only talk about when she was ready, or something she'd never talk about at all.

All of a sudden Coa-Coa's humming turned into singing. The sound of her voice instantly stopped my weeping. I listened attentively to her mellow, calming voice, a voice that I never knew she had inside her. It was so angelic. God must have allowed her to borrow it from one of his angels to share with me just for that moment and that moment only.

I drifted off to sleep listening to Coa-Coa singing the words, "Sometimes I feel like a motherless child, a long way from home, a long way from home."

Chapter 16
It's Hard Out Here
for a 'Ho'

"Tonio? Tonio?" I said, waking up on the couch and looking around.

"It's me," Coa-Coa said. "It's not Tonio, it's me. You fell asleep, so I brought you over here to the couch, remember?"

"No, I mean, Tonio was supposed to be here. He was supposed to come take Brandy and me out to dinner. Did he come by? Did he call or anything? He was supposed to be taking me and Brandy out to dinner."

"Uh-uh." Coa-Coa shook her head in the negative. "But just relax. I cooked that cheeseburger hamburger helper you had in there. There's some left for you."

I yawned and looked around. It was dark outside. "What time is it?"

"About seven."

I jumped up. "Where's Brandy? Where's Brandy?"

"Chill, ma. She's upstairs with Naya. Matter fact, I'm 'bout to snatch Naya up, and we gon' head out 'cause I got that stupid class in the morning that the county makes me go to in order to get that check. You gon' be okay?"

"Yeah, I'll be fine."

"All right then, girl."

Coa-Coa stood up and called Naya down the steps.

After they left I called Tonio's cell phone but didn't get an answer. I called him all night long and never got an answer. *Maybe Penny is right. Maybe a week of laying up was all he wanted out of me. Maybe nobody would ever want me.*

"I hate to keep being the bearer of bad news," Coa-Coa said through the phone, "but turn to Channel 10 right now. Don't hang up; I'm going to stay on the phone with you."

I could tell by the sound of Coa-Coa's voice that something was wrong, very wrong. I picked up the remote and turned to Channel 10. "What?"

"Shhh . . . just listen," she said as a picture of Tonio's face appeared on the screen.

"Antonio Jamal Mackey was found dead with a gunshot wound to the head and the chest. His body was found at a known drug house . . ." was all I heard the newscaster say before I dropped the phone.

As I sat in the church sanctuary, not necessarily mourning the death of Tonio, but pretty much just paying my respects, not one tear fell from my eyes. Although Tonio and I had a connection because he was my first and also the father of my child, we still had never really developed the relationship we needed to have in order to make something special out of it. On top of that, I was just jaded with niggaz. I know that was wrong for me to say as he lay dead in a casket. Don't get me wrong, I loved Tonio because of the role he played in my life. But once again, I think I was more in love with the idea of what we could have eventually become rather than what we were. I wasn't about to sit up in that church, crying the blues and putting on a show, acting like some of the broads I saw.

I guess you could say it was the typical funeral of a dope boy—All his women on the side were looking around to see what other girls were crying, picking out who all of his fuck buddies were, according to who was crying hardest or loudest. It was ridiculous.

His main girl, who he'd had two kids by, which I had no idea about, had put a remembrance in *The Columbus Dispatch* newspaper for him. It was a big picture of Tonio and a message from her and their kids together. It was her way of letting all them other bitches out there know who his bottom bitch was, his main squeeze—the bitch who cooked his food and washed his drawz, and whose name was on the lease at the place he called home.

In all honesty, I wasn't fazed by any of this. Matter of fact, I got up right in the middle of the funeral and left the church. At that point, all the bitches had their eyes on me. They must've thought that I could no longer bear to sit through the funeral. I got all kind of "who-the-fuck-is-she?" looks.

That's not why I did it though. I just couldn't sit there and look at all those girls who were just like me. Girls who had no direction as to where life was taking them, and were willing to jump on and ride the coattail of any man who told them they were pretty. I could no longer sit there and see a reflection of myself, so I blew Tonio a kiss, and rose the fuck up out.

When I got that check in the mail for $10,000, I was shocked. It was like a miracle. I didn't believe it at first. I thought it was a trick. I even called the number of the insurance company that was on the check stub, and they confirmed that Tonio had listed Brandy as one of the beneficiaries on a life insurance policy he had. He had listed Brandy along with six other kids listed as his children. *Whoah wee*! I know some baby mamas was heated to find out about all them damn kids he

had. I ain't know that nigga was doing that much fucking. I
was glad all I ended up with was a baby by that nigga and not
AIDS. Thank God we had used condoms when we were together those few days.

The next time Hallow's ass came by the crib, I was glad to
inform him that I was going to start paying rent. I hit him off
with the first six months, a total of $3,000. I figured that
would buy me enough time to get the fuck up out of there
and get a place on my own, where the landlord didn't feel
like he could just drop by my shit whenever he felt like it. I
paid off all of my overdue bills and hit Coa-Coa with a grand
on GP.

I got a reliable little hooptie to get me around, to keep me
from having to take public transportation. I bought Brandy a
fresh new wardrobe, shit I normally wouldn't have considered buying, but I felt that my baby deserved it. Needless to
say, the money seemed to have vanished as quickly as it had
come. By the seventh month, when rent was due, I was back
in the same boat again—down to my last dime, literally.

As my finances dwindled, I started treating my utility bills
like they were layaway plans, putting twenty dollars down
here, twenty dollars down there. Finally I had disconnect no-
tices left and right.

That lousy high-school diploma wasn't worth the paper it
was printed on. What a fucking waste. The most I could get
was a job flippin' hamburgers. Can someone please tell me
how a woman takes care of a child with a weekly paycheck
from McDonald's? Hell, some rich white kids get more than
that per week from their parents for lunch money. I knew
shit was on its way from bad to worse. When I wasn't able to
do for Brandy the simple things some mothers easily did for
their children, like a happy meal here and there, go to the
movies, or something simple like that, that just made it all
the more difficult.

Brandy crept into my bedroom one night. "Ma, I'm still hungry."

"You already ate. Go on to bed."

"But that was a little bit of food. That wasn't dinner. I wish we still lived with Daddy. There was a lot of food there. We only got a little bit here."

Of all the emotions I could have experienced at that point, it was anger. I wasn't mad at Brandy, I was mad at myself for not being able to provide for her. I was mad at myself that she was starting to notice and call me on it. It made me feel like a failure, like a bad mother.

" 'A little bit of food'? 'A little bit'?" I jumped out of the bed. "Some kids don't even get that. Some kids don't get shit!" I grabbed her by the arm. Never, unless I was showing her affection or comforting her, had I put my hands on Brandy before. "Take your little ungrateful ass to bed." I hit her on the butt and slung her out of the room by her arm.

She cried as she hit the floor in shock. She was hurt, not by the lick I gave her on her butt; her heart hurt. Her mommy, her protector, the one she could come to if anyone ever hurt her, was the one hurting her now.

I wanted to go tell her I was sorry. I wanted to go tell her I was sorry for hitting her, for being broke, for not being able to provide enough food for her, but I couldn't. I was so embarrassed and ashamed.

Uncle Sam cut me off from that funky little check and food stamps when I missed all of those stupid classes that I was required to attend in order to get benefits. I either had to work or go to that stupid class. I no longer had Penny to take care of Brandy for me, and Coa-Coa was going to those classes herself, in-between working as some cashier at some carry-out, where she got paid under the table. There was all that Title 20 bullshit that I didn't understand. I was just so depressed that I didn't even want to go out and try to do shit.

But now my poor Brandy was suffering for it. She had to suffer because of the fucked-up decisions I had made in my life.

I couldn't block out the sound of her cry that night by burying my head under the pillow. I did drown out her cries, though, with cries of my own. I made it up in my mind that night that I would do whatever I had to do in order to take care of my child, whatever I had to do!

"What the hell do you know about being a goddamn bartender?" Coa-Coa asked as I kissed Brandy goodbye and headed towards the door. "You don't even drink—how the hell you gon' mix drinks for other people?"

"Look, I need the money," I snapped, tired of Coa-Coa's meddling.

Ever since I asked her if she would baby-sit Brandy at nights if I took a job bartending, she had been asking me a hundred and one questions.

"I need the money. I gotta do what I gotta do, you know. Brandy's gotta eat, and it's my responsibility as her mother to make sure that she does. So if that means bartending from nine o'clock at night until two o'clock in the morning, then so be it."

"Damn, yo." Coa-Coa snapped her head back and put her hands on her hips. "Forgive me for just wondering how Little Fuckin' Red Riding Hood is all of a sudden the big fuckin' bad wolf. I mean, come on, ma, a bartender? You? Please . . . don't sound right."

"So are you calling me a liar? You think I'm lying to you, Coa-Coa?"

"Whoa, whoa." She held her hand up. "I think you better just go on to work before this conversation goes in a direction that neither one of us wants it to . . . for real."

I closed my eyes and took a deep breath. "Sorry, Coa-Coa, I'm just nervous. I'm just frustrated, you know." I thought for a moment. "You got anything to drink?"

"I got some juice, or Coke." Coa-Coa turned and headed towards the kitchen.

"No, I mean a real drink. Something strong."

Coa-Coa stopped in her tracks. "You? A drink? A real drink? Hold—"

"Look, forget it. I gotta go anyway. Sorry for snappin' at you. I gotta go." I exited out of Coa-Coa's house and headed for my car.

I guess Coa-Coa sensed something was up because she watched me head down the street until she couldn't see me anymore. I know this because when I turned to look back, I could see where the curtain was pulled back on her front living room window as she stood there watching, watching me drive away into a world I had never experienced before.

"Hey, Hallow," I said over the song that was playing on the jukebox.

"What's up, Baby?" He planted a long, wet, juicy kiss on my cheek. "Welcome to Club Paradise." He then turned his attention to a girl walking by, grabbing her by the arm. "Hey, Cream, this is Baby. Baby, this is Cream." He leaned into me and said, "And she is creamy." He then turned and licked her up the side of her face.

She rolled her eyes up in her head and wiped his wetness off her face. "Hey, Baby." She shook my hand.

"Nice to meet you," I said, shaking hers.

"You wanna come in the back with me and I'll show you your locker?"

"Sure."

"Come on."

I nervously began to follow her. Medium build, with curves in all the right places, Cream was a knockout. She introduced me to a couple of regulars, as we made our way through the bar. Even though I still had on my street clothes, I felt naked walking through the room full of horny guys throwing money at women for shaking they sweaty asses in their faces. They looked at me like I was an uncooked meal that would be just right for the tasting, once I cooked in the oven a little longer.

"Is that okay with you?" Cream asked.

"Excuse me?" I hadn't heard a word she had been saying as she chatted all the way to the dressing room.

"Baby, you okay?" she said as we stood outside of the dressing room.

"Yeah, I'm fine."

"All right then. Let's do this." She pushed the door open and led me into the back.

All I saw was ass and titties behind that door. There were dancers of all shapes and sizes—some brick houses and a couple of broads who weren't any bigger than the poles they had to slide down.

After giving me a brief rundown of how things worked in the club, Cream said to me, "Did you bring something to dance in?"

"Yes." I pulled the swimsuit I had bought at Waterbeds & Stuff from out of my duffle bag I had carried into the club with me and held it up for Cream to inspect.

A couple of the other girls she had introduced me to began to laugh.

"Don't pay them no mind. It's just an inside joke we have how you can always tell the girls who've never danced before because they always try to wear the full backs."

" 'Full backs'?"

"Yeah—costumes that cover your entire ass up. It's the ass that gets you tips, so Hallow only goes for thongs here, girly." She walked over to her locker and pulled out a fluorescent green two-piece lacy, thong set that still had the price tags on it. "You can pay me back tonight after you count your tips, 'cause you gon' get paid swell tonight. When the DJ announces you as the virgin to the stage—and your name is

Baby too—oh, girl, you gon' need four, five Crown Royal bags to hold all them dead prez they 'bout to be throwing at your ass. Plus drinks money is a 50/50 split. Girlfriend, it's on. But don't get spoiled. This shit you 'bout to experience tonight ain't no everyday thing, so take advantage of it. Shake dat ass, ya heard me? Now go on and get dressed. I'm up next. I see you when you get out there." Cream disappeared to the other side of the door.

I stood there looking around, trying to figure out where I was supposed to go to change into my costume. The only other room was a stall with a toilet in it.

"Whatsamatter, Baby?" one of the dancers asked. "Ain't no private dressing rooms in this bitch. If you scared to take it off in front of us, what the fuck yo' ass gon' do when you get out there and got to take it off in front of a room full of strange men? You better take that shit off." The girl licked her lips and massaged her crotch, all the while watching me.

The other girls began to laugh and chant, "Take it off, take it off," as I removed my clothing and put on the fluorescent green costume.

"Baby, what's taking you so long?" Cream stuck her head in the door. "You up next. The DJ 'bout to introduce you."

"Okay, I'm on my way out." I put on the clear four-inch heels I had purchased and took a deep breath.

"Look, it's okay, mama," the girl who had been taunting me said. "I was scared my first time too, but this seemed to help." She handed me a bottle of Hennessy.

I took a gulp that burned the shit out of me when it went down, and then I made my way out the door.

"And here she is," I heard the DJ say, "the one all you perverted pedophiles been waiting on, tonight's virgin, the one and only . . . Baby!"

There was thunderous applause. Some men even stood up. As the song "One in a Million" began to play, I made my way to the stage. I was nervous as shit. I swear on everything,

I was so scared that I wanted to break down and cry right then and there; that, or make a run for the nearest exit. But just thinking about Brandy kept my ass right up there on that stage.

I don't know what the fuck I was thinking when I saw this as an easy way to make money. There wasn't anything easy about this shit. I don't know how chicks did it, but I was about to find out . . . the hard way; at least, I thought I was.

I hadn't wiggled my titties or shook my hips but a couple times before I reached over to grab the first bill I would ever make from stripping out of this older gentleman's hand. Just as my fingers clenched the bill, someone clinched my wrist with a death grip and dragged me off the stage.

The Final Chapter

"Let go of me," I said to Coa-Coa as she pulled me by my wrist out of the club and into the parking lot.

"Back the fuck up. This my girl," Coa-Coa said to the bouncer who contemplated interfering.

Had Coa-Coa been a dude, he probably wouldn't have let her slide; plus, I gave him a look that it was cool. He shooed his hand at us, like we were wasting his time, and went on about his business.

Coa-Coa said, "What the fuck do you think you're doing?— And if you tell me bartending, I'ma bust you in your lying-ass mouth."

There I stood outside in the parking lot of Club Paradise like some little girl who had been busted by her mother and was now getting the scolding of her life. I was so embarrassed, glowing in the dark in that damn costume. "Look, Coa-Coa, I'm not going to stand out here arguing with you in this parking lot where everybody is looking at me."

"Oh, what? You embarrassed? Your ass embarrassed now? A couple of minutes ago you was hoping everybody was looking at your ass, but now you don't want nobody to see it?"

Coa-Coa poked my shoulder with her finger. "Huh, answer me, whore. Am I right, whore?"

Although it was Coa-Coa standing there calling me out of my name, to me it was like Penny saying it. I could hear Penny's voice instead of Coa-Coa's."

"Shut the fuck up!"

"Oh, now you're a mad whore."

"I swear to God——"

"You swear to God what, whore?" She poked me in the other shoulder.

That's it right there. I just snapped on her ass and charged her. Unfortunately, me and those clear stilettos did not agree on which direction to go in, so I landed flat on my ass before I could even get to her. It hurt like hell too.

Tears began to fall from my eyes, from the pain of the fall, and from sitting there half-ass naked and being called a whore by someone who I thought was my friend.

"Your momma sure did name you right. All you do is sit around crying like a big ol' baby."

I could not figure out where all of Coa-Coa's anger was coming from.

"You ain't done nothing but cry from the minute I fuckin' met you."

"So I lied to you, big fuckin' deal." I got up off the ground and brushed my butt off. "That is no reason for you to come up here on my job, showing your ass."

"From the looks of things, that's what they do at your place of employment—show ass."

"What are you doing here anyway? Where are the girls?"

"They home in bed. I caught the bus up here while my neighbor, Kee-Kee, is sitting with them until I get back." Coa-Coa gave me the once-over, eyeing me with disgust. "Look at you—I can't even stand to look at you." She turned away.

"Then don't look at me. Why did you come here anyway?"

"No! The question is, Why did *you* come here?" Coa-Coa

turned back around and screamed at me, pointing her finger at me. "You lied to me! You lied to me!" Coa-Coa's face turned beet-red as she balled her fist and started shaking them. "You lied to me! Liar!"

"Coa-Coa, I'm sorry," I said, confused at the outburst she was having. I slowly approached her. "Calm down, please. I didn't mean to lie to you. I just didn't want to tell you what it was I was actually doing here. It's nothing to be proud of, you know."

"Then why are you doing it?" She gave me a look like I'd betrayed her.

"I needed the money, goddamn it!"

Coa-Coa looked me up and down and nodded her head. "And you think you're cut out to be a stripper? You think you so tuff, you think you so street. Bitch, I'm street. You think you know these muthafuckin' streets? You might have been adopted by the streets, accepted because yo' mama or somebody might have been raised by the streets. But a bitch like me was spit straight out the streets' muthafuckin' pussy. Damn it, my mama was what you trying to be—a 'ho'—that's right, a goddamn 'ho'. And you know what? I was even dumb enough at one point in my life to try to be one too."

"I don't know what your mama may have been, or what you may have been, but I'm not a 'ho'. The only damn thing I was doing in there and was ever going to do was dance."

Coa-Coa walked up to me and grabbed me by my face as if I were her child. "Baby, that's what they all say, trust me. I said it too." Coa-Coa's eyes began to water, and she slowly backed away from me, releasing my face.

For the first time since I had known her, I saw tears fall from her eyes. "Coa-Coa." I put my hand on her shoulder.

"Don't." She turned her back towards me.

I slowly removed my hand from her shoulder.

After a moment or two, she turned to face me again. "Look, Baby, I know why you're doing this. I know it's because of

Brandy. You've seen it. You've seen that look in her eyes. See, I know that look because it's the same look I used to have in my eyes when my mama would look at me when I was a little girl. See, that look your child gives you when you can't provide for them the way you want to"—Coa-Coa broke down in tears as she continued— "that's the look that pushes you to do the unthinkable. That look will make a mother do things she never imagined herself doing. That's the same reason why my mom started dancing, but it was her addiction to heroin she picked up from one of the girls she danced with that was the reason for her continuing to dance. Pretty soon, just showing a little tail and tits wasn't enough to feed both me and her veins. That's when she started sleeping with men for money. Hell, sometimes bitches too. I knew this because she'd take me with her sometimes. I knew that she was selling her body, and she knew that I knew. But every time we left from one of her gigs, she'd buy me a Happy Meal or something and promise me that she'd stop doing it." She paused for a moment and then continued. "But still and yet, it was that look I'd give her when there wasn't enough food in the house or the times that she couldn't buy me a Happy Meal that started the downhill spiral in the first place. I remember the look of humiliation on my mother's face when we'd go to the grocery store and she didn't have enough money for all the shit she had piled into the cart.

"We'd stand in line, while she was having the clerk remove stuff from the bill until the balance got down to how much money she had in her pocket. She knew she only had twenty dollars when we came in the store. She knew that when she put beer in the cart, and cigarettes and shit. You know what, though? The first items she'd have the cashier take back off the bill was shit like the bologna and the milk." Coa-Coa chuckled. "It damn sure wasn't the beer or the cigarettes. No, that was what she needed in order to coast between her fixes . . . 'cause Mama couldn't fly unless she was flying high.

I remember on Christmas, she would be so fucked up that she couldn't even get the presents under the tree before I woke up to see what Santa had brought me. I'd go down the steps, and she'd be sitting right there on the couch, nodding off her high, head jerking back and forth. On top of that, she'd have a lit cigarette in her hand. I'd gently remove the cigarette and put it out. Then I'd go back upstairs and lie down in my bed and wait a little while longer, hoping the next time I came back down she'd have the stuff under the tree.

"After coming down the steps two or three more times, she'd finally get up and put the toys under the tree. I can say this much, though—at least she did have something to go up under the damn tree. But you know what?" Coa-Coa started to cry and whimper again. "I'd give anything to stand in line at the grocery store with her again and watch her put groceries that she couldn't afford back. I'd give anything to be able to run up and down the steps on Christmas, waiting for her to sober up enough where she could put the gifts under the tree. But I can't . . . because some fuckin' hundred-dollar trick sliced her up in our living room because he was so drunk that he couldn't bust a nut and blamed her. Get this— then the fucker had the nerve to want his money back. But Mama wouldn't give it to him. So he killed her. He killed my mother with her own kitchen knife, and I found her cut up and dead when I came home from school." Coa-Coa fell to her knees and wailed. "Mommy! Mommy! She told me that she wasn't doing that shit no more, that she wasn't dancing and selling herself anymore. But she lied, and I know she lied because I found her." Coa-Coa hit her hands against her head. "She lied. She said she wasn't doing it anymore, but she lied. And because she lied, she's dead."

I wanted to comfort Coa-Coa, like she had comforted me so many times, but at first I couldn't. I just stood there crying right along with her, thinking of how lucky I was. Penny may not have been anywhere near the best mother in the world, but she had her reasons. And 'spite all of that, she was my mother. I loved her. She was alive, and I loved her. I had always loved her; she just had a problem with loving me back.

"I'm sorry. Oh God, I'm sorry, Coa-Coa," I said to her after finally going over to her and putting my arms around her.

At first I didn't know if she was going to receive me or not, but then she looked up at me and just threw her arms around me. We sat there for I don't know how long bawling like two big babies. There we sat in the parking lot of a strip club, two grown women, crying and not caring about who saw us.

After a minute, when we realized how crazy we must have looked to passers-by, we both busted out laughing. We stood up, laughing hysterically. We were really laughing to keep from crying, but we were laughing nonetheless.

"So why did you do it then?" I said, after I stopped laughing.

"Huh?" Coa-Coa said, as her laughter ceased.

"Why did you start dancing then?"

She sniffed, looked up and then replied, "I don't know. Just following in Mama's footsteps, I suppose. But when I went from stripping, to giving lap dances, to sucking dick in the champagne room to straight-out trickin', I knew I had to change. I was gonna die out here in these streets. I was truly gonna end up like my mother. At first I didn't give a damn. Fuck it—I wanted to die, but I knew my mother wouldn't have wanted that for me. I mean, living on welfare ain't what she would have wanted for me either, but it was up a step-up from this type of shit." She pointed to Club Paradise. "And you know what, Baby?—I don't have the fancy clothes that I used to, the nice hairdos from having a standing appointment in the salon, the car or the laid-out apartment that I had when I was stripping. But you know what I do have? Dignity. I have dignity and self respect." She looked at me. "I don't have a mother anymore, but I have a beautiful daughter . . . and I can say that I have a best friend now." She smiled at me as her eyes watered again. "And all of that is worth living for."

"Baby! Baby, what the fuck, yo?"

I looked up and saw Hallow standing at the door yelling for me.

"Look, I know you new and all and this shit takes some getting used to, but you fuckin' up my money. Rent is due, baby—mine and yours. So, in other words, you and your girlfriend gon' have to finish y'all's little talk when you get home. But for now, I need you to get your ass in here and make this money."

I took a deep breath and turned to look at Coa-Coa.

"If you choose that in there, Baby, as much as I love you, I can't be your friend anymore. I won't watch you die. I won't. I can't. But I know you gotta do you, so that's a choice you have to make on your own. I probably shouldn't have even come here. Anyway, I know you've gotta find a cure for 'the look.' But in my own personal opinion, Baby, I don't think you're going to find it in there." And with that, Coa-Coa started to walk away, headed for the bus stop.

Although Coa-Coa walked away, my problems didn't. I still had rent that was due. I still had to eat. I still had to take care of Brandy. I had to do all of these things now, so I needed money now.

"Coa-Coa."

She stopped in her tracks and turned around to look at me.

"I really do want to leave with you right now, but I can't."

I turned back and looked at Hallow who wore a smile of victory on his face.

He nodded at me. "You're doing the right thing. There's too much money in here to walk away from tonight."

Coa-Coa just shook her head at me. "I'm sorry to hear

that, Baby." She turned back around and continued to walk away.

"I can't leave with you right now. All of my shit is still in there, and I'm not wearing any clothes. If you wait five minutes, I'll give you a ride home."

Coa-Coa quickly turned back around. "Yes!" She jumped up and threw her arms up.

I headed back towards Club Paradise. "Consider this my thirty-day notice," I said to Hollow. "I'll be moving out the first of the month."

Hollow stood at the door, his mouth dropped open, no longer wearing a smile of victory.

I couldn't get back to that dressing room to get my stuff fast enough. Hollow couldn't have been more on point—for once in my life I was doing the right thing. And no amount of money was worth my soul.

EPILOGUE

Even though I gave Hallow a thirty-day notice that I was moving out of his property, he gave me a three-day eviction notice. I was sure it was in retaliation for me not working for him at his strip club, and for not fucking him for all those times he tried to get at me. But it was cool. Isis and I ended up becoming roommates, so now Brandy and Naya became the best of playmates. (Oh, yeah, Coa-Coa went back to going by the birth name her mother had given her.)

Our apartment was nothing fancy, but it was ours. And we paid for it with money we earned from lots of hard work, not money our former "Uncle-in-law" used to give us in order to keep us under his thumb.

That friend of my mother's, the one who I'd overheard her having a conversation with about my father that day, turned out she owned a chain of bookstores. Well, due to a predicament she found herself in, she had to take a break from running them. She had her boyfriend—well, he became her husband later on—get a hold of me and offer me a job. Of course, I accepted it, on one condition—that Coa-Coa got put on too. So, not only did we live together, but we worked together too. And more importantly, we even prayed together.

The woman who managed one of the other stores was really into church and had hounded us about visiting her church until we finally gave in just to get her off of our backs. That day, we accepted Jesus Christ into our hearts as Lord and Savior. I started going back to my old church, the one Penny attended. Penny and I still didn't have much of a relationship, but I allowed her back into Brandy's life. I pray every day that God will put it in her heart to someday learn to love me back. Until then, I'll just love her enough for the both of us.

As far as Duke and Celeste, I really didn't hear too much about them. I wasn't really trying to either. When I closed that chapter in my life, I didn't intend to ever revisit it; I was too busy working on the sequel. One that didn't include any Duke's or Tonio's.

My main focus in life was to be an honest, hardworking mother, making sure that I played the necessary role in Brandy's life to ensure that she grew to be a strong, self-supporting young lady and to never, ever, become dependent on a man . . . or man period. It was my job and my duty to break the cycle now. So instead of wasting my life and time seeking someone to replace the Daddy I never had or somebody to be a Daddy in my child's life, I was building a relationship with God, the one who always was and always will be my true Father.

THE END

About the Author

Joy, a native of Columbus, Ohio, after thirteen years of being a paralegal in the insurance industry, finally divorced her career and married her mistress and her passion, writing.

In the year 2000 she formed her own publishing company, END OF THE RAINBOW projects. Her sole purpose with END OF THE RAINBOW was to introduce in all those she encountered the quality of sharing her grandmother had instilled in her. This domino reaction would incite those with a passion in life to envision and manifest it, and for those unaware of their passion, to unearth it. Joy shares what she has learned in the literary industry by instructing a workshop titled **"Self-publishing: The basics you need to get started."** In this informative workshop, she touches on everything from copyrighting and bar coding to ISBNs and economical print-on-demand.

In 2004 Joy branched off into the business of literary consulting, in which she provides one-on-one consulting and literary services, such as ghost writing, professional read-throughs, write behinds, etc. Her clients consist of first-time authors, national bestselling authors, and entertainers. The end result of a couple of her clients' projects resulted in Joy being able to present their manuscripts to a publisher and land book deals for them.

Joy has come a long way since the debut of her first title, **Please Tell Me If the Grass Is Greener.** Since then she has published a diary of poems titled **World On My Shoulders**, she has collaborated on the publication of an erotica anthology titled **Twilight Moods**, in which her contribution is titled **"Daydreaming at Night"** and she was also featured in **The Game: Short Stories about the Life**, in which her contribution is titled "**Popped Cherry.**"

Joy has also written a children's story titled **The Secret Olivia Told Me,** which will be published Spring 2007 by Just Us Books. Joy self-published her first full-length novel titled **The Root of All Evil.** It was eventually picked up by a major publishing house and re-released. In addition, they signed Joy to two other novels, her Essence magazine bestseller, **If I Ruled the World,** and **When Souls Mate** (the sequel to **The Root of All Evil**). They also signed Joy to a novella deal titled **An All-Night Man**, in which Joy's contribution is titled "**Just Wanna Love Ya.**" Joy's triumphant street novel titled **Dollar Bill** is also an Essence magazine bestseller.

In another of her works, Joy was able to shine with two of the brightest stars in the literary industry, Nikki Turner and Kashamba Williams, in the anthology **Girls From Da Hood 2** in which Joy's contribution is titled **"Wanna Be."** In 2006 her short story titled "**BEYATCH!!!**" will appear in **Street Chronicles Volume 2 ... The Girls in the Game Edition** and her short story titled **"Life of Sin"** will appear in an Urban Erotic anthology presented by Noire. She also has a short story titled "**Behind Every Good Woman**," pending publication. Her full-length novels, **Mama, I'm in Love (. . . with a gangsta)** and **WET** are due for release in the winter of 2006.

Not forsaking her love of poetry, just this year Joy had several of her poems published in a book of poems entitled **Traces of Love**. "I plan to turn my focus back to poetry one day soon," Joy says. "I still write poetry and have another diary of poems titled **Flower in my Hair** waiting in the wings. But lately my spirit has been moving in another direction."

Needless to say, Joy will no longer be penning street lit,

erotica, or adult fiction after the release of the above-mentioned forthcoming titles. Joy is now working on a Christian fiction piece titled **Me, Myself, and Him**, which will debut under Urban Christian in fall 2007. In this novel, a woman struggles in her walk with God because she's trying to hold on to the love of a not-so-God-fearing mate. She realizes the difficulty of trying to live the Word while walking in the world. Finding herself trying to please man and God, she encounters the tough issues of reality. Of course, this novel pushes the envelope of Christian fiction, but it wouldn't be Joy's true literary style if she didn't. "I have matured both as a writer and spiritually. My walk in life has changed; therefore my writing has changed. I just hope that the dedicated following of readers I've been so blessed to have earned will decide to take this spiritual journey in the written word with me, as I shift to pen what God has called me to do."

Joy continued by saying, "When God called me, I had to be obedient and say 'Yes, Lord.' My intent is not to switch up to a different audience. Hopefully I won't lose the readers I already have, but gain the readers I don't have. I know I might have to give up a few, but my soul still says YES!"

You can visit JOY at www.JoylynnJossel.com